THE MILLIONAIRE'S MECHANIC

LUCY LEROUX

❀ Created with Vellum

TITLES BY LUCY LEROUX

The Singular Obsession Series

Making Her His

Confiscating Charlie, A Singular Obsession Novelette

Calen's Captive

Stolen Angel

The Roman's Woman

Save Me, A Singular Obsession Novella

Take Me, A Singular Obsession Prequel Novella

Trick's Trap

Peyton's Price

The Spellbound Regency Series

The Hex, A Free Spellbound Regency Short

Cursed

Black Widow

Haunted - Coming Soon

The Rogues and Rescuers Series

Codename Romeo

The Mercenary Next Door

Knight Takes Queen
The Millionaire's Mechanic
Burned Deep - Coming Soon

Writing As L.B. Gilbert
The Elementals Saga
Discordia, A Free Elementals Story
Fire
Air
Water
Earth

A Shifter's Claim
Kin Selection
Eat You Up
Tooth and Nail
The When Witch and the Wolf - Coming Soon

Charmed Legacy Cursed Angel Watchtowers
Forsaken

CHAPTER ONE

Rainer Torsten looked down at the security monitor, frowning at the woman on screen. She was wiping her hands nervously on her pants, her small frame dwarfed by the oversized plush chairs his decorator insisted projected strength and gravitas to his clients.

"This is the security problem you alerted me to?" he asked skeptically.

"The woman doesn't have a legitimate reason to be here," Stewart Powell, his head of security, said repressively. "She lied to get access to this office."

Rainer's company, Torsten Investments, occupied the entire top floor of the high-rise building. For the woman to be sitting in his waiting room, she had to run the gauntlet of two reception desks, his own and the one on the lobby level. Both were manned with trained staff who would have turned away anyone without an appointment who wasn't on a pre-approved list.

"How did she get admitted?" he asked.

This was a secure building, one of his first major acquisitions. The other businesses that rented space from him appreciated the excellent security his people provided. To be sitting in that chair, the woman had to have presented a plausible reason for it. Otherwise, she would have been turned away at the lobby level—discreetly, of course. The other enterprises that occupied the remaining floors didn't enjoy a spectacle. That sort of thing was bad for business.

"This woman misrepresented herself to the reception desk downstairs and our own here," Stewart said, his ever-present scowl magically gone.

If Rainer didn't know better, he'd believe the man was thrilled to have a breach. But he didn't call Stewart on it. Instead, he let his man earn his six-figure salary.

Powell tapped the figure of the woman on the screen. "Downstairs, she identified herself as an employee of Elite Motors, waving a set of keys as if she were making a delivery. They let her right up," he added with a sniff.

Well, that explained the overalls the woman wore, and why she'd made it to the twenty-first floor. Rainer was a well-known car enthusiast. He had multiple vehicles in every city that he kept an apartment. Since he had permanent quarters in over a dozen major cities, that put his car collection in the mid-forties.

His taste was eclectic. Rainer owned the latest hybrids, modded especially for him by the manufacturer. But he also collected rare antiques and vintage muscle cars—anything special that caught his eye. It was his favorite indulgence.

His friends Garret and Mason joked that he was turning into Jay Leno, with his car collecting proclivity. "Pretty soon you're going to need to buy yourself an airplane hangar just to house them, just like him," Garret had said.

Rainer hadn't told him that he'd already purchased a warehouse outside of San Diego instead. Except now it looked as if his favorite hobby might be becoming a hole in his security.

"I haven't done any business with Elite Motors in the last year," Rainer mused. "It could be they acquired something recently that they'll think I want. Maybe they sent this girl to offer it."

Even as he said it, he knew it was unlikely. The woman in the waiting room was young and black, a touch petite but his type overall. It was possible someone at the dealership had noted his preferences in women and sent her to make an offer. But that was too desperate a move by a business such as Elite Motors. That place tried to live up to its name.

Elite was a full-service boutique car dealership that took great pains to project an air of rarified luxury and exclusivity. An in-person drop-in at his place of business, one without an appointment, smacked of desperation. This was a rookie maneuver made by a new business, or one circling down the drain. As far as he knew Elite was doing fine but doubtless one of Powell's people was checking on that now.

"If Elite had something new for you, they would have called first, made an appointment. Even if they wanted a face-to-face so they could do a hard sell, they would have sent a real salesperson, not one of their junior mechanics."

Powell held out a tablet with the Elite website. It was too fancy a place to list every member of their support staff by name. Only the high-performing salesmen had that distinction, but buried in the 'About Us' section was a group photo with all the staff. The smallest woman on the left appeared to be a physical match for their uninvited guest.

"It could just be a woman trying to get your attention. Maybe she saw you at the dealership and developed a crush," Powell shrugged. "It's been a while since one went to this length to throw herself in your path, but it's not impossible. Given how quietly you've been living, she might have felt the need to go to more dramatic lengths."

Neither acknowledged *why* Rainer had been living like a monk. Powell still blamed himself for what happened last year, what they now collectively referred to as 'the incident'. It explained his overreaction to a minor security incursion.

Rainer took a second look at the woman on screen, trying to identify the same threat Powell recognized. But he didn't see it. Also, he had a stack of contracts waiting for him on his desk. He'd wasted enough time.

"Talk to her in person," he said finally, turning away from the screen. "If you don't like what you hear, call the dealership before you call the police. If it's just some girl with a crush, I'd rather not get her fired—but I also won't tolerate another unscheduled drop-in."

The last thing he needed was a stalker.

Powell nodded at Waters, his large and most intimidating second-in-command. Waters grinned, rubbing his hands with glee as he exited the door leading to the reception area.

CHAPTER TWO

Georgia wiped her hands on her coverall pant legs again, wincing when a streak of oil spread across her palm.

Damn it, I knew I should have changed into street clothes before coming here.

But she hadn't worked on any cars at all today—not even an oil change. That didn't seem to matter, though. Mechanics were magnets for grease and grime, especially the low man on the totem pole at work. In fact, her subordinate status was what had gotten her into this mess in the first place.

She shifted uncomfortably, trying to hide the stain. But the movement just called attention to it. The perfectly coiffed receptionist gave her another supercilious death stare, making her feel two inches tall.

Clearly, Georgia wasn't going to get in to see Rainer Torsten today.

Why did I think coming here in person was a good idea? She should have emailed the recording. That would have been the smarter play.

Or maybe not. What made her think they would take an email seriously? They wouldn't even open it. It would be just another bizarre bit of spam, lost in a business inbox that likely received hundreds of emails a day. Biting the inside of her cheek, she resisted the urge to bury her head in her hands.

Why don't I think these things through?

Rainer Torsten used to be a big-time Wall Street guy, a hedge-fund manager who made millions of dollars a day. At one point in time, his face had graced the cover of every business magazine in the country and probably all the European ones as well. But sometime in the last couple of years, he'd seemingly lost his taste for empire building. He still ran a successful angel investment group, but according to the very flattering magazine profile she clutched in her sweaty hands, he had also become one of the country's major philanthropists. One who didn't like to brag about how much of his wealth he was giving away.

Most of that money had gone to charities for women and children —enough that he'd gone from billionaire to multi-millionaire in the last couple of years. *By choice.*

That was why she had come in person. She had wanted to make sure the man who did so much for others had a chance to protect himself. But just because Rainer Torsten was the rarest of combinations, a rich man who appeared to care about others, that didn't mean Georgia could just waltz into his painfully posh office and *talk* to him.

The fact that she was holding one of those glowing magazine profiles of Torsten, along with the picture of the '49 Talbot Lago she was restoring, had also been another misstep. It just made her look like a crazy fan.

And judging from the entrance of an exceptionally large man in a dark suit that screamed *I-am-security*, the receptionist agreed.

The hulk turned to her. Her mind did that funny and completely whacked-out thing it did where everything slowed down, her heart beating in time with the man's footsteps.

She watched wide-eyed as the guard came to a stop in front of her. He was even bigger up close. *Why don't I think these things through?*

"Miss, would you come with me, please?"

Georgia's breath got stuck in her throat. She cleared it, the sound both squeaky and strangled. "Err… I must speak to Mr. Torsten. I have some information he needs to hear."

The man crossed his thick arms, his face creasing as if he were about to start laughing, but it was gone in a flash. The stern expression reasserted itself as if settling in for a long winter. "Sure, you do."

His arm lifted, the fingers twitching in a 'come with me' gesture.

Georgia didn't move to follow him. She couldn't. If they booted her out of this office, she'd never get back in. They'd slap her face on a watch list like they did on TV.

She would never get another chance to save Rainer Torsten's life.

Gripping the damp magazine, she sucked in her stomach, bracing herself. "I cannot stress this enough—it's *vital* that I speak to your boss."

"Actually, my boss is Stewart Powell, Mr. Torsten's head of security."

Georgia gaped, mouth open. "*Wait*... can you take me to him?" she asked incredulously.

The man blinked as she jumped to her feet, reluctantly drawling out an answer. "Yes..."

"All right. *Please* take me to Mr. Powell instead."

❧

Rainer looked up from his computer screen, then rubbed his eyes. "She did what?"

"The woman—Georgia Hines—no longer wants to talk to you. She was happy to speak with Stewart instead...something about a threat to your person."

Waters shrugged his massive shoulders. "I'm not sure why he's taking her seriously, but Powell decided to hear her out. He's interviewing her in the small conference room. I thought you'd like to know."

Rainer pushed his laptop away. "Well, *that* is an interesting approach."

Water's brow creased. "Sir?"

"Nothing. Forget it," Rainer said, not bothering to explain Powell's theory that their visitor was here to somehow entice him into dating her.

That scenario was still possible, but the fact that she was settling for a sit down with Powell instead of him, suggested it was something else.

She's probably some crackpot. But Rainer's curiosity was piqued. And that was a bad sign. He had been living too quietly if some office crasher was enough to get him to drop everything to listen to Powell's interrogation.

Yeah, I need to get out more, Rainer thought as he made his way to the small security office—a satellite of the main hub on the ground floor. He'd been a hermit for the last year and a half. He rarely went out—not to his favorite restaurants or the theatre. No parties. Not even to the fundraising events hosted by the many charities he supported.

No wonder Powell was bored out of his mind. Rainer wasn't much better.

The girl was cuter on the high-resolution monitor in the security office.

"Turn the volume up," he told the woman manning the control panel.

His timing was perfect. Stewart was just hitting his stride.

CHAPTER THREE

The head of Rainer Torsten's security was only a head taller than her, but Georgia knew appearances were deceiving. This man, who introduced himself only as Powell, was infinitely more dangerous than the much larger one who'd deposited her in this room.

It was the way he moved… as if he were seconds away from leaping over the table in a slick ninja maneuver. There was also the way he sat, with the sharp edge of watchfulness practically flaying her skin open as he paced in a half circle on the other side of the table.

"Why don't you take me through it again?" he asked, pausing and cocking his head to the side in a move that echoed the Terminator in 'T2'.

Georgia gave him a tight smile. "As I told you before, I work at Elite Motors."

She scratched her nose, and Powell's mouth pulled up at the corner. Sighing, Georgia took a crumpled napkin from her pocket. After she found a clean spot, she wiped her face. The smear was thankfully small.

She shrugged. "I'm the low man on the totem pole in the mechanics bay. I mostly do oil changes or deal with the occasional carburetor problem. Some light bodywork."

Powell waved her on, telling her to get on with it.

"Anyway, being the newbie means I get stuck doing the crappiest jobs—literally. Like helping clean the showroom bathroom when the janitor calls in sick or there's an unexpected mess outside of their work hours."

It hadn't always been quite so bad. Yes, she was the newest hire and the other mechanics had always assigned her the worst tasks, but when her foster brother had worked there, he'd watched out for her. Mack had made sure they rotated their duties, so she wasn't the one stuck scrubbing the toilets every time. He also made sure she'd had the chance to work on some sweet rides that challenged her skills.

Things were different now that he was gone.

She cleared her throat to dispel the sudden tightness. "Some VIP's kid had stuffed an entire roll of toilet paper down one of the commodes right after opening, making it overflow. Since the janitors only come in just before closing, I was the one tapped to clean it. I was standing on the toilet when I heard the men talking."

"The pair who made the threat?"

She nodded. "Yes, they were talking about their plan and when to grab him." Georgia grimaced. "At first, I didn't know who they were talking about, but then they mentioned Rainer Torsten by name."

Powell pursed his lips, appearing to consider that. He sat across from her. "And why were you standing on the toilet?"

That confirmed it. *He thinks you're full of shit.*

She clenched her jaw, straightening her spine. "There's a cabinet over each stall. It's where we keep the spare rolls of toilet paper. I can't reach it without standing on the lid."

Her height was a curse. Georgia was the shortest employee at Elite. Even Judy, the receptionist, and Samantha, the only female salesperson, towered over her.

Powell still studied her as if she were a paramecium under a microscope. "Other than his name, was there any other details you can share?"

"They mentioned having a chance to grab him on Thursday, outside the bank. Does that mean anything to you?"

The man's face darkened. "As a matter of fact, Mr. Torsten does have an appointment at a financial institution next Thursday."

The words came out hard and clipped. It might have been her imagination, but the room suddenly felt colder, as if Powell had suddenly turned into Mr. Freeze. The cold wafting from him made her want to squirm. *Someone just cranked up the AC. Stop being silly.*

"Mr. Torsten's schedule is not known to many," Mr. Powell continued in that same clipped tone. "We keep it confidential for safety reasons. Unfortunately, we can't always guarantee the people we meet will do the same."

She frowned. "You think someone at the bank told me about his appointment?"

Powell inclined his head. Georgia stifled a sigh. "I didn't hear about his meeting from a bank employee. I don't even know what bank we're talking about. The men I overheard never mentioned it by name."

"Convenient."

Georgia scowled. "I'm not making this up. I overheard someone threatening to kidnap your boss."

Powell leaned back with exaggerated casualness. If she didn't know better, she'd have thought he was enjoying this. "It's an entertaining story, I'll grant you. But there's no way to verify your story."

Georgia leaned forward, setting her cell phone on the table next to the magazine. "I recorded what I could."

Powell blinked. "Oh."

"I started my recording app after I heard his name. Mr. Torsten is a highly valued customer at Elite, so I recognized it."

Bending forward, she pressed play. A man's voice filled the air, the sound resonating in the tiled room where it had been recorded.

"...not going to be easy. Torsten's a big guy so be ready with the stun gun," a man was saying.

After a pause, a deeper voice rumbled, "Just handle your end, and I'll handle mine."

There was a shuffling sound and a grunt.

"Are you sure the guards will fall for it?" the first voice asked.

"It'll work. This was planned by a genius, remember?" The tone was oddly sarcastic, but the other man merely grunted before replying.

"It better. His appointment at the bank next Thursday is the cleanest shot we're going to have for weeks."

There was more background noise, a muffled voice that came from outside the bathroom.

"Let's go," the man with a deep voice said as if he were spooked.

A squeak indicated a door being opened, then the sound of it closing. The voices faded, but the recording kept going because she'd been frozen on top of the toilet for an entire five minutes after—an eternity at the time.

Georgia pressed the stop button. "Sorry, that's all I got. I missed the beginning. I didn't start the memo app until after I heard his name."

Mr. Powell's eyebrow twitched. "Did you recognize either of the voices?"

She shook her head. "No, sorry, I don't. I assume they are customers, but I spend most of my time in the garage during business hours. Sometimes, we see clients if we're handing them their keys back, but we usually just park the cars in a designated section of the lot and leave the keys in the ignition. I'm not on the sales floor much."

"Unless you're cleaning the toilet."

It wasn't a snide tone, but Georgia bristled. "Yeah. Exactly."

Except for Mitchell and Dale, the two head mechanics, most of the grunts in repair and maintenance didn't see Elite's well-heeled customers. Georgia had only caught a single glimpse of the elusive Rainer Torsten during his last visit—or, more accurately, of the back of his head. And the only reason she saw that much was because Judy had run out to the back to get her. The receptionist had a massive crush on the man, and she'd wanted someone to gush over him with. But Georgia wasn't the type to moon over a stranger, much to Judy's disappointment.

Aware that Mitchell would chew her out for taking too long for lunch, she swiped her phone off the desk. "If you give me an email address, I can send this to you."

Powell raised an eyebrow, but he reached into his pocket for his wallet. He withdrew a small card with a phone number and email on it. It bore nothing else, not even his name.

She sent the recording to both, assuming the phone could play voice files, too. When a beep sounded, Powell took out his sleek cell, acknowledging receipt of the files with a crisp nod.

"And that?" he asked, gesturing to the magazine as he put the phone away.

Georgia lifted a shoulder. "One of the salespeople had that interview Mr. Torsten did a few months ago in her office. He mentioned some rare cars he's always wanted. I think the owner was having her try to hunt them down, but Sam hasn't had any luck yet. I happen to be restoring a '49 Talbot—one of the cars he mentioned. I thought pretending to sell it might be a good way to get a face-to-face, but after talking to you, I don't have to see him."

Powell put his phone away, considering her with those cold, dark eyes. "This could still be an elaborate story. The men on that recording could be your friends, helping you get Rainer's attention for your song and dance about this Talbot you want to sell."

Groaning, Georgia rolled her eyes. "Look, I read some nice stuff about your boss, how much he gives to charity. Samantha at Elite says he's charming and has never hit on her—not that she'd mind. He's a stand-up guy, by all accounts. That's the only reason I came down here to warn him—and the car is not for sale."

She picked up the magazine before rising. "Now you have the recording. As far as I'm concerned, I've fulfilled whatever obligation I had by making sure you heard it. Act on it... don't act on it. That's all up to you. But judging from your nice suit, Mr. Torsten pays you well to keep him safe. I hope you do it."

Spinning on her heel, she strode toward the door in preparation of a dramatic exit. Unfortunately, someone had moved the wall.

CHAPTER FOUR

Rainer didn't budge when the woman crashed into him. She was so small that he barely felt it. But he couldn't help but grin when she blinked her big hazel eyes up at him. The light color was a striking contrast to her thick fringe of dark eyelashes.

Mechanic Georgia Hines was adorable. About five-one with skin the color of coffee with a splash of cream, she had her tightly curled hair pulled into a severe bun, but one or two stray curls defied her. They haphazardly framed her face, glints of red glowing in the dark brown strands.

Not African American, he mentally revised. Dominican maybe?

"Whoa there," he said, taking her by the arms and guiding her back a step.

The girl took two, putting enough distance between them to force him to drop his hold. A pity. She had felt good in his hands.

Georgia blinked up at him with parted lips, her expression slightly dumbfounded. Had she been looking at his hair, he would have understood the reaction. He sported a fresh dye job—his hair a bright cobalt blue shade not found in nature. It was one of several exotic shades he'd been trying. Before the blue, it had been lots of different colors—purple, peacock green, and yellow.

He'd even tried a bright scarlet a world removed from his natural red.

But the petite woman in front of him didn't even register the outlandish hair color. Those incredible eyes were glued to his face, flatteringly so.

He suppressed a wild impulse to stroke her lush rosebud mouth with his fingers. *You can look, but no touching.*

But that didn't stop him from using his other senses. His smile widened. "You smell like gasoline. I like it."

And he did. Rainer was one of the few people who genuinely enjoyed pumping his own gas. It might have been one of the reasons he liked cars so much.

But little Georgia didn't take the compliment in the spirit it was intended. Her lush pink lips pressed tightly together. "Oh, um, sorry."

She glanced down at herself before narrowing her eyes at his suit front as if checking for stains, her expression panicked.

"No harm done," he assured her.

Georgia nodded jerkily.

The name suited her perfectly. Petite, but rounded in all the right places, she was a ripe peach ready to be plucked. He blinked, realizing he'd been staring a touch longer than was socially appropriate. Georgia looked as if she wanted to hide behind the nearest chair.

Her eyes skittered to his face, then quickly away. "Uh...well, I just came by to pass on some information, so I should be going."

"Just one second," he said, ruthlessly shutting down another smile.

Rainer reached for the photograph tucked in the pages of the magazine she held. His eyes widened as he examined the snapshot. "I'll be damned. You *do* have a Talbot."

The snap was of Georgia next to the vintage vehicle, which was in mid-restoration, her arms up like a game-show hostess demonstrating her wares. A stoop-shouldered man with thinning hair gave the camera a thumbs-up from beside her.

Georgia hesitated, but then her little hand snatched the photograph back. "Sorry. If you heard anything I just said, you know that mentioning it was a ruse so I could deliver my message."

The smile he'd been fighting broke free. Even the woman's words were adorable. When was the last time someone had used the word *ruse* around him?

Somehow, this exchange was the most fun he'd had in months. *Hell, I do need to get out more.*

"A threat against me. I heard," he said. "And don't think Powell and the others aren't thrilled by it. They've been pretty bored lately. You've livened up their day."

He took back the snapshot, studying it. "As for this, it's a damn good ruse. I have been looking for a car just like this for years."

He'd said as much in public. Maybe more than once if memory served. The people they'd sent to interview him—the few he granted these days—were aware that talking cars was a reliable way to kick things off on the right foot.

Rainer admired the vehicle in the picture. "It was obviously in rough shape, but you seem to be doing a good job with the restoration."

He paused to stroke the sleek line of the hood. The back end bore quite a few dings, but the hood had been smoothed out by an expert hand. *Smooth as silk.* "It is all your work, isn't it?" he guessed.

She was small, but she looked lithe and strong, the bit of forearm visible beneath the sleeves of her overalls noticeably muscled. That kind of definition only came with hard work.

Georgia's expression eased, softening. He suspected most people didn't give her work the recognition it deserved.

"Yes, it's all me, a project I'm doing on my own time. My dad inherited the car from his father, but it never ran, so I'm restoring it for him—it was supposed to be a retirement gift."

"Supposed to be?"

Her expression fell before her shoulders straightened determinedly. "Dad's postponing retirement. But that just means I have to get my butt in gear to have it ready for Christmas."

At the word 'butt,' the Pavlovian lizard part of Rainer's brain took over and he glanced at the fine derriere he'd clocked when she'd risen from her chair. Snapping his eyes back up at her face, he hoped she hadn't noticed. But something about this woman was pushing all his buttons, turning him into the chauvinist he used to call out his friends for being.

Trying to save himself, he decided to indulge his curiosity. "Why is he postponing retirement?"

His question seemed to catch her off guard. Her lips parted and she hesitated, but then shrugged. "He just is."

Money problems, his brain supplied. Rainer gave the snapshot back with a winsome smile. "In that case, are you sure your dad can't be talked into selling? I can make it worth your while."

For a moment, his instinct said he had her. There was a flicker, the tiniest bit of hesitation, before she shook her head. "It's a gift for my dad," she repeated, a trace of resigned sadness in her tone.

Rainer assumed she meant the sad older man in the photo. There was zero resemblance to the luminous girl in front of him. But he didn't ask if she'd been adopted. That would have been rude.

The mechanic began to edge around him, but she stopped. "I *did* hear those men plotting to kidnap you—I'm not making it up."

"I appreciate the heads-up, I do," he said, his head tilting to the left. "Despite the sizable charitable donations that get me written up in magazines like the one you're holding, I remain an extraordinarily rich man. It makes me a target for a lot of crackpots and would-be criminals. But very few people act on their harebrained schemes. For the foolish who do, I have Powell."

On cue, the sleek shorter man appeared on his right. Georgia's eyes widened, telling Rainer that she hadn't heard Powell approach. His head of security moved like an assassin.

"All right, then," she said, her head snapping to Powell and back again. Her cheeks deepened in a lovely blush. "Um, uh, good luck."

She slipped around him, then was out the door as if her shoes were on fire.

Rainer watched her go. Yes, he'd been right about the ass. *A ripe peach.*

Sighing, he turned to Powell. "Any chance that the threat is real?"

"Slim to none, but we'll look into it."

Nodding, Rainer left, deciding to order lunch in. As pleasant a diversion as Georgia had been, he still had quite a bit of work to do.

❧

Seventeen minutes after the official end of her lunch break, Georgia ran into the garage bay.

"Damn it," she muttered, checking the time on the dash.

She opened her mouth, ready with the excuse she'd formulated on the fast drive back. But Mitchell didn't give her a chance to use it.

Without glancing up from the Bentley engine, he pointed at her. "Docked an hour."

"But—"

Straightening, he twisted to give her a flat look, that supercilious single eyebrow raised. "Would you rather get a write-up for your file?" he asked, wiping his hands on a rag.

Flushing, Georgia took a deep breath so she wouldn't swear at him. Promoted to the supervisor position when Mack died, Mitch enjoyed flexing his power over her. He wasn't above giving her a write-up either. As far as he was concerned, Georgia had gotten away with murder when Mack was in charge just because he'd made sure everyone had split their duties, good and bad, evenly.

Mitch gave Judy a lot of shit, too, but the receptionist didn't work under him. Neither did Samantha, but Mitch wasn't stupid enough to mess with one of Elite's biggest moneymakers. Georgia was the only female who had the unfortunate privilege of answering to him.

"I had to run an errand for my dad," she said, eyes on the ground.

She wished that her diffident voice and cowed posture were a conscious response to dealing with Mitch's dick behavior—because standing up for herself only made him worse. But her pounding heart and the desire to crawl into a hole was nothing so calculated. She hated being singled out, her visceral desire for flight exacerbated by Mitch's larger size and smug swagger.

Rainer is taller and broader, her brain pointed out. But her reaction to him hadn't been remotely similar to this.

Also, Georgia couldn't afford to not stand her ground. Not with what was happening at home. "I can make up the time after hours," she said, trying not to sound like an unsure teenager. "But I had to go to Ephraim's bank while it was open, and there was a long line."

Mitch considered that, his eyes flicking to the side. She knew Dale and Alfredo were watching them, but, in this case, it worked in her favor. Everyone at Elite knew Ephraim. Thanks to Mack, they were aware of the problems that Ephraim's business was going through.

"Fine. But you better do an entire hour," he said, tossing the towel on a nearby bench before disappearing into his office.

Dale walked off without commenting, but Alfredo—Fredo for short—nudged her in commiseration. "Forty minutes of unpaid overtime. That sucks."

"Yeah," Georgia muttered, but she was aware that it could have been worse.

"Sorry Ephraim is still having a shitty time," Fredo said, not rubbing it in that he'd been late yesterday morning, but Mitch had only given *him* a warning.

Georgia knew better to expect Fredo to stick his neck out for her. Mitch didn't treat Fredo as badly as he did her, but Fredo had taken enough shit from him over the years. She wouldn't ask him to set himself up for more.

"Ephraim will be okay," she said. "He just needs a little time to figure some stuff out."

Fredo made a sympathetic noise before walking away. Sighing, Georgia put her bag in her locker, getting to work before Mitch docked her another hour of pay.

CHAPTER FIVE

Two weeks later

Georgia shuffled the heavy paper sacks in her arms, swearing when one ripped. The contents spilled all over the worn welcome mat of her childhood home.

"Damn it." That had been the sack with the glass jar of pasta sauce. Twisting, she spotted the jar in the dirt next to the concrete path. Picking it up, she thanked the stars it was still unbroken. Friday evening was spaghetti night, and her dad hated when their routine was upset.

It took two trips from the car to the kitchen to get everything unpacked and organized before Georgia could start dinner. After starting the water for the pasta, she bustled around the small kitchen, opening and closing cabinets as she prepared dinner for two.

The worn wooden cabinets needed a new coat of lacquer, but, otherwise, this place looked the same as the day she had arrived in Casa Levi-Jones when she'd been a damaged eight-year-old without hope.

She certainly hadn't expected this to be her forever home. Georgia had been burned too many times before to believe something as absurd as that.

The modest four-square house, nestled deep in suburban San Diego, hadn't been Georgia's first foster placement. More like the seventh or eighth, but she only had clear memories of the last two. But recalling that skinny black girl who clutched a garbage bag of her belongings no longer hurt—thanks to Diamond and Ephraim, the foster parents who had claimed Georgia as their own.

By the time Georgia had been assigned to them, she'd met enough new 'parents' for several lifetimes. Her unspoken skepticism had been in her refusal to unpack her things and her monosyllabic answers to any questions she was asked.

It didn't help that she wasn't their first foster child. They had a boy in the past. The social worker had told Georgia that as if it were a *good* thing instead of a huge red flag.

Georgia would later find out that the Levi-Jones' hadn't willingly given their foster son up. Mack, whose real name was Shane Mackenzie, had a mom who wanted to keep him, at least she did when she was sober. Unfortunately for Mack, his mother's clean periods were few and far between. But she tried, and Mack was fiercely loyal to her. He deeply resented the efforts of the conscientious social worker, who would repeatedly pull him out of his mom's house to stick him back in the system.

Mack was a problem child who had gotten kicked out of more than one foster home before being assigned to Ephraim and Diamond. Being goodhearted, they had done their best to make sure Mack knew he was wanted—even when his mother asked for him back. And they always welcomed him home when she inevitably messed up, even when he'd made it clear he didn't want to be there.

Being forced back two or three times a year messed with Mack's head, but he'd never taken it out on Georgia. Not once she'd told him her mother didn't want her.

Taking out the pasta strainer, she stroked the little planets on the wallpaper her foster mother had covered the shelves in because she loved the stars.

Diamond had been larger than life. Black, voluptuous, and garrulous, she had taken Georgia by the hand and shown her so much love it had broken through the thick walls she'd had built around herself.

Georgia had been more doubtful about Ephraim. Quieter than his chatty and loving wife, he'd stayed in the background during those first few weeks. He'd been perfectly nice and welcoming, but he rarely spoke, letting his wife do all the talking. Ephraim was the quintessential nebbish Jewish accountant.

Thin and buttoned-down, Georgia's first impression of her foster father had been of a lanky human scarecrow. But she had liked how he would be there, working or washing dishes in the background, frequently smiling at something his wife said or did without actively engaging.

Then Mack, her foster brother, had come home, and Georgia's family had been complete. For a while anyway.

"You didn't have to make dinner," her dad said, appearing at the threshold to the living room. Except for his thin hair and a more prominent bald spot, Ephraim hadn't changed at all in the last sixteen years.

Well, that wasn't exactly true. He no longer stood as tall, and his clothes were a little more wrinkled even though Georgia ironed them now. She even sprayed them with starch the way Diamond had taught her, but they never stayed crisp and smooth the way they had when her foster mom was alive.

They had lost Diamond four years ago to breast cancer. And then Mack had died in a car wreck last year. Now she and Ephraim were alone.

But you have each other, she reminded herself. *And you both need to eat.* Ignoring him, she clucked her tongue and waved him to the table.

Ephraim sat at the small four-person table with a slow movement, grunting as he folded himself into the chair with effort. Taking off his glasses, he began to polish them, staring off into space.

She continued to prepare their meal, letting the music from her phone take the place of conversation. Georgia drained the hot water from the pasta before taking the plates and glasses from the cabinet and setting them on the table.

"Leftovers would have been fine," Ephraim said, rousing enough to track her movements. "You didn't have to go to any trouble."

"All that's in the fridge was stale Chinese," she pointed out, taking a seat after loading up their plates. "But that was my fault. I couldn't get to the shopping until today. It's been busy at work."

She handed him the plastic bottle of shredded parmesan. "I hope you don't mind spaghetti again so soon. I wanted to do something fast so I can put in a few hours on the Talbot."

His small smile was more than enough to warm her, making the effort worth it. "Not to worry. You know it's one of my favorites."

Since he said that about every dish she made, Georgia didn't really, but she simply dug in, telling him about her day in between bites. But Ephraim simply nodded when she spoke, his mind a million miles away.

Her dad was always a little unfocused, but this was another level of abstraction. Even when Diamond had finally passed, he'd been there for her and Mack.

But that was because he'd been prepared. Her mom had been sick for a long time. Diamond had known the end was coming. They both had time to prepare. It had been tougher when Mack died. There had been some very dark days for them both, but they remembered what Diamond had told them over and over during her last few months.

Family is everything. You have to be there for each other, no matter what, because no one will be there for you like your family.

Georgia finished her plate, noting that her father's was almost untouched. "Is everything all right?"

Ephraim wiped her mouth with his napkin. "Everything is...well, things are not good, *ziskiet*. I've decided to sell the house."

Startled, Georgia fumbled her fork. It clattered to the floor, leaving little red stains on the cream and blue linoleum.

"It's because of him, isn't it?"

Eight months ago, her father had been ripped off by his business partner. Abraham had been Ephraim's closest childhood friend. They had set up a small accounting firm in their mid-thirties. Things had gone very well for the first decade, their business had been small but stable. But Abraham had hidden the fact he had developed a gambling habit. He'd ended siphoning money from their client accounts—nearly a hundred thousand dollars.

It would have been a much larger amount, but Ephraim was an incredibly good accountant. He noticed the missing funds in a matter of weeks, although it had taken him another month to finger Abraham as the culprit.

That was because he'd tried so hard to convince himself it was one of the support staff. Ephraim had even considered the cleaning lady as a suspect before finally confronting Abraham. Guilt-ridden, the man had voluntarily retired from the business to avoid being prosecuted.

Ephraim, being who he was, had forgiven his friend.

"I thought things were fine now," Georgia said, trying not to sound as dismayed as she felt. "That you put everything right without endangering the business."

Ephraim took off his glasses again, wiping them needlessly. "I managed to replace the missing funds. But it was only a matter of time before word got around that Abraham left the business under a cloud."

Georgia put her head in her hands. "The rumor mill at the synagogue."

Her father sighed. "It was naïve of me to believe they wouldn't find out. These old birds are better than the CIA. I've lost half my clients."

All the air left her lungs in a rush. "*What*? But you put the money back."

Ephraim had raided his retirement fund and mortgaged the house to do it, but he'd replaced every cent Abraham had stolen.

Her dad rubbed his eyes with the back of his hand. "Confidence is everything in the accounting business. We were charged with handling people's money, the fruits of their labor, their very future. Abraham violated that trust."

"But they're punishing *you*. He doesn't even work there anymore!"

Sighing, Ephraim put his glasses back on. "It doesn't matter. Even the rumor of malfeasance is enough to make people pull their accounts."

His stooped shoulders rounded a touch more as if he were drawing into himself. Anymore and she'd have to convert a car door into a shell because he'd be a turtle.

"But some of those people have been with you for years," she protested.

"And a few clients did choose to stay. As for some of the others, it may have been the push they needed to go elsewhere. There are newer, flashier firms in town. Our operation has never been trendy. We gained our clients mostly through word of mouth because we were steady…dependable. But we aren't that anymore."

Wishing she hadn't eaten her entire meal, Georgia put her hands on her stomach. "Can you sell a house that is mortgaged?"

"Yes. And we should make enough from the sale to pay off the bank and put a down payment on a two-bedroom condo—if you still want to live with your old man, of course."

Unlike Mack, Georgia had never lived on her own. And she wasn't about to start now, not when Ephraim needed her so much.

"You're kidding, right? Do you know how expensive rent is in this town? I'd never be able to afford my own place, not without a roommate—that may as well be my favorite guy in the world."

Ephraim snickered, giving her a patently skeptical glance. But he didn't suggest she go off on her own. They'd had the 'young people need to live their own lives' conversation before. He knew Georgia would never move out. She had inherited her stubbornness from Diamond, a fact he liked to remind her of despite the fact she and her foster mother didn't have a drop of blood in common.

"What will you do about the office?" she asked.

"Close it."

She winced.

He wiped his forehead with his tablecloth. "It's not that bad. Without the office as overhead, things are more cost-effective. I can run a one-man operation out of our home with the clients who choose to stay."

"What about your secretary? The other staff?" There were two other junior accountants in addition to Margaret, his longtime assistant slash receptionist.

"They're already looking for new jobs." Ephraim gave her a tight smile. "I wrote them excellent letters of recommendation. It was the least I could do."

Knowing her father, he was ripping himself into little shreds for not being able to do more. *But maybe you can.*

"Dad...what about the Talbot?"

Ephraim blinked. "What about it?"

She took a deep breath. "What if we sell it?"

He reached over to pat her hand. "You're the one who insisted on fixing the old clunker. It's yours to do with as you wish—you never had to give it back to me."

The Talbot had originally belonged to Ephraim's grandfather. He'd passed the vehicle onto his son, who had promptly wrecked it. But Pop-Pop hadn't disposed of it. Instead, he threw a tarp over it and stuck it in the back of his garage, always intending to fix it up one day.

When Mack had become a mechanic, Ephraim had hoped he'd start the restoration of the classic car. But while Mack loved to tinker on his own projects, his frequently adversarial relationship with their parents meant he rarely touched the Talbot, much to Ephraim's disappointment. But he always held out hope Mack would change his mind, and it would be the thing that brought them together.

In many ways, Ephraim was naïve. But his once-placid and optimistic nature had taken too many blows.

Despite her intense desire to get her hands on the Talbot, Georgia hadn't touched it until after Mack was gone. One day, she'd come home from work, removed the tarp before pushing the car to the center of the garage as a sign that she was going to start working on it. Then she'd gone to take a shower before Ephraim arrived home.

She'd held her breath, anxious over her father's reaction. But he'd been so happy that she wanted to work on the car, he'd given it to her as a gift.

Georgia hadn't accepted. No, the car was going to be a present to

Ephraim for always being her home and her rock. A nerdy, socially inept rock, but her everything, nonetheless.

Except now the house was at stake.

"I might know of a buyer," she shared. "One of Elite's customers expressed an interest in the Talbot after he heard I was restoring one," she said, deciding not to mention her harebrained visit to Rainer Torsten's office.

It had been two weeks since she'd busted in on the man. She'd set up a Google alert on his name. The date of his appointment at the bank had come and gone without any mention of him in the news or gossip sites. Georgia assumed that meant he was all right.

There's a separate God for beautiful people. The way she had gaped at the man continued to send her into a shame spiral even now, all these weeks later.

It was especially disconcerting because her reaction had been so damned unexpected.

The business mogul who graced magazine covers was a handsome suit. Yes, Rainer was young and had striking features, but he was no different from the pretty men who graced the gossip rags at the checkout counter. Before meeting him, she'd thought his charity work was the most attractive thing about him.

However, in person, Rainer Torsten was devastating. No picture could convey the impact of those cheekbones or the intensity of his dark eyes. Someone like that didn't belong in an office. A master artist had carved every line, but what would have been cold perfection was softened by a generous mouth and sun-kissed skin with its own portable luminosity.

Rainer could have walked into a dark room, and she would have known where he was by the subtle glow he seemed to emanate.

Was it any surprise that Georgia's composure had crumbled? One look at the flesh-and-blood man and her stomach had nosedived to her feet, weakening her knees along the way.

She had never understood the word 'dumbstruck' until that moment. Georgia had been paralyzed under his hands, lips parted as she stared at him like an idiot. Judging from the amusement in his dark eyes, he'd been aware of her reaction. In his defense, it must have been hard to miss. But it still embarrassed her in retrospect.

She told herself it didn't matter. It wasn't as if she were ever going to see the man again—not even to offer the car. Instead, she could call his office and ask for Mr. Powell. The security man could function as a go-between if Rainer still wanted to buy the Talbot.

But her plans to offer the car to the venture capitalist had a major flaw.

Ephraim finished chewing his large bite of spaghetti. "Absolutely not," he said, coughing and reaching for his drinking glass. "I gave that car to you."

Georgia opened her mouth to argue, but Ephraim's lined face sagged. He reached over, squeezing her hand.

"Georgia, I was never sorry that you didn't get a degree, because cars are your life. But that's why you have to keep the Talbot. I couldn't pay for your college, but you will have a legacy from me. The Talbot stays in the family."

And that right there was what Mack had never understood about Ephraim. He wasn't just a foster father. To him, the relationship was real. To Mack, it had always rung false. But Georgia knew Ephraim considered her a daughter in every sense of the word. It was why she'd do anything for him.

From experience, she also understood that his tone meant 'case closed'.

"All right, Dad," she whispered, tears that she wouldn't let him see making her eyes burn. "We won't sell the Talbot."

CHAPTER SIX

Georgia set her body hammer down on the garage floor and knelt to stroke the Talbot's door panel. It had taken most of the afternoon, but it was finally as smooth under her fingers. Humming she walked around the car, inspecting it from every angle. A little switch in her head flipped, a pleasing rush of endorphins sweeping through her brain as she admired her handiwork.

She had spent every spare minute of the last week beating out the last lingering dents in the Talbot's body. Even though she had agreed not to sell it, she felt an urgency to get as much work done on the vehicle as quickly as possible. The prominent 'For Sale' sign that now graced the lawn was the reason.

Georgia turned her back to the offensive square of corrugated plastic, focusing on the sleek steel curves in front of her. If she hurried, she had just enough time to sand the hood and front panels before dinner. The rest of the car would have to wait for the weekend because she was pulling a double shift at Elite tomorrow and the next day—a string of oil changes and a tune-up.

Hopefully, there would be no overflowing toilets today. *And no criminals,* she tacked on mentally.

Georgia had cleaned the showroom bathrooms multiple times

since overhearing the kidnapping plot. At first, her heart had pounded, her body tense as she expected the men she'd overheard to come back and punish her for foiling their plans.

In reality, Georgia knew there was little chance of that. They hadn't seen her, and had no way of knowing she warned Torsten, but she hadn't been able to help her reaction. Georgia had been fight-or-flight ready, imagining every person who came in was them.

It had taken three or four shifts that included bathroom-cleaning duty for her to stop expecting a confrontation. The men hadn't returned.

Georgia still had no idea who they had been or if their plans had been real. However, as time went on without Rainer Torsten mentioned in the news, she grew increasingly convinced the security man had been right. There might have been a plan, but the parties involved had chickened out. More likely, there had never been a genuine intent to carry it out.

In retrospect, she was embarrassed to have gone to Torsten with the outlandish claim. She'd replayed the scene in her head every night since, dying a thousand deaths every time she'd crashed into the man's long, hard body. Even worse was the way her brain had shut down, leaving her gaping at him like a lovestruck fangirl.

As it turned out, he had quite a few of those.

After her visit, Georgia had done an internet deep dive on all things Rainer Torsten. In addition to all the glowing business profiles, there were dozens of mentions on celebrity gossip sites, the ones that stalked the rich as well as the famous.

There she'd seen pictures of Rainer at movie premiers and entering nightclubs, always with a gorgeous woman on his arm. She assumed they were models from their perfect bodies and faces. Meanwhile, Georgia was a short, skinny nobody, her body boyish in comparison to the often-voluptuous vixens Rainer preferred. Only one thing about them surprised her. More often than not, the models Rainer dated were women of color—mostly black.

From her search, it was also clear Rainer had a legion of female followers who tracked his every move, or they tried to. This last explained a great deal about the treatment Georgia had gotten from the security guys. She was surprised they'd bothered to hear her out at all.

It didn't help that her overactive brain dissected every word they'd exchanged, repeatedly and on a loop. Georgia had spent more than one night hugging a pillow as she talked herself down. Even if it had been a false alarm, she had done the right thing by reporting the threat. Wasn't 'see something, say something' still a thing?

Even if you did sound a false alarm, you weren't wrong to go. Yes, the security men had been suspicious, but they hadn't laughed her out of the room.

Georgia kicked one of the spare tires stored in the corner. *That's because they waited until you left.* Another wave of heated mortification swept over her, but she didn't have time to wallow. The past was the past. Even if she'd made a fool of herself, she'd done it for the right reasons. Which was why she now counted to ten, pushing the memory of Rainer's smirking mouth away.

The items on her to-do list were piling up. Next on the agenda—find boxes so she could start packing up her bedroom. No one had made an offer on the house yet, but there'd been a few inquiries. The realtor told them that housing was in such demand that they could expect an offer above their asking price, even in this older neighborhood.

That was good news, of course, but Georgia had still cried herself to sleep after the woman had shared that tidbit.

Because Ephraim was still at work, shuttering his office, Georgia allowed herself a few tears now. *A house isn't a home,* she assured herself. Home was family, which meant as long as she and Ephraim stuck together, she wasn't losing that. But it still hurt to think of losing the house. This was the place where Diamond, a librarian and mechanic's daughter, had taught Georgia how to cook *and* how to change her own tires.

Her foster mother had been the one to show her and Mack the ins and outs of car maintenance. Diamond kept her mechanic skills up because she considered it a cost-saving measure. Books were her first love, and she'd been a dedicated librarian for forty years.

As a child, Georgia used to spend hours in the kids' section while Diamond worked. Then, as a teen, she loved being able to read how-to manuals, to figure out how things worked. Books that broke down how to work on engines had been revelations.

"You can find anything in a book," Diamond had said when an astonished Georgia had run to the circulation desk to show her the glossy pictures in the hardback.

Thinking about that day brought a lump to her throat. But Georgia embraced the memory. Diamond wouldn't want her to look back at any of their time together with regret or melancholia. Her foster mother had been strong and sure of herself. Even cancer hadn't destroyed her innate sense of self or core competence. She tried to teach Georgia that, telling her that she had to learn to roll with the punches. Georgia liked to think she'd succeeded, although she would be the first to admit that all the years Diamond had spent coaxing her out of her shell were a spectacular failure.

Wiping her face on a clean spot on her sleeve, Georgia began to prep the sander to remove the lingering traces of rust and old paint.

The original color had been black, but she had sourced a deep rich burgundy that was era-appropriate. Painting the vehicle would normally be the last step for her, but she'd decided not to wait for those last few parts she needed to finish rebuilding the engine—Georgia had a few leads on where to find them.

If those didn't pan out, she would repurpose something a little more modern. It wasn't as if she were going to sell the car to a picky millionaire who insisted on complete authenticity. Not after Ephraim's reaction to the suggestion.

When Georgia moved her foot, a piece of metal bounced away with a tinkling sound.

"How did you get here?" she asked, picking up the round bolt she'd nudged with her boot. She was normally very meticulous when it came to taking engines apart—not a screw or nut out of place. "You're slipping, G…"

With many other mechanics, the engine parts would have been a scattered mess, but Georgia's compulsion for order reigned supreme in her garage. The bulk of the Talbot's engine block was spread out into partially assembled piles on the table, which she had made out of wooden pallets. The surface was the top of a metal desk someone had sawed off and left at the junkyard.

Walking around the engine block, she placed the missing bolt next to the carburetor she planned to install after the new fuel line came in. "Now don't run off again," she warned it.

"Do you always talk to your machinery?"

Gasping, Georgia snatched up the nearest object. Whirling around, she threw it at the voice. Belatedly, she recognized the tall man who stood just outside the garage's threshold.

Shit! She had just thrown her heaviest socket wrench at a millionaire.

CHAPTER SEVEN

Georgia's terrible aim saved the day. The heavy tool clattered to the floor a few feet away from Rainer's feet.

"Sorry. I didn't mean to scare you," he said, lifting his hands to show her that he was unarmed.

Then Rainer turned to the Talbot, his appreciation and admiration warming his expression. The transformation took him from cool sophisticate to luscious Greek demigod on the prowl. Even his hair was different. The stunning blue was brown now, taking him from a modern masterpiece to merely unapproachable. Perseus in blue jeans searching for his next conquest.

Her brain promptly short-circuited. Until she realized he hadn't come for *her*. He had come for the car.

Rainer moved toward the Talbot, crossing the threshold and officially invading her domain. Her eyes swam as it shrunk in size, going from a roomy two-car garage to a cramped shed, almost like a sci-fi effect in a movie.

"It's even more impressive in real life," he said, stroking the sleek curved hood.

"Thanks," she managed, her eyes roaming over him helplessly.

Rainer was dressed casually today, wearing a plain white t-shirt under a simple but expensive black leather racer jacket. It was paired with jeans that hugged his long legs so faithfully they had to be custom made. Either that or Rainer possessed the form designers pretended all men had but so few were blessed with.

The man in question didn't seem too distressed at having a wrench flung at him. It lay forgotten on the floor as he walked around the car.

Dazed, she watched as the space around him shifted like a kaleidoscope with a fixed center. *Damn*...I man must have been larger than life because he was bending reality around him, like an ultra-dense neutron star that sucked in all the matter, warping their surrounding space.

Blinking to clear her head, Georgia snapped her mouth shut after realizing she stood there gaping, openmouthed. *Girl, get a grip. He's just a man.*

But her brain kept telling her otherwise. She and this perfect specimen of humanity didn't live on the same plane of existence.

Luckily, Rainer was too preoccupied examining the vehicle to notice her awkward response to him. He ran his hands over the newly smooth doors, opening the passenger side to get a look at the leather interior and the refinished spoked steering wheel.

By the time he finally ripped his attention away from the car, she had regained some semblance of control.

"I'm sorry to drop by unannounced," he began. "I was visiting a friend who lives not far from here, and I decided to check if you were home."

Turning his head, he glanced at the 'For Sale' sign on the lawn. "Is this a bad time?"

A loud snort escaped. Mortified, Georgia clapped a hand over her mouth and nose. Okay, perhaps she wasn't as in control of herself as she believed.

Rainer shifted position, leaning a shoulder toward her. "I apologize. I should have called."

"You don't have my number."

He raised a brow.

"Oh." Georgia felt like an idiot. Of course he had her number.

Rainer was at her house. By now, he likely knew everything about her, down to her social security number. "I guess Mr. Powell found my address."

"Before you left the office," he confirmed. He shrugged when her eyes opened wide. "You did give us your real name and where you work. It was easy to find your information after that."

"Of course," she murmured, picking up the wrench on the floor.

"This is a nice setup," Rainer said, gesturing to the creeper ramp that allowed her to work on the Talbot's undercarriage. He reached up to touch the chain of the pulley and sling system she'd jerry-rigged to move engines by herself. "I take it the Talbot isn't the first engine you've taken apart in here. It's not your first restoration."

"No, I've done a dozen or so over the years, projects I teamed up on with friends or acquaintances who had a car in the family they wanted to fix up and sell. Also, a couple of junkyard salvages."

Those projects had earned enough for her to buy the Crown Victoria she drove. That model Ford was more popularly known as a cop car. Georgia liked it because it was easy to repair, and parts were easy to find. Also, she rarely got speeding tickets.

"I also do some work on the side for friends and other people." She waved at the open garage doors to encompass the neighborhood. "Our neighbors come here first if their cars start making weird noises."

"And I bet you fix them for free." There was that grin again as if he were amused by her small acts of charity.

"When I can," she said, her face heating in a Pavlovian response to his smile. "But people pay for their parts and give me something for the labor when they can. Muffins and brownies are standard. Sometimes casseroles."

"Casseroles?" he echoed.

She shrugged defensively. "Ephraim likes noodles."

Putting in some distance to try to get away from his gravity well, Georgia turned her back to set the wrench in its designated spot. "I guess the kidnapping didn't happen. I checked the news just in case, but I didn't see your name mentioned."

Rainer put his hands in his jacket pockets, leaning a hip against the sink counter fixed to the wall.

"Yeah, I'm safe and sound as you can see."

Georgia's eyes flicked to him, then away, as she pretended to rearrange her tools.

"Nothing happened, right?" Surely he would have said 'thank you' or something similar had there been an attempt to kidnap him.

But Rainer surprised her. "I don't think so."

She turned back to him with a frown. "*Think*?"

He lifted a shoulder. "We pushed the appointment at the bank back by half an hour. Aside from someone opening a fire exit door, which triggered an alarm, it was business as usual."

Georgia pursed her lips. "And Mr. Powell agrees—about the alarm being nothing?"

He chuckled, the rich sound traveling down from her ears with a frisson as if she'd been stroked with fur. "Well, for a while there, he was *extremely excited*. The extra security guys we brought swarmed down there very impressively. But there was nothing to be found. That particular door gets opened without authorization a lot so the few smokers in the building can sneak a cigarette outside. All the stairwells have a smoke detector."

"Oh." Her shoulders dropped a fraction.

Rainer laughed again. "Sorry to disappoint you."

This time, she joined him, snickering lightly. "Of course, I'm glad you're safe. But I was so sure that those men were serious. I would never have gone to your office like that otherwise."

"I believe you." Rainer shifted to stand a bit straighter. "There's nothing in your background to suggest you're an attention seeker. Quite the opposite."

Now Georgia was just weirded out. "Just how deep did Mr. Powell go snooping?"

Rainer bit his lip. "He's pretty thorough. You got the full workup, I'm afraid," he said, a slight trace of apology in his voice. "As did your foster parents."

Georgia took a deep breath. *Wow.* He didn't even try to hide digging into her past. But she reminded her she had asked for it.

"I guess you know all about Ephraim's partner stealing from him," she muttered. "That must have been a big red flag."

Rainer nodded, but his face remained open, not unkind. "Powell did bring it up as a possible motive. He thought you concocted the story to try to get some reward money out of me. Maybe got some friends to playact that recording."

Georgia's heart skipped a beat. "Wow. That is...very plausible."

He dismissed that with a wave of his hand. "It would have been, had you come back to try again. Also, you don't appear to have any men in your life who would conspire to make that audio recording."

She burst out laughing. "Ouch."

It was Rainer's turn to blush. He winced. "I didn't mean it the way it sounded—it's just that the other mechanics at Elite have different voiceprints. We checked."

The sheer effort that had gone into investigating her was staggering. "I do have other friends," she blurted, a touch indignant.

"Girlfriends, yes. But the only real man in your life is your foster father."

Georgia rocked back on her heels with an amused laugh. The man didn't pull any punches.

Hey, your sad sack of a life is an actual bonus here, she chided herself. She wasn't a suspect in his eyes. Powell was another story.

Speaking of... "I'm surprised your security people let you out on your own, sans bodyguard."

The twitch in his cheek told her Powell had argued about letting him do just that. But Rainer was the boss. "We're not at Defcon one anymore," he said with a shrug. "I told him we could stand down."

"That's good, I guess."

"I do think you heard something real," Rainer added generously. "But like I said in my office, most people don't carry out their threats."

Georgia nodded. "Well, keep being careful just in case. Vigilance and all that..."

It was what her mother would have said, albeit more boldly and with greater confidence. Diamond would have convinced both Rainer and Powell that a threat existed on the first try.

"I will," he said. "However, I didn't come here to discuss the plot you overheard."

"I know. But nothing has changed. I still can't sell you the car."

"Are you *very* sure?" The look that accompanied the question could have melted butter. Georgia had to resist the urge to fan herself.

"I *can't*." She threw up her hands. "I spoke to my father after I saw you, floated the idea of selling… It didn't go well."

"What if I spoke with him?" Rainer's gaze moved covetously over the Talbot. "I'm sure I could talk him around."

The mental image of the 'For Sale' sign blazed across her mind. "Well…he technically gave it to me as a gift. But he wants it to stay in the family."

Ephraim would forgive her for selling it, but if she tried to give him the cash to save the house, he might not take it.

Scenting blood, Rainer didn't say a word. He simply waited, displaying a patient cunning that must have served him well during business negotiations.

You can't afford to pass this up. "Let me talk to him again."

Rainer beamed at her. That small, pathetic part of her that was greedy for his smiles panted like an eager puppy.

"Don't get your hopes up." She scowled, turning to the driveway at the sound of a car engine. "He's pretty set on the car staying in the family."

"Leave that to me," Rainer promised, rubbing his hands together in anticipation. "Is that him? I can talk to him right now."

But he didn't get a chance. Georgia squinted at the drive. The engine she heard wasn't Ephraim's. She knew what his sedan sounded like it, and this wasn't it.

She was about to check it out—the car was idling at the mouth of the drive—when there was a popping sound. The next thing she knew, she went flying through the air, a heavy weight crushing her to the ground.

Rainer had tackled her. His big hand had moved up to protect her head, but it didn't work. The back of her skull rapped on the sealed concrete floor twice in quick succession. Pain, too much to process, bloomed. Her ears began to ring, the high pitch drowning everything else out.

Rainer leapt off her. His body was silhouetted against the dying evening light as everything closer to her darkened. Two other massive forms appeared in the threshold. They moved inside, going for Rainer.

Dazed, she blinked at the three men who seemed to struggle in slow motion. Her vision blinked in and out, catching one shadowy form trying to hold two off.

Two against one, Rainer should have had no chance.

My phone. She had to get her phone to call the police. Or Powell. Why the hell had Powell caved and let Rainer come out here on his own?

She tried to crawl to the table in an attempt to reach her phone. Before she could, Rainer stood over her. He held a bloody crowbar, which she numbly realized belonged to her.

His lips moved, but she couldn't hear any words coming out. Rainer turned to look behind him. It appeared as if he were shouting at someone.

Then he picked her up, cradling her in his arms before hustling her out of the garage.

CHAPTER EIGHT

Rainer crossed his arms, tapping his foot impatiently as his private physician examined Georgia.

"I'm okay now," Georgia protested, trying to get up from the exam table for the second time.

Finally losing it, he crossed the room to hover over her.

"Lay back down or I will physically restrain you," he said sternly. "I don't want you to move until the doctor says you can."

Behind Georgia, Dr. Bennett did a double-take. His personal physician had never seen Rainer behave like this. *Fuck it*. Rainer had never *felt* like this.

Georgia settled back in the bed, her fine features tightening, a hand over her stomach as if she felt nauseated. *Because I broke her damn head.*

Rainer hadn't protected her well enough when he threw himself over her, removing her from the line of fire. Now her skull might be fractured.

Georgia hadn't even been able to pick herself up off the floor, not answering his anxious inquiries about her health. She'd just blinked at him owlishly. It had taken more than seven minutes—a fucking eternity—for her to reply coherently, but still far too sluggishly.

Powell had tried to insist the doctor take a look at him first, but Rainer had shut that down with a single blistering glare. *He* was fine—a little bruised, and one of the bones in his hand might be cracked from throwing punches before he picked up the crowbar—but it was Georgia who needed immediate medical attention.

"Where are the X-rays you ordered?" he asked the doctor while watching Georgia like hawk.

"Let me check." The physician stepped into the hall, returning with a large envelope. He slipped the X-rays out, then placed them on one of the illuminated boxes fixed to the wall. "Good news. There's no fracture. A minor concussion at worst."

"*Minor*?" He scowled. "Are you sure?"

"Would you rather I have a fractured skull?" Georgia asked.

The hint of amusement in her tone made the tight twist in his gut start to unravel. She was beginning to sound normal again.

Bennet clapped him on the shoulder. "I recommend close supervision and a little TLC—along with a course of painkillers to be taken as needed. Also, no sex for at least a week."

Georgia's cheeks flamed, but Bennet excused himself to organize the prescription. "Why did he tell you that, and not me?" she asked, her lips twitching.

"He assumed we were a couple."

One of her brows raised. She gestured at the coveralls she wore. These were a plain grey, not the black that was the standard Elite company issue. "Was it my glamorous outfit that decided him?"

Rainer passed a hand over his face, leaning against the exam table until they were almost touching. "I'm sorry you were hurt."

"Not your fault." A fine line appeared between her brows. "At least, I don't think it was. I'm not entirely sure what happened."

Georgia reached up to touch the back of her head, wincing. "One minute, we were talking. The next, I was on the ground."

"So, you don't remember me tackling you?"

Her rosebud mouth pursed. "You *did* knock me down," she said, her disbelief mingling with indignation.

"You don't remember being shot at?"

Her eyes flared wide. "Someone shot at me?"

"No." He shook his head. "Someone shot at *me*."

It took a moment for that to sink in. "Oh. *Oh…*"

A tiny nod as she began to piece everything together. "You fought them off."

"The bullet came first. One of the men shot wide, into the garage. The bullet hit the wall."

It had been a small caliber—something meant to scare and possibly incapacitate him. But it wasn't a bullet that would do a lot of damage. The kidnappers hadn't wanted to kill him. Not before they got their ransom.

His instincts about Georgia's inherent kindness were proven right when she didn't say 'I told you so'.

Rainer pulled up a chair, dragging it next to the exam table before sitting. "I want to apologize for bringing those people to your door. Because of my visit today, the kidnappers know where you live."

Georgia's lips parted, and she tried to scramble up. "*Ephraim*."

A hand on her stomach, he urged her back down. "He's fine. Ephraim arrived shortly after we left. Powell had a man waiting for him."

Her lashes fluttered. "Why?"

This was the part that could get sticky. "We're relocating him."

Lips parting, she gaped. "Oh."

"The house has been compromised," he said, echoing Powell's assessment. "The kidnappers could come back at any time."

She nodded slowly. "Did you take him to a hotel or something?"

"No," he said. "To an apartment in a building that I have part ownership in."

She shuddered at the word *ownership*, her glance flicking down. Abruptly, he straightened, removing the hand he'd splayed across her abdomen.

Georgia's breathing slowed. "So, he's safe?"

"Yes." Rainer hesitated. "Please don't take this the wrong way, but, luckily, you're moving. I would hate to leave you in a vulnerable position. I think it best that we move all your things into the same apartment as Ephraim. It has four bedrooms and an office—there's plenty of room for you both. Any furniture that doesn't fit can go in one of the basement storerooms if necessary."

Her face fell, silent confirmation of his suspicion. Selling the family home hadn't been voluntary. They were being forced to do it because of the shutdown of Ephraim's business.

"Are you sure moving is necessary?"

He studied her face. Powell still had his doubts, but Rainer's instincts said that she wasn't involved. After a year or more of second-guessing himself, he was going to listen to his gut. Hell, Georgia's innocence might be the only thing he *was* certain about in this mess.

She had tried to help him, to warn him that he had a target on his back. She had been in the wrong place at the right time, and now she was hurt, her safety compromised. Rainer was responsible for her because of it.

One of the reasons Rainer kept getting written up in the trade mags was the way he treated people, the employees under him, and the professionals he did business with. Rainer demanded excellence and rewarded loyalty.

Even when his staff messed up—royally in one instance—he hadn't fired them. As long as they made the effort to fix their mistakes, he dealt with them fairly. And he didn't fire anyone without cause. He'd also never leave his people to hang for someone else's mistakes. It was his fault the kidnappers had found out about Georgia. He wasn't going to abandon her to deal with the consequences on her own.

She was his people now.

"Yes," he told her, the weight of responsibility settling on his shoulders. "But don't worry. I'm going to make sure you're safe."

Judging from her pale and clammy appearance, his words were little comfort. "If it's the men I recorded in the bathroom, how did they find you?"

"I was followed from my office."

Rainer had planned to make an offer for the Talbot since Georgia had first come by. Powell had found her social media accounts. She'd documented a fair number of previous restorations—and a few mods —of all types of vehicles.

Not that Rainer needed proof of her skill before making an offer for the Talbot. He would have taken it as it was. After seeing the quality of her work, though, he'd decided to hold off and give her a chance to make more progress on the classic car.

Part of him had also been waiting for the threat against him to materialize. But when weeks passed without anything happening, he grew complacent. So, he'd gone to see her. But the actual time and date of the visit had been unplanned.

Fortunately for him, his head of security had successfully argued against pulling his security detail. Though Rainer had chosen to drive himself around, a discreet sedan carrying two of the junior security guys had followed him.

Eager to reclaim his independence, Rainer didn't allow them to enter buildings with him, not unless he had an engagement that would take longer than an hour.

Waters had noticed Rainer had a tail as soon as he left his office, but the car—a black Honda with tinted windows—was soon lost in traffic. Waters reported the incident, but he'd dismissed it when the car didn't pop back up. When he got to Georgia's, his people parked a little down the street, keeping the open garage door in sight.

They hadn't expected the kidnappers to come back.

The black Honda had crept down the street at a normal speed before abruptly turning in Ephraim's driveway. The gunshot had been a warning, something intended to scare Rainer into going quietly. His assailants hadn't known his people were watching everything from down the street.

They also hadn't counted on him fighting back.

Thanks to 'the incident,' Rainer had taken the steps to prepare himself for a physical confrontation after his buddy, Garrett, had talked him into investing in Auric, a private security firm.

The company had been founded by Elias Gardner, a friend of Garrett's who had gone the military route. Elias had tapped his cousin, Ian Quinn, another former soldier, as his partner in the venture. When the former Army Ranger and Navy Seal decided they had wanted to expand their operation, Garrett had jumped at the opportunity to be a part of it, bringing Rainer on board at the same time.

They were supposed to be silent partners with minority stakes, but Rainer had been feeling insecure since the breach. That was why Garrett had suggested they both train with the new team their investment dollars had allowed Auric to field.

"You can surround yourself with bodyguards, but you aren't going to feel secure until you learn to defend yourself," his friend had pointed out.

Rainer had reluctantly agreed. Mason, the team leader, had whupped his butt. Big time. He made Rainer run army-grade obstacle courses, taught him weapons, and a variety of hand-to-hand fighting techniques. Mason also became a good friend in the process.

Thanks to that training, Rainer had been able to hold off the two men who came after him.

Today's fight had been short and brutal. Once he'd pushed Georgia out of the way, Rainer rolled and sprang to his feet with a move that would have made Mason proud. He'd blocked the first man who'd gone to pin his arms, kicking up to push away the second. Spinning, he'd lunged for a wrench from the rack of tools. His hand found a crowbar instead. Rainer had used it to break one of the fucker's arms.

But the kidnappers had a getaway driver in the Honda. The third man had seen Waters and his companion come barreling down the street. When he'd honked to warn them, the men had broken off their attack, making it to their vehicle before his people could stop them. Ephraim's driveway had two huge black tire streaks left by the Honda as it pealed out.

There was a knock at the door. Powell opened it, signaling for Rainer to step out.

Murmuring his excuses to Georgia, he joined his head of security in the hall.

"Did you find the Honda?"

Powell shook his head.

Rainer growled. "Keep looking."

"I will, but it's the most common car on the road, down to the make and the color," Powell warned. "And they've probably changed the plates."

"What about traffic cams? Can we track them that way?"

"Already on it," Powell assured him.

Sighing, Rainer rubbed his face. Once Powell left to keep coordinating the search, he turned back to Georgia. She appeared lost in thought, her eyes fixed on the wall.

She looked so small and vulnerable lying there. Pity warred with an intense feeling of protectiveness. It would be so easy for the kidnappers to tie the address of the house back to Georgia and Elite motors. She couldn't go back to work any more than she could go home.

But she'll insist on it. The girl who quietly worked in a field so heavily dominated by men would want to go back to work. Georgia would want to get as many hours in as she could to help Ephraim.

Unless you get her out of town.

Returning to her side, he hesitated. He didn't have the right to comfort her physically. But when she turned those big hazel eyes up at him, suddenly *not* touching her seemed wrong.

Wrapping an arm around her, he leaned her against his side. "Georgia, I'm going to need you to trust me."

Her response blindsided him with its simple faith. "I do trust you. What do you need?"

CHAPTER NINE

Georgia buckled her seatbelt with a sense of awe and disbelief at her luxurious surroundings. This plane could comfortably hold a dozen people. Two couches faced each other with a leather chair at either end. Each of these had a fancy control panel that would elevate the footrest and lower the back, turning each chair into a fully reclining bed.

Rainer told her the jet wasn't his—it was a charter from a company he contracted to fly him all over the world. But it was still private. Aside from the crew, they were the only people on board. Not even that terrifying man, Stewart Powell, was aboard.

"We're not going to need security where we're going," Rainer said when they first boarded the plane.

The response had puzzled her, but she'd been too overwhelmed at the time to argue or ask for more details. But after a few hours of flight, reclining in the plush leather chair while sipping on the endless fruit juices the air hosts kept bringing, she felt better. Less muddled now, she started to doubt her actions.

Georgia had put herself in Rainer Torsten's hands. She didn't even know where he was taking her.

He'd also told her she couldn't go back to work, arranging for her to take a leave of absence from Elite. "They won't fire you," he assured her when she panicked, concerned Mitch would use the leave as an excuse to let her go. "I'm too good a client for them to offend."

"What did you tell them?" she asked curiously.

"Just that I needed to borrow you for a special project." When she frowned, he added. "I may have strongly implied it had to do with the Talbot. I think they assumed I came across it on your Instagram, and I didn't correct them—they have no reason to think you came to me. Not unless you told them."

She assured him that she hadn't. "What about Ephraim? Why couldn't he come with us?"

He lifted a shoulder. "Because it's easier for two to drop off the grid than it is three. Also, Ephraim expressed concerns about going dark. He wanted to keep in touch with his remaining clients. If he doesn't stay available to them, he might lose them, and I didn't want to add to his stress levels."

Her leaving had done that already. But Rainer was right. If Ephraim disappeared right now, he would lose those last few clients. And that would irreparably damage what was left of Ephraim's self-esteem. So much of his sense of self came from pride in his work and having his clients' trust. Not that he had been thinking about them at all this morning.

"Don't worry about me, Georgia," her father had told her just before they left for the airport. "You just stay safe."

It was strange that Ephraim hadn't questioned Rainer's ability to do that. But then he might have assumed the man's many bodyguards would be accompanying them.

Beat, Georgia took a deep breath and closed her eyes, but that proved to be a mistake as the world beyond her lids began to spin with vertigo.

She opened her eyes to find Rainer leaning over her. He held the bottle of prescription painkillers his doctor had given her. "It's time for another dose."

It was at least an hour ahead of schedule, but Georgia wasn't about to argue. The pounding in her head had resumed and what little breakfast Rainer had coaxed her into eating was starting to swirl unpleasantly in her stomach. She didn't want to throw up on these nice leather seats.

Too weak to argue, she meekly held out her hand. He shook two pills out onto her palm, then fetched her a bottle of water from a hidden mini-refrigerator next to her seat.

Georgia sat up in surprise. Unless you were aware of it, you'd never know the tiny compartment was there.

"That is seamless," she marveled, briefly distracted from her pain. She stroked the sleek panel with her fingers. "The fridge doesn't even hum."

Georgia looked up to find Rainer watching her with an amused expression.

"What?" she asked, heat creeping up her neck.

He leaned back in his chair. "You're the first woman to admire the fridge, not because it holds bottles of Crystal in addition to water and soda, but because of its design."

She snorted. "Had a lot of women in this plane, huh?"

"Once upon a time," he replied. "But I think it was a different plane. This appears to be a newer model. It's been a while since I went anywhere with anyone."

"I see," she said, desperately trying to convince herself that she wasn't jealous of those women, no matter how far back in the past they were. "Taking a dating hiatus?"

"Of a sort." His expression unreadable, Rainer looked around him. "Where is that attendant? I could use a coffee."

Georgia turned to her other side, randomly pushing on the other panels.

Hand halfway up, Rainer froze, studying her. "What are you doing?"

"Looking for the coffee machine."

The corner of his mouth pulled back. "I'm afraid the fridge is the only hidden compartment we can expect."

"Hey, I'll have you know that I once had to redo the dash of an '89

Ford Fiesta because the owner wanted me to install a mini-Keurig under the radio."

"I don't believe it." He laughed. "Why would anyone mod a Fiesta?"

She held up a hand, imitating a Girl Scout. "I swear it's true. The car belonged to an old friend of my foster mom. She was sentimentally attached to it."

Chuckling, Rainer pulled out a laptop from his satchel, his attention already elsewhere.

"So…are you going to tell me where we're going?"

The mirth bled from his expression, transforming him into someone stern and forbidding. "We're going dark."

Her pulse quickened at the ominous words. "What does that mean?"

Leaning back in his seat, Rainer crossed one of his long legs over the other. "You're in this mess because of me. I'm responsible for you now. So, I'm taking you someplace where no one can find us. This will give my people time to find the men who came after me. Until they do, we're keeping communication with the outside world at a minimum. It is also best that you don't know exactly where we are, just in case monitored. For that reason, I'm not giving you back your phone, not right away."

Her lips parted. Until that moment, Georgia hadn't even realized she didn't have the thing on her. "But I'll need to talk to my dad."

He nodded. "Of course. I'll arrange it through Powell. Once we get where we're going, you'll be able to talk to him every day."

Georgia stilled, telling herself that the sensation of the walls closing in around her was only in her head.

"But only through you?" Would he be there, listening to her conversations?

Rainer must have been able to sense her apprehension. "It's temporary," he assured her. "My people are the best. They're going to catch these guys in a couple of days—a week tops."

He waited for a response.

Georgia smiled weakly. "Who am I to doubt your Mr. Powell?"

❧

Rainer knew Georgia was upset with him. Her face gave away her every emotion, enough for him to see the trace of resentment she felt over his high-handedness. But the lingering effects of her head injury and innate shyness meant she didn't argue. She simply withdrew, becoming noticeably quiet for the remainder of the flight.

Of course, part of that was the medication. It made her sleepy. She nodded off during the last hour. When the landing failed to rouse her, he gathered her in his arms and carried her out to the Jeep himself.

The four-wheel drive was necessary for the trip up the mountain.

Forty minutes later, he pulled up in front of a cabin surrounded by pines on three sides. The sprawling log structure was just as Garret described. Nudging Georgia awake, he murmured. "We're here."

Her long lashes fluttered. She blinked, sitting up with a dazed expression. One look at their surroundings and she undid her seatbelt, scrambling outside.

Georgia sucked in a breath, the cold enough to make her exhale into fog. "Snow!" she exclaimed, bending over to scoop up a handful.

A light but dirty dusting covered the ground. "It's not very clean," he pointed out with a wince. "It hasn't snowed here for over a month, but with the cold temperatures, it hasn't had a chance to melt."

His friend Garret warned him that it could make the road a little hazardous if it got below freezing, with hidden patches of black ice. But Rainer had driven well below the speed limit on snow tires.

His guest was precious cargo.

And, apparently, that guest enjoyed the snow. *Well, at least someone does.* Rainer sighed, wishing he could have used his property in the Bahamas instead. But retreating to a known haunt would have defeated the purpose.

"Holy shit," Georgia murmured as he ushered her toward the six-bedroom cabin lodge. She had been so distracted by the snow that she hadn't looked at it. "I thought we were supposed to be in hiding?"

Rainer dropped their bags just inside the threshold. One step below them was a large open space with a living room on their left and a shiny chrome kitchen on the right. The two areas were separated by a bar that doubled as a kitchen island.

His mouth pulled down. "We are."

She raised her arms as if trying to touch the ten-foot-high ceiling. "This is hiding?" She laughed. "It looks like a freaking hotel."

Rainer smiled at her enthusiasm, even if he didn't share it. "This place belongs to my friend Garret. No one knows he owns it, so they can't trace it back to him—or me by extension."

He stopped in front of the massive fireplace across from the couch. "I'm sorry it's not going to be all that much fun. Garrett only uses this place when there's a good snowfall projected. He likes to ski."

Georgia's lips twitched. "You are apologizing because you brought me to a luxurious mountain lodge?"

Rainer lifted a shoulder. "I've never been one for winter sports. I would much rather be at my place in the Bahamas, lounging at the pool."

Georgia sidled up to him, peeking out the window next to the fireplace. There wasn't much of a view—a short distance away, the pines began to crowd the house. "*Oh.* Well, now I'm sorry we're not in the Bahamas, too."

"Well, Garrett did mention a hot tub."

He'd meant the words to be commonplace, but even he heard the undercurrent of innuendo that somehow got away from him. Judging from her blush, so did Georgia.

"For the residual bruising," he explained with an awkwardness he hadn't felt since he was a teenager. "You can use it as much as you like. The solar panels on the roof mean we'll never run out of power. Many of the bedrooms also have a gas fireplace, supplied by a big tank outside."

But despite the nap in the car, Georgia was starting to fade, wilting before his eyes. "I think the grand tour can wait until after a nap," he said. "Unless you'd like to eat first?"

"Not hungry." Sitting on the armrest of the couch, she sighed, slumping over. "I don't get why I'm so tired. I hurt my head, not my body."

Her words managed to keep his eyes from roaming over that tight curvy figure—but only just. Georgia was small, but that just meant Rainer could pin her against the wall with ease.

Stop that. She has a head injury, he reminded himself. But his mind flashed back to that moment in his office when they'd first met. The way she'd looked at him—a slightly shocked visceral appreciation normally reserved for great works of art.

Powell had noticed, too. "She looked at you as if you were made of gold."

Of course, that had just made his head of security suspicious, but Rainer had read the genuine discomfort in her face. Georgia was embarrassed by her reaction to him. She still was, judging by the way she'd turn away or duck her head whenever he caught her watching him.

Fuck it. I like the way she looks at me—like she can't help herself.

He liked that a lot. But now was not the time. Rainer was responsible for Georgia. Not to mention the fact that they were being targeted by kidnappers with unknown resources. Once they were out of danger, he'd reevaluate the Georgia situation.

"It takes time to recover from a blow to the head," he said. "But I don't want you to worry. Even though we're here alone, we're not cut off from civilization. I have a direct line to Dr. Bennett's office, and there's a fully equipped medical lab a short drive down the mountain if you need it. We have an appointment tomorrow morning."

"We do?"

Resolve crumpling in the face of her honest bewilderment, he moved to put his hands on her shoulders. "Georgia, I would never take you to the middle of nowhere with a head injury without a plan."

He moved his hands to stroke gently, liking how dainty she felt under his palms. "This area may not be extremely popular in the off-season, but when the snowy season officially starts, it will be full of rich people getting their rocks off by hurtling down the mountain on sticks. This means all the proper amenities are in place—including a full-time rescue chopper. If you have a bad reaction to the medication or your symptoms get worse, I can call that helicopter to come get us if we can't make the drive down."

"Wow," Georgia breathed. "A helicopter. That's intense."

She smirked suddenly. "You really hate the snow, don't you?"

"I hate the cold, period." He held out his hand. "C'mon, let me show you where you'll be sleeping."

Her small hand fit itself into his as she followed him to the guest room next to the master suite. If she needed anything in the middle of the night, all she had to do was call out to him.

CHAPTER TEN

The local medical clinic was at one end of a low-key strip mall off the main road of the small town located down the mountain. Rainer told the staff they were a married couple, last name Smith. He even had a fake ID to present to the receptionist.

The doctor took her vitals, asked her a few questions. Her answers apparently satisfied him, because he soon clapped his hands and sent them on their way with a complimentary bottle of painkillers. The entire appointment took thirty minutes.

After agreeing to go for coffee, they took a short walk down the tiny strip that boasted itself as the downtown area before climbing into the Jeep to make the return trip. She took the fake ID from Rainer, comparing it to her state-issued driver's license.

The counterfeit in her hands was flawless. Except for the fake name, the two were identical. "Where did you get this made?" she asked, tracing the holographic symbols with her finger.

Rainer chuckled. "Honestly, I have no idea. I have a 'don't ask, don't tell' policy with Powell. But it's part of the whole traveling incognito thing."

Something in his tone made her wonder. "Is this the first one he's made for you?"

His hands turned the wheel with deft, expert movements. "No. He's had a few others made for me, pre-kidnapping threat."

Georgia frowned. "Why?"

"To check into hotels under assumed names mainly."

Her stomach did a sharp nosedive to the floor of the Jeep. "Why would you need to do that?"

For women, her mind whispered. Either to avoid them—and he did have fans. Had one stalked him? Or maybe it was for another reason... like hiding an affair with a married woman.

But Rainer's reason was far more prosaic. "We mainly use them when we go overseas for business to places where kidnapping is a threat." He sighed. "I never thought I'd need them here at home."

"Oh," she said, biting her lip. "Sorry."

"Not your fault." He glanced over, his eyes dark.

He reached over, then patted her hand. The small gesture spread heat radiating out from her hand to the rest of her body. Suppressing a groan, she wished she could lower the heat without being obvious.

"You can keep the ID," he said. "You know, after."

"I don't know what I would need one for, but thanks." She examined the forged ID again, turning it over in her hands. "If I'd had a fake this good in high school, I could have done some serious damage," she murmured.

"Why Georgia, I had no idea you were a bad girl."

She wanted to imagine there was a touch of sexual suggestion in the comment, but Georgia knew that playful huskiness she heard was just in her head.

Rainer wasn't flirting. He was simply a kind man, concerned for her well-being. It made her sad little crush on him all the more pathetic.

It didn't help that he was also protective. Rainer hovered attentively, helping her in and out of vehicles. That close proximity kept pushing her off balance. Not that she needed to be near him to react. Her body flushed whenever Rainer entered the room. Georgia lived in a constant state of blush. She sometimes wondered how he could stand next to her and not feel the heat she generated.

But at this moment, his eyes were on the road. She could drink him in to her heart's content. "Sadly, no. I was a giant nerd, of the gear-head variety," she confessed. "But a fake ID could have come in handy getting beer to trade for parts."

"Parts?" He frowned.

"Car parts."

"Oh." He laughed. "I didn't realize beer was a valid currency for those."

"It was at the local junkyard where I used to scavenge for parts."

He hummed. "I see. So, the interest in cars came early?"

"Yeah. My foster mother taught me. Her dad and grandad were both mechanics. She taught Mack first because he was older, but she only showed him basic car maintenance. Then, I started tearing lamps and my alarm clock apart to figure out how they worked."

She smiled, staring dreamily out the window. Those childhood memories of her and Mack puttering around the family sedan were good, untainted by what happened later.

"When I went after the vacuum cleaner, Diamond decided to channel all that energy more productively. She said it was okay to mess with anything in her car as long I could put it back together afterward."

"And did you?"

"Well...eventually. But there was more than one occasion when Ephraim had to drive Diamond to work."

Rainer grinned. "I bet he didn't mind."

"No, he didn't. Ephraim used to worship the ground she walked on," she agreed. "They were really sweet. She used to tell him he was better than Rain man, saying he was both Dustin Hoffman and Tom Cruise rolled into one."

"Aww..."

"Yeah, she tended to gild the lily. But nicely..."

"And what did Ephraim call Diamond?"

"He used to call her his emerald. They're technically rarer and more precious than diamonds."

"Well, fuck. My parents were nowhere near that nice to each

other."

Georgia straightened in her seat. "Oh. Sorry to hear that."

He shrugged. "Eh. It is what it is." The tone was flippant, but there was a dark, deep undercurrent there.

Deciding discretion was the better part of valor, she changed the subject. "I'm a little surprised the clinic was so well equipped for such a tiny, nondescript place," she added after a minute of silence. "It even had a helicopter."

The shiny white and red machine had been sitting on a helipad a little behind the building and to the right.

"I'm not sure if that one is theirs or if it's the one that belongs to the emergency services," Rainer said, looking through the Jeep's windshield around at the mountain as if it had personally offended him. "Occasionally, a couple of hikers get lost in the woods. That's why they need the chopper. Also, to airlift anyone who skis into a tree."

He glanced at her, noting the amusement on her face. "It happens more often than you'd think," he added darkly. "That's how Sonny Bono died."

She inclined her head. "Tell you what, the next time we go into hiding, we'll do it at a beach."

The teasing words were meant to nudge him into a smile, but he only grew grimmer.

"We are going to get these guys. And when we do, they're going away for good." Hands tight on the steering wheel, he shook his head. "I'm not letting this happen again."

Georgia's head jerked to stare at him. "*Again*? Have—have you been almost kidnapped before?"

"Not exactly," he said after a short, sharp silence. Rainer's cheekbones were starkly prominent. "Let's just say I have a security team for a reason."

The atmosphere in the car grew heavy, enough that she decided not to ask what had happened—despite her avid curiosity. Georgia was hungry for every morsel of knowledge about him, but she also wouldn't hurt him for the world. And whatever had happened to him had hurt, deep enough to leave scars.

And you know all about those. Better leave well enough alone.

Because while Rainer was nice enough to take care of her while she was injured, he wasn't as open as he appeared. He wouldn't ever confide in her.

After returning to the cabin, Rainer announced he was going to do some work in the office. Worn out by the short trip, Georgia retreated to her room, too tired to take advantage of the insane amenities.

The king-sized bed had some sort of space-age mattress topped with a cozy comforter and a mound of pillows she wanted to keep. There was also a huge flatscreen mounted to the wall opposite that appeared to get every channel under the sun.

In addition to the satellite television, there was a full bookshelf crammed full of bestsellers, which made her like Garrett despite the fact he had bought a secret cabin to hide from the wife he was divorcing.

Rainer insisted it wasn't a move to hide assets. "Both sides come from money," he explained. "In amounts that mean buying a place like this isn't going to make a dent in his bottom line."

Georgia was skeptical, but Rainer explained that his friend *was* a good guy, going through a nasty divorce. "He just needs a bolt hole when things get too tense."

Bolt hole? More like a party pad, Georgia sniffed internally. The hot tub Rainer had mentioned turned out to be half a dozen. Each room had one just outside the sliding doors that led to the deck wrapped around the back half of the lodge. Garrett appeared to entertain a lot, and he'd renovated the lodge to maximize its house-party potential.

You forget Rainer has his own party pad in the Bahamas. Georgia tried not to find that thought depressing. But it was.

❧

The following days fell into a regular pattern. Georgia would sleep in, a luxury she couldn't afford in her daily life, thanks to the fact Mitch dictated her schedule at Elite. He gave her all the late night and early morning shifts—all the ones he didn't take himself.

After a leisurely morning, she'd join Rainer for lunch before going back to her room to read or study new-to-her car manuals online. At least she tried to. Easily fatigued by her head injury, she'd end up sprawled on the bed, passed out. It was as if she were catching up on the last five years of sleep.

While she did her best *Sleeping Beauty* impersonation, Rainer worked remotely. She wasn't entirely sure what a venture capitalist did. According to Google, the simple answer was funding new startups, but it had to be more involved than that, judging from the amount of time Rainer spent in his office. He didn't emerge until dark when he would come into her room to wake her for dinner.

It wasn't until the fourth evening that she realized all the delicious meals he served were frozen.

"Did you have a gourmet restaurant prepare all of this for you?" she asked, pretending they were sitting across from each other at a chic romantic French bistro.

"I think it's a catering service. Garrett uses them every time he comes up here. He's not much of a cook."

"I guess you're not much of one either," Georgia teased, tasting her dish, a hash Parmentier made with scallops and lobster mixed with cod in a cream sauce.

"No," he admitted with a smile. "I'm only decent at making breakfast. I can fix pancakes from scratch and my hash browns are *tight*, but, beyond that, I'm crap in the kitchen."

It was another tidbit of him that she ate up, despite her dismay at the realization she didn't rate homemade pancakes. Those were reserved for all those ladies he'd been photographed with.

C'est la vie, she thought, trying to shrug off her melancholia. After all, she was with him now. She would soak in his words and movements like water on parched earth. The memories would get her through the drought ahead.

She didn't speak much the rest of her meal, prompting him to keep asking the occasional question so she could hear the sound of his voice.

Then he mentioned that it had started to snow outside.

Excited, Georgia sprang up to check the nearest window. "It's true, look at them!"

The delicate flakes were falling sparsely, each delicate crystal reflecting the light from the window like a fire's ember as it drifted down.

Squealing despite herself, Georgia ran out to the larger back deck that wrapped around the side and backs of the cabin.

The first snowflake hit her forehead. Opening her mouth, she shuffled until she caught one on her tongue. It melted immediately. Giggling, she went for another one.

Footsteps sounded on the wood floor. Georgia turned to find Rainer leaning against the jamb of the sliding glass doors. His face was distinctly amused. But she didn't care if he'd caught her being childish. She was going to be herself if it killed her.

"You act as if you haven't seen snow before."

"I have." She sniffed. "Granted, it was already on the ground as I drove past, but I'm still counting it."

"Ah," he said, putting his hands in his pockets. "Well, enjoy your first snow*fall* while it lasts. It's only a few flurries. According to the forecast, we're not due for more than an inch or two in the coming weeks."

The unspoken 'and we'll be gone by then' didn't dampen her mood.

Georgia tsked. "Don't harsh my groove here," she said, proceeding to catch more snowflakes before a thought occurred to her that made her snap her mouth shut.

"I know acid rain isn't a thing anymore, but what about acid snowflakes?"

Laughing, Rainer shook his head. "Ever heard the expression 'as pure as the driven snow'? You're safe."

"Good," Georgia said, rubbing her hands. "Does your friend have any grenadine in that hidden bar?"

All the booze was discreetly tucked into a cabinet next to the dining table. Like the panel in the plane, it was disguised to blend in. But Rainer opened it before dinner every night to pour himself a few inches of something brown and expensive, almost always apologizing because she couldn't partake while she was on painkillers.

"Planning to make snow cones?" he teased.

"As a matter of fact, I was," she replied pertly.

He grinned again, but then his smile died. "I have some news from Powell."

She could tell from his expression that it wasn't the good kind. "What happened?"

"Nothing." Rainer scowled. "A whole lot of nothing."

Despite the snow slowly gathering in her hair, Georgia took a seat on one of the wide wooden chaise lounges covered in plastic to protect it from the elements. "So, he hasn't found the kidnappers yet?"

"No," Rainer confirmed. "The vehicle they drove was abandoned at a supermarket not far from your house. It had been stolen a few days earlier from a mall parking lot across town. Powell and his men are still combing through all the traffic-cam footage in the vicinity."

Georgia absorbed that in silence.

"We will get them," Rainer promised. "You'll be able to go home, just not as soon as you hoped."

But as long as she was with him, that part didn't sting. Nope, that came when she remembered what was awaited her back in San Diego. "I almost forgot... I don't have one of those anymore."

No longer enthused about the snow, she brushed off the flakes that had settled in her hair. "We're going to have to go condo-hunting when I get back." Hopefully, the proceeds from the sale would be enough to get them a nice one, someplace Ephraim could use to meet clients.

Rainer stirred. "Yeah...about that. I'm part-owner of the building where we stashed Ephraim. You're welcome to stay in the apartment with him until you two get back on your feet—no charge."

Georgia bristled. Diamond hadn't raised her to take charity. "We'll be fine."

Rainer sighed. "Georgia, don't do that. I'm part of the reason you're in this mess."

She was tempted to stick her tongue out at him. "Ephraim's old partner is the reason we had to sell the house. The move was coming —your situation just sped it up."

"That doesn't change the fact you had to move before you were ready." He peeled himself off the doorjamb, sitting in the chaise lounge opposite her. "And the apartment I arranged is a nice one. Plenty of space and natural light. It's on the waterfront. Gorgeous views of the Pacific."

She groaned. "That only makes it worse. Ephraim won't ever go for living at your place rent-free."

The corner of his mouth kicked up, making the butterflies in her stomach take flight. "So, I'll charge him rent. Something reasonable."

Georgia could tell from the calculation in his expression that it would be pennies on the dollar.

She pointed a finger at him. "Don't think he won't know it won't be market price. He's very savvy."

Bracing his weight on his hands, he leaned back, stretching sideways on the lounger.

"All right. So maybe we don't tell him exactly when Powell gives us the all-clear. We'll catch the kidnappers, but tell Ephraim there might be a known associate in the wind. We can tell him there's no chance of them making a play, but that it will be better to stay put just in case."

She frowned. "Why?"

"Because the building he's in is safe, with plenty of cameras and full-time security guards."

He leaned forward. "Ephraim will stay if there's even a hint that your safety is still in question. You know he will."

Georgia narrowed her eyes. "Sneaky."

He winked. "It will work if you don't rat me out."

Damn the man. She knew he was manipulating her and her father, but he was doing it openly and with so much charm that she was considering going along with his plan. It didn't hurt that doing so would keep her in his sphere longer.

God, you really are pathetic.

"I'll think about it," she promised before allowing herself to be coaxed back inside to finish dinner.

CHAPTER ELEVEN

Georgia read a dozen bestsellers and watched more reality TV than was healthy before admitting the truth—relaxing was *boring*. Five days in and she was feeling loads better, sleeping only at night and experiencing only the occasional minor twinge. The headaches were gone, and she was chomping at the bit to do something...anything.

She knew she had to get out of the lodge when she started fiddling with the kitchen appliances. The itch to take them apart was like a burr under her skin. Plus, there was all that pristine snow to play in outside.

Despite Rainer's earlier contention that it wouldn't stick, there had been a steady snowfall the last two nights. The thick coat of fresh white snow covered the ground like an extra thick dusting of powdered sugar on chocolate cake.

Georgia played like a child near the lodge. She made her first snowman. Two sets of snow grandparents and one very misshapen snow dog soon joined a snow wife and snow kids.

Rainer took one look at her creations before laughing his ass off. She didn't take it personally, not after he ran back inside to get the family hats and scarves that he'd found in the guest room closets.

"You're not going to make me take them down?" she asked as he settled an oversized pair of sunglasses on one of the kids.

"Why would I do that?"

"You're so concerned about safety that I thought you'd be upset since I cut down the visibility outside the windows, giving the bad guys a place to hide."

He looked at her as if he hadn't considered that. After a minute, he rubbed his chin. "Well, even if they manage to find us out here there's enough cover for them in the trees. Our best bet is to turn on the alarm and hide in the panic room."

Georgia dropped the snowball she was rolling to make Spot, the snow cat. "There's a panic room?"

He straightened, nose wrinkling. "Well, it's more of a panic closet and there are two—one at either end of the house. You haven't seen them because they look like regular closets. That's a thing—a panic room disguised to be something else, like a pantry or a bathroom. They have a hidden cabinet full of food and medical supplies, and a SAT phone. They also have bulletproof doors."

"Wow." She had been aware the lodge had an alarm system because they had to punch a code for every entrance. The only way to avoid this was to flip them off at the main control panel or via the app Rainer had installed on his phone.

She hadn't realized he had control of the entire house until she accidentally left her morning bacon on the stove too long. She'd thrown open the kitchen window to ventilate the smoke, bringing Rainer running because a silent alert had gone to his cell.

"I didn't realize," she'd apologized as he'd pressed a button to cancel the alarm.

"Don't be. It's a little aggressive, but I decided to leave it in this hyper-vigilant mode. It doesn't send off the warning to the authorities right away, giving you a window to cancel it."

Aware the extra hoops helped him rest easier, she didn't argue against keeping it on. Even if it meant she had to warn him every time she had to open a window or a door.

Naturally, someone that paranoid about security didn't approve of her plan to go snowshoeing on her own. She had found the snowshoes and skis in the garage, along with an ancient-looking generator that must have belonged to a previous owner, before the cabin was expanded and renovated.

"What if you get lost?" he asked, looking up from his desk where he was no doubt perusing some convoluted business deal.

"I have my phone," she said, holding up her battered Android, the one that had been free with her contract. He'd given it back a few days into their stay.

It was slow as hell in the mountains—her carrier must not have had a cellphone tower in these parts, although Rainer didn't seem to have any problems with his reception.

He frowned. "I'm not sure that's good enough."

She was warmed by his concern, but there were only so many snowmen she could make. "I have to get out of this house or I'm going to start taking apart appliances. I don't think either of us wants that. I promise not to go farther than a half-hour from the lodge," she added, putting her right hand up like a Girl Scout.

He considered that for a minute before pushing his laptop closed. "Why don't I go with you?"

Her heart did little loop-de-loop in her chest. "I don't want to interrupt your work."

"It's all right," he said, getting to his feet. "Nothing is that pressing at this point. I'll make up the time after dinner."

"Are you sure?" she asked, feeling a touch guilty for making him go with her. But she should have expected as much. Rainer had a too finely honed sense of responsibility.

"Don't worry about it, Georgia."

When he grinned, her knees promptly turned to jelly. He may as well have tackled her, the end result was the same.

"I am starting to get a little antsy without a proper gym, too," he continued. "But I guess it doesn't make much sense to have one since Garrett's sole purpose is to come here to ski. He loves it—the snowshoes are for guests. I've never tried it before, but a workout is a workout."

Georgia was too hungry for his company to keep arguing with him. Whoever said familiarity bred contempt had never met Rainer Torsten. She'd had a vague expectation that her crush on him would fade the better she got to know him. *What a joke*. It would have been funny…had it not been at her expense.

If anything, her admiration for Rainer had only increased. He wasn't just a pretty face. Rainer possessed a razor-sharp intelligence and eloquence that was apparent every time he opened his mouth. There was also an innate elegance to him, the kind very few people were born with. Georgia loved watching him, soaking in the grace with which he moved. She even enjoyed watching him eat, picking up and imitating his flawless table manners so she wouldn't look like an uncultured swine next to him.

They got ready for an afternoon outdoors, dressing warmly in thick parkas they found hanging in the guest rooms—hers was two sizes too large—before helping each other strap on their snowshoes.

It was the first time for them both, and they didn't get the fastenings right on the first try. Georgia walked right out of hers in a few steps, and Rainer bent over her feet to redo the ties.

The temptation to reach out and touch his silky hair was so strong that she had to sit on her hands.

"Ready?" he asked, rising and holding out a hand.

"Sure," she said, hoping he didn't notice her blush. She felt the touch of his hand long after he let go. Having him to herself like this was a fluke, a million-to-one chance akin to winning the lottery.

She ignored the voice in her brain, the one whispered that a nobody like her didn't deserve a place in his life.

Don't think about tomorrow, she told herself as they set out under the snow-dusted trees. He was with her now. Once they left this cabin, she'd never get this opportunity again, so she had to make the most of it, cramming as many memories of Rainer into her brain as she could.

It was a little pathetic, but Georgia couldn't help herself. So, she would play in the snow with a handsome millionaire, tucking away each reminiscence so she could pull them out later, maybe after a hard day's work, to savor like the memories of a fine, never-to-be-repeated, meal.

They trudged all around the lodge, checking on her snow family before venturing farther out, stamping the fresh powder down with their tennis racket-like appendages. The layer wasn't thick enough for them to have trouble, but she'd had no idea how difficult walking would be or how quickly she would feel the effects in her weak muscles.

"My thighs are burning." She laughed, panting and leaning against the rough bark of a thick pine tree. "I'm definitely going to be feeling this in my butt later!"

Rainer glanced down, his eyes lingering on the curves of her ass a beat longer than was strictly polite. Realizing she'd caught him staring, he flushed before turning away.

Georgia told herself not to read anything into his reaction. *You practically asked him to look.*

"Yeah, I can skip leg day after this," he said, turning toward the cliff face they had just come across. "I think we've almost circled back to the house. The rock face above us is the near the bottom of the tract Garrett skis down."

"How does he get up to the top of the mountain? Does he hire a helicopter?"

"Well, I wouldn't put that past him. In this case, though, he uses the snowmobiles in the garage— I know you saw them."

"I did," she admitted. Two Arctic Cat ZR's had been stored under a tarp on a small trailer that could be attached to a four-wheel drive.

Having never seen one before, Georgia had been itching to peek under the hood, so to speak, up until the moment she'd Googled the makes and models of the snowmobiles and found out how much they cost. Since Rainer's friend Garret would probably object to her taking one apart, she'd given them a wide berth, deciding to admire them from afar.

"When the powder is fresh and thick, Garret drives those up to the top of the mountain and skis down."

Georgia looked up, watching him navigate the snowshoes like an expert—because of course, he did everything well. "How does he get the snowmobile back down?"

Rainer's mouth quirked. "You know, I never asked. But he doesn't ski alone so someone else must drive it back down."

"The buddy system?"

"Something like that." Rainer took one last look at the cliff face as if trying to figure out a path up.

"Do you rock climb?"

He put his hands on his hips before turning to her. "I have a few times, but only in a gym. Swimming is my go-to sport."

She should have guessed that. Rainer had the broad shoulders of a swimmer.

"I'm a terrible swimmer," she confessed, examining the rock face. "I can't make it across the pool without stopping to touch the bottom with my toes—which is impossible unless I'm in the lane against the wall." She scoffed. "Or a kid-sized pool."

She knew she had shocked him by how quickly he turned around, the snowshoes not impeding his speed. "Didn't Ephraim or Diamond teach you how to do a proper stroke?"

"They don't swim either."

Rainer straightened, seeming to take that as a personal affront. Closing his eyes, he shook his head. He opened his mouth, closed it, then opened it again. Finally, he slashed a hand through the air and shrugged. "This cannot be allowed to pass—I'm going to have to show you."

"Where?" She chuckled. "Cause as soft as this snow is, I don't think diving in the snowdrifts would be all that similar."

He appeared to consider this before throwing up his hands. "Damn it," he swore. "I knew we should have gone to the Bahamas."

Laughing, she was already turning away before Rainer shouted and a wall of white came crashing down from the heavens.

CHAPTER TWELVE

Rainer didn't know whether it was their voices causing too many vibrations or just bad luck, but he watched helplessly as the snow on the ledge above them suddenly broke loose, crashing onto Georgia's little body.

It happened so fast—too fast for him to help her.

She saw it at the last moment and tried to jump back, but she didn't get far enough to keep the mass from overtaking her. It flowed around her like a rogue wave, trapping her body. Fortunately, the snow didn't cover her head.

But his relief was short-lived because it was his turn. The rest of the unstable drift fell on him. It thumped him in the back and shoulders, the deceptively soft-looking stuff hitting like a shower of rocks. He was quickly buried over his head.

"Rainer!" Georgia's voice was muffled under the snow, but he *could* hear her.

I can't be buried that deep if I can hear her, right? At least, that was what he told his racing heart. The lizard part of his brain was jumping up and down, screaming at him to move, but his entire body was immobilized, like a fly in amber.

Fuuuuck. He needed to calm down. *I can't be that deep.* But the lizard brain didn't buy that.

But then he heard Georgia's calling to him. All at once, his world realigned. She could be hurt, her head injury re-aggravated if some of the snow that had buried him had hit her in the second wave. He had to get to her. She needed him.

But despite his best efforts, he could barely move. Rocking his head back and forth, Rainer managed to wiggle enough to give him some breathing room—literally—but little more.

Then he heard Georgia start to dig. A moment later, she uncovered his head. He rewarded her efforts by swearing a blue streak in her face.

"Sorry," he apologized after he took several deep, gulping breaths. "*Shit.*"

"That's okay," she replied in a warbling voice. Georgia's eyes were rimmed with red. Her hands shook as she scrabbled, trying to push the rest of the snow away from his face.

"Are you hurt?" he asked.

Her little fingers brushed the snow away from his neck. "No, not really. I was only buried to the chest."

"Are you sure you didn't hit your head?"

"Nothing's wrong with *me.* You're the one who's buried," she snapped before sobbing aloud. Twisting her head, she wiped her cheek on her sleeve. "I'm sorry. Let's just get you out of here before you freeze to death."

"You're fine," he soothed, feeling pretty shaky himself about the near-miss. And he was nowhere as cold as he should have been, warmed by her concern.

And here I thought that was just an expression. But Georgia was distraught, her concern for him apparent in her frantic digging.

She kept pushing at the pile until she'd freed one arm, then the other. Thankfully, neither was broken. After that, he was able to help. With both working, he was soon able to bend over and undo the snowshoe straps. Georgia had been stripped of hers. He could see one half-buried in the rucked-up snow next to them.

Once his were untied, Rainer put his hands on the ground and half pulled, half-kicked the rest of the snow off.

Finally free, he staggered to his feet. Georgia tucked herself under his arm, helping support his weight as he wobbled unsteadily. She was surprisingly strong.

Must be moving all those engines. She couldn't take one of those apart without some muscle.

He tightened his hold on her. "I don't know about you, but I think I'm done playing in the snow for the day."

"Me too." Georgia tugged him in the direction of the cabin. "Let's get the hell out of here.

❧

They had surprisingly few bruises, and they didn't have any broken bones. Despite Rainer's concern for Georgia, she had gotten out of the mess relatively unscathed. The large bruise on his back was the worst of their injuries. It sat just under his shoulder blade where the snow must have carried down a big rock along with the fresh powder, with enough force to leave a mark.

"I am going to have Garret's ass on a platter," he muttered as Georgia examined the spot.

He had stripped down to the waist to check for bruises and possible fractures. But she was fine, something he kept repeating to himself like a mantra.

"I'm not sure it's his fault we were buried. It was a bad idea to stand under a ledge that sloped down like that."

"Please don't be reasonable right now. I want to be mad, and Garrett makes a good scapegoat. That ass assured me there would be no snow up here."

"In that case, you're right. Damn Garrett. How dare he fail to control the weather properly?"

He threw her a baleful glance, but she just smiled. Rainer had to resist the urge to rub his head against her shoulder like a cat—up until her fingers probed too close to the bruise.

When he hissed under his breath, she murmured an apology. "You're lucky this didn't hit your spine."

She was right, but he couldn't think about that right now. He was too focused on Georgia, on her husky voice and delicate touch.

"Are you sure you don't want to go down to the doctor? You might need X-rays."

"I don't think anything is broken," he said, rising and turning to face her. "Besides, those small-town doctors keep regular business hours. There's no point in dragging them back into the office when I feel fine."

He waited for a response, but he didn't get one. Georgia's eyes were fixed to his chest.

His mouth twitched, but he didn't call attention to her distraction. She must have realized he'd spoken, because her gaze slid up to meet his guiltily. "Err…no doctor. Are you sure?"

The devil climbed on his shoulder, whispering and nudging. "I just need a long hot soak in the tub," he said, keeping his face as expressionless as possible.

A tiny little whimpering noise escaped Georgia's lips. Suddenly, Rainer felt no pain.

"G-good idea," she said, backing away with the towel. Catching herself, she cleared her throat. "Well, if you're feeling too stiff—I mean sore—in the morning, we should drive down."

Then she turned tail and hurried to her room.

"*Well, shit,*" he muttered aloud. His Georgia problem was getting bigger.

❧

The knock on his door was so tentative that he almost didn't hear it. He lifted his head off the pillow, his body aching everywhere. *Damn snow.*

"Just a second," Rainer called, his brain registering the fact that it was morning.

He glanced at the bedside clock. It was after nine. He didn't usually sleep this late, which explained Georgia's knock. She wouldn't seek him out unless it was important.

Quickly pulling on some sweatpants, he went to the door. "Georgia?"

"I'm sorry to wake you," she said. Her face was tight.

"I should have been up," he apologized, realizing he'd worried her. "But I'm fine. Just overslept. No need to rush down the mountain for X-rays."

Georgia twisted the kitchen towel she held in her hands. "That's good because I don't think we could get down there if we tried. Have you looked out the window?"

What now? With a sinking feeling in his stomach, Rainer rushed to the main patio doors.

The snow had piled up overnight. It stood at least three and a half feet deep, and it was getting deeper with every minute. The dreaded white stuff was coming down fast and hard.

"I checked the weather report." Georgia joined him at the window. "The forecast said we can expect another four feet at least."

He groaned aloud. "But I checked the report before we came. We weren't supposed to get more than a few inches, a foot tops."

She grimaced. "I guess it changed because now it says we're in pre-blizzard conditions.

Rainer swore under his breath. His forehead hit the cold glass of the window. "*Fuck*. I hate the snow."

Georgia nudged him gently. "At least we don't have anywhere to be, right?"

"Yeah." He laughed, giving the snow a dirty look. "I guess our plans haven't changed much."

"C'mon." Georgia touched his arm before tossing the kitchen towel over her shoulder. "I'll make you eggs and latkes."

He blinked before remembering that her foster dad was Jewish. His stomach rumbled. "Throw in some bacon and you have a deal."

The latkes were first-rate, far superior to hash browns. But aside from Georgia herself, the latkes were the only bright spots in his day.

The snow kept coming. By nightfall, it had piled up so high they couldn't open the doors.

But still, he didn't worry for their safety when it kept snowing the next day, or even the day after that. Not until the power went out.

CHAPTER THIRTEEN

"How does it look?" Rainer called out the window.

The floor of the master bedroom was a mess, a thick layer of snow turning to slush on the carpet. But he didn't care about that. He was worried about Georgia's precarious balance on the roof just above him.

The power had cut out sometime during the night. He and Georgia had woken up to a freezing house. Georgia had been sure that they could simply clean off the solar panels to get the power back. They had scoured the house and garage for a ladder, without success. As it turned out, the snow had piled high enough for her to climb up without one.

Rainer hadn't wanted her to go up alone, but she had pointed out that it made little sense for them both to do it. Plus, she was lighter and strong enough to muscle her way through whatever hurdles climbing around up there might entail.

But she had been out there too long. The melodic swear that filtered down a moment later confirmed his gut feeling. There was a problem.

More snow falling into the room signaled her return. Rainer caught Georgia as she scrambled inside.

"I have bad news," she said, working off the ski gloves. "The solar panels themselves are not the problem. It's the thing they feed the power into—the controller that processes the energy was damaged somehow. I think the snow broke a branch off from that tree up against the side of the house. It busted the converter box on the way down. I can't make it work without a replacement."

Rainer swore, shoving the excess snow falling in through the window back outside before forcing the sash closed with brute force. "Something tells me Garret doesn't have a spare lying around."

Georgia raised her hands, rubbing them together to warm them up. "I don't think that's the sort of thing people keep spares of. A specialized technician will have to come out to install a new one."

"Who knows when that will be," he murmured, taking her hands and rubbing them between his much larger ones. They had already checked the phone lines. Whatever cell tower was servicing this corner of the mountain must have gotten knocked out.

"Damn, your fingers are frozen. Those gloves must be crap. I'm sorry."

He blew on her fingers to warm them up.

Her mouth pulled down in chagrin. "I didn't have enough dexterity wearing them. They were too thick…so I took them off."

His mouth tightened. "You could have fallen off the roof." The gloves had sticky pads that should have helped give her hands traction.

Smirking, she gestured to the window and its partially obscured view. "All this snow would have broken my fall."

"Not funny," he groused.

Rainer scrubbed his hair roughly with his hand. But he wasn't a CEO for nothing. "All right, we have to take stock. The temperature inside the house is going to keep dropping. We'll have to hole up in a smaller space, in one of the rooms with a fireplace."

Georgia glanced at his mantlepiece. "Most of the fireplaces in the bedrooms are gas. Are you sure we can trust the gas lines?"

"They run those underground, don't they?"

She shook her head. "The fuel is one of the big propane tanks outside, and it's almost empty."

Rainer closed his eyes. "*What?*"

A small calming touch above his elbow. "We didn't know to check the gauge. Your friend might not think about that until he gets up here."

"More likely it was one of Garret's people who forgot to check the gauge. They prep the place so everything will be ready for him and his guests to drop in." He scowled. "At least they stocked the kitchen with canned goods in addition to the frozen meals. We won't starve."

"We'll be fine." Georgia took her hand back. He immediately missed it. "The fireplace in the living room burns real wood, and there's that pile in the back of the garage. It'll be nice and dry, so that's not a problem."

They had discovered the chest-high pile of logs early on, had even used a few to make a cozy fire when the snow first began to fall, but he was regretting that. What if they needed to conserve that fuel, too?

Then you'll find a fucking ax and you'll cut down the damn tree that took out the solar power. Two birds—keeping Georgia warn and sweet revenge.

"That's a much bigger room to heat," he pointed out.

She lifted a shoulder. "We'll have to camp close to the fireplace. Let's move the couch back and drag our mattresses there. We can pile every blanket in the house on them."

Rainer nodded. Her plan was their best bet to stay warm for the next couple of days. "Think we can cook on the fireplace?"

"I'm sure we can jerry-rig something up."

He swore. "We're surrounded by snow, but, if our plan works, everything in the freezer is going to melt."

The kitchen and living room were one big room. If they managed to keep the temperature up, then all the pre-prepped meals would spoil.

Snickering, Georgia jerked her thumb at the window. "Voila, Mother Nature's freezer. Let's unload everything and put it in a snowbank on the east side of the house, where the sun doesn't hit."

"Sounds like a plan." He followed her out of the room before a thought occurred to him. "*Shit*. Won't it attract bears?"

She stopped short, consternation on her fine features. "Ugh, let's hope they're all hibernating."

They spent the next few hours executing her plan. The food was the easy part. To prevent frostbite, Rainer grabbed a snow shovel from the garage, using it to carve out two holes in the drift outside. If a bear was untimely roused from his nap, then maybe he or she would only find one.

Georgia stacked the prepared foods into the holes, keeping the more fragile things like the eggs and juice cartons on the right side. Then they sprinkled the contents with fresh powder to keep them as cold as before. Finally, they used spare plywood they found in the garage as makeshift doors.

The nest in front of the fireplace proved more problematic. The six-piece sectional in the sunken living room wasn't one of the modular kinds that could be taken apart. It was one single massive piece of furniture, too heavy for them to move more than a few inches.

"Stop," he said when Georgia's feet almost slid out from under her. "We'll just leave it and sleep on it."

But when they tested the arrangement after nightfall, the couch was too far from the fireplace for them to feel the heat.

They ended up grabbing a mattress from the nearest guest room. After moving the coffee table, they found there was just enough room to fit the queen-sized bed between the fireplace and the couch, leaving a foot or two of space as a buffer.

"Do you think that's sufficient? What if the fire throws out sparks and the blankets catch fire?" Georgia asked as they prepared to bunk together for the first time.

"It should be enough of a gap for any sparks to die," he said, hoping the mattress was the fire-retardant kind. "But we'll keep the screen up when we sleep, just in case."

Nodding, she curled up on his right, her feet closer to the fireplace.

She snuggled under the comforter from his bed, getting cozy for the night.

Rainer stretched out next to her, laying on his side so he could prop his head on one arm. "This is not exactly the glamorous getaway I promised you."

A little pucker appeared between her brows. "When did you promise me glamour? The only thing you said was that we'd be going someplace safe."

He let his head fall back on the mattress, snorting. "I'm not sure this place qualifies."

The mattress shook a little as she laughed. A hand reached out, resting on his bicep. "The lodge construction is very sturdy, and the snow will melt. And at least now, I'm going to have a story to tell my girls when I get back. This is probably the most exciting thing that's ever happened to me—please don't point out how sad that is."

Rainer smiled, tempted to gather her up in his arms, but he was determined to stay a gentleman.

"Actually, this may be the most exciting thing to happen to me, too," he said, deciding the incident last year didn't qualify as 'exciting'. *More like fucked up and demoralizing.*

Georgia rolled, turning to face him. She held out a hand. "Well, here's to adventures with new friends."

Charmed to his toes, Rainer reached out to clasp the offered hand. "To new friends."

And maybe more someday.

CHAPTER FOURTEEN

He woke up in the middle of the night to find Georgia burrowing into him. The room was freezing. The fire had gone out, a few embers all that was left of the blaze that had been burning when he'd dropped off to sleep.

Groggily, he got up and added more logs, carefully replacing the screen before hightailing it back to the bed.

He pulled the covers back over him, tugging Georgia's lax body against his chest and curling around her. She made one of those cute sleepy sounds and wiggled backward, instinctively trying to get closer to his body heat.

Damn. Her rounded tush was rubbing against the front of his sweatpants. Gritting his teeth, he tried to think of anything else—baseball stats, stock market figures—anything to keep from getting hard.

But it was hopeless. Georgia kept wiggling, shooting shotgun-sized holes in his self-control.

Then she turned around. Her eyes opened, and she smiled at him dreamily. Reaching up, she put her hand on the back of his neck even as her lashes fluttered shut.

"Georgia, are you awake?"

"*Hmm?*" The pads of her fingers stroked his neck.

"I need you to be awake so you can tell me it's okay to kiss you."

There was a pause as she froze in his arms. Her lashes fluttered open. Oh yeah, she was wide awake now. *Good.*

"And after I kiss you, I'm going to fuck you—a long, hard fuck. Is that all right?"

Her hand spasmed against the back of his neck, gripping him a little tighter.

Rainer grinned. "You know it's too dark for me to see your face, so I'm going to need a nod or verbal consent."

He waited, holding his breath. Then, there was a tiniest of head movements, followed by a definitive and eager nod. Several of them.

"Thank you, God," he muttered, bending his head to take her mouth.

Her lips were as soft as he had imagined. Plush and delicate. Rainer felt the urge to bite them, a feral impulse he'd never experienced with anyone else. Teasing those lips apart was one of the greatest experiences of his life.

And still, that didn't compare to her taste. Her lips parted under his questing tongue, and her essence hit him full force—pure ambrosia. Sweet but with a hint of something more, some nameless spice he was instantly addicted to.

The cold was quickly forgotten as he stripped out of his thick layers, his blood pumping so hot he could heat the whole damn room. He was naked before she was. Georgia had just worked off her top layer when he remembered all the condoms were in the bedroom.

"*Shit.* I'll be right back." He got up and ran out of the room without pulling any of his clothes back on.

That was a mistake. The rest of the house was so fucking cold that it felt like he was going to freeze his balls off. He ran faster, stumbling in the dark of his room on nothing at all. Picking himself up off the floor, he rounded the bed and found the box of condoms his people packed in every suitcase.

He hadn't needed them in over a year, but he hadn't had the heart to tell them that. Well, his self-imposed drought was over. He planned to feast.

❧

Georgia had woken up plastered against Rainer's long body. Even covered in warm layers, he'd been so hard and muscular, like a living statue. She almost died a thousand deaths when she realized she was stroking him, and probably had been for some time.

Then he said he was going to fuck her, and her nether regions had exploded.

The coarse words should have been off-putting, but Georgia's body had the opposite reaction. She was a full-grown woman with the normal desires and needs that accompanied that state, but she'd gone without for so long she ached. That and she'd never wanted anybody the way she wanted Rainer. Her needy body wanted to crawl all over him, pressing every inch of her skin to his, to consume him.

Then he'd jumped up and run away. The shock of it was more jarring than the cold in the room. But he came back before her brain could process his absence, slapping a long strip of condoms on the mattress next to her.

Her back hit the mattress as he tugged her sweatpants and underwear off in one go, more enthusiasm than grace. Hair roughened skin brushed hers, and she threw her arms around his neck.

"Hi." His voice was muffled because his mouth was against her cheek.

"Hi," she giggled back as his big body rubbed against her like cat. Not the tame domestic kind, of course, but one of the lethal and predatory variety. A leopard or mountain lion that had, for some reason, decided to get in bed with her.

That whimsical train of thought sputtered and died the moment his hand worked between them. Fingers stroked between the hot seam between her legs. Rainer groan drowned out her whimper. "You're so wet."

He put on the condom with flattering speed. Then he pressed her down into the mattress. "I'm sorry," he apologized, his voice guttural. "I can't wait."

That was fine with her. "I don't want you to," she whispered, her hands clutching his shoulders.

His mouth covered hers, his tongue sweeping past the seam of her lips at the same time as he fit himself to her opening. Rainer didn't lift his head as he possessed her, that rough invasion coinciding with their first kiss.

His thick length pushed at her entrance, the broad head of his shaft catching at the constricted ring of muscle and then pushing past. But it had been a long time and she was tight enough to make him hesitate, his cock just a few inches inside.

He raised his head, a question in his tone. "Georgia?"

"I'm fine," she panted. It felt as if every nerve ending in her body was firing at once, as if her body wasn't capable of processing his invasion.

"Are you sure?" he whispered. "This isn't your first time?"

"No," Georgia said, shifting so he slid another inch. "It isn't. Is that disappointing?"

"Hell no." She felt more than saw his scowl. "I just don't want to hurt you and you're so small, so tight."

He buried his face in the pillow next to her, muffling his words. "Dear God, you're so tight."

She knew Rainer well enough to realize he was thinking of pulling out and stopping. That stubborn noble streak was going to ruin everything.

Desperate and determined to keep him exactly where he was, she tugged his head down, licking the inside of his mouth, drawing in the taste of him while she wrapped her legs around his waist, undulating her hips up while urging him down with her mouth and hands.

Rainer swore, throwing his head back as his length slid deeper. With curses that sounded like endearments, he lost the fight with his better angels, burying himself to the hilt in her heat.

Georgia held on, her sensitized inner flesh slowly stretching around his thickness. Rainer was large and she was small and needed more time to get used to him, particularly in light of her long period of abstinence. But that helpless hunger that overtook her every time she looked at him made her impatient, and she tried to pull his hips down with her hands.

Her stiff nipples brushed against his chest. The tingles sent little shocks of pleasure to her core. Greedy she rubbed against him for more contact, an act that made him suck in his breath.

Rainer pushed up on his arms, looking down at her. Then he took her hands and pinned them over her head. "Be careful what you wish for, baby."

Georgia knew she was playing with fire, but she couldn't help herself. She raised her hand and bit his lower lip, undulating her whole body up this time, eager to touch and stroke. Her skin sparked against him, almost painfully.

Rainer's free hand fisted in her hair, his lower body pulling back.

Georgia gasped, her fingers digging into his back as he pulled his shaft out until only the tip of him was nestled inside. After an exquisitely anticipatory pause, he plunged back in, the reins on his control snapped.

Rainer began to move, the wet heat and rough friction burning away any rational thoughts. Gasping with pleasure, Georgia managed to swallow the high-pitched cries he elicited from her as he made good on his promise to fuck her long and hard. Well, most of them anyway.

But this 'fuck' felt like more. Her body instinctively found and mimicked his rhythm without a trace of the awkwardness that had defined her only other physical relationship.

Whatever short-circuited her brain around him also bypassed it, with its overthinking tendencies. With Rainer, she was a creature of instinct, her body attuned to his. When he thrust, she softened, taking him greedily, and shuddering when he withdrew only to delve back in deep.

The tight, twisting coil of pleasure broke more than once. Georgia's first orgasm made her scream, a breathless cry that died under his mouth as Rainer took another soul-stealing kiss. The next made her buck so hard he pinned her hips down. The last was a grinding dance that made her pussy clamp around his cock so hard she finally took him with her.

Pulsing, he drove into her repeatedly, his breath so fast he could barely swear.

"Holy shit," he gasped as he came with one last convulsive wrench. He collapsed on top of her, his sweat-soaked skin hot to the touch.

Still shaking from the residual aftershocks of his passion, Georgia wrapped her arms and legs around his body, holding him close as he softened inside her.

❧

Rainer was still trying to recover from the hardest, most intense orgasm of his life when he realized he was crushing Georgia. Flipping over on his back, he pulled her on top of him without breaking their connection.

They lay that way together for long minutes, touching and exploring until the fire ignited again and he urged her on top to ride him for what he promised himself would be the first of many times. She was hesitant at first, requiring guidance. It made him think that his initial guess of her being inexperienced wasn't that far off. There hadn't been too many lovers in her past.

But where he led, she followed, utterly responsive.

Georgia adapted to him like she could read his mind, and when her tight little pussy clamped down on him, the smooth globes of her ass rubbing his thighs, he exploded with enough force to make him nearly pass out.

Spent and sated, he pulled the covers over their rapidly cooling bodies. Georgia nestled against him, fitting like she'd been made for him. She soon dropped off to sleep. He cuddled her to him, feeling happier and more at peace than he had in a long time.

But the feeling didn't last. Try as he might, Rainer couldn't sleep. He lay next to Georgia, holding her, a sinking feeling in his head and stomach.

Something was wrong.

CHAPTER FIFTEEN

Georgia was a little surprised to wake up alone. Telling herself that it wasn't a big deal, she got up and dressed. Perhaps Rainer's laptop still had some battery and he'd gone back into the office to do some work. But when she checked the office was empty.

Feeling chilled, she went to dig through the pile of clothes they'd pulled out for the night. Adding a second sweatshirt to the one she'd pulled on, she found Rainer in the master bathroom, rubbing his glorious pecs with a wet washcloth.

"I think the pipes may have frozen over or they're in the process of freezing," he said with a teeth-bearing grimace as he swiped under his armpit with a dry towel. "Only a trickle is coming out."

The bad news was tempered by the sight of his beautiful body. *Damn girl, this is serious shit. You gotta focus.*

"We should start gathering fresh snow in buckets and bowls," she said, after shaking her head to clear it. "If we have to, we can melt it in the fireplace."

"Maybe we should fill the tubs, too."

"That's a good idea."

She shuffled her feet, intending to get to work immediately, but his hand snaked out, snagging and pulling her to him.

"Hey." The full force of his gaze pinned her to the spot.

"H-hi," she stuttered, heat inexplicably creeping up her neck.

A corner lip quirked up. "Not so brave in the daylight, are you?" he teased.

"I…"

"Close your eyes."

Startled, Georgia hesitated—until Rainer brushed his fingers over the top of her lids, a gentle nudge. When her eyes were closed, he took her hands and put them over his chest. It was still bare despite the cold in the room. But he didn't shiver. Rainer's skin was hot to the touch. And it felt like heaven.

Moaning a little despite herself, Georgia rested a cheek against him, rubbing it against the muscled landscape of his chest. Her breath fanned across his satin skin, and he tensed.

Ever so slowly, he peeled her hands off his chest before taking her shoulder and setting her half a step back. She opened pleasure-drunk eyes, satisfied to see he was breathing as fast as she was.

"First, we gather the snow. Then we pick up where we left off."

Lips parted, she nodded before turning to leave. But she was unsteady on her feet. Chuckling, Rainer wrapped his arms around her from behind, pressing a kiss to the hypersensitive spot next to her ear. "Georgia, you are so good for my ego."

She leaned into him, unable to stop herself. "The way you looked at me, just now. That was good for mine."

He groaned aloud, but let her go. They gathered buckets and bowls of snow, filling as many receptacles as they could—including several of the bathtubs in the unused bedrooms. Then Rainer secured all the doors and windows while Georgia anxiously watched the snow fall from the living room windows.

If they went out right now, it would be waist-high for Rainer and almost to her chest.

Hands closed over her shoulders. "Everything is going to be fine. This storm can't last much longer. Once the snow stops falling, I'll be able to call up a repairman, get the solar fixed."

She swallowed, straightening her shoulders. Now was not the time to panic. Rainer needed a partner, someone practical who wouldn't freak out on him. "Should we start rationing food?"

"*No.*" He hugged her to him. "We're not all that low. We have enough for three or four more days and after that, there's always the stock of emergency rations—energy bars and freeze-dried meals from the panic room. There's a week's worth of food in each."

Weak with relief, she leaned into him. "So as long as the fuel holds out, we'll be fine?"

His voice lowered, the tone intimate. "Well, we also discovered an excellent way to keep warm."

Turning around, she smiled, her arms reaching to stroke as she pressed herself against him.

"I like how you rub against me." He tapped her nose. "Like a little cat."

"Cats bite," she said, nipping at his fingers. She caught one between her teeth. Rainer took a deep breath, his eyes widening as her tongue stroked the pad of his thumb.

Georgia found her clothes stripped off her in short order. Giggling, she tried to help, but he stopped her. Then she was naked, but her entire body was flushed, so much that she didn't feel the cold.

Strong arms hauled her up. This time he set her gently on the mattress in front of the fire, before he pulled her pants and panties down in a single smooth maneuver.

Georgia expected him to move up her body. But Rainer surprised her, his head settling between her legs.

Not expecting that intimacy, she tried to dislodge him. To her, oral sex was more intimate than intercourse, and she was embarrassed that he just went for it. But Rainer didn't give her any room to withdraw in shyness. He was too hungry, licking and sucking at her lips and clit like he'd been presented with a favorite meal. Trapping her raised legs with his arms, he held her down as he ate her out until she was begging for mercy.

But Rainer didn't have any—not even after he made her orgasm by grinding his palm against her opening and clit until she shuddered. He relentlessly drew out every delicious sensation in her until she collapsed into a mindless heap of pleasure. But still, she somehow had the wherewithal to stop him when he reached for the condoms they'd left next to the bed.

"But I want to taste you, too," she whispered, her cheeks heating at her forwardness. But she didn't let her shyness deter her as she urged him up and over her until he straddled her chest.

"You're too small for this," he breathed. "I'm going to crush you."

"Don't worry about me." Georgia rocked, rubbing her sensitive nipples against the sweet spot between his dick and his balls. Sucking in a sharp breath, Rainer pressed his lips together as he braced himself over her. When she curved her fingers around his length, his entire body tensed. She grinned at his reaction, pumping him with her hands before opening her mouth.

"Christ," he hissed as she darted her tongue out, making sure to pay special attention to the seam under the flared head. She hummed in response, savoring his taste. Rainer allowed her to lead, holding still as she guided him in deeper. She experimented, stretching her lips wide and opening her throat as they both learned how much of him she could take. Then he took over, pistoning in and out until he was fucking her mouth, while still carefully observing her limits.

More enthusiastic about this act than she'd ever been before, Georgia relished the experience. As he slid in and out, she held his hard-as-steel shaft at the base, savoring his taste on her tongue. She spent a pleasurable few minutes worshiping him with her mouth until Rainer finally threw his head back, neck corded, and slid free of her lips with a pop.

When he pulled away, tearing open a condom, she didn't stop him. She just held on as he surged into her heated flesh, stretching her in a way that should've been uncomfortable, but instead just made her want to twist and scream and dig her fingernails into his skin until she climaxed. Which was exactly what she did thanks to his hard thrusts, ones that shook the mattress and pinned her underneath his satisfyingly heavy weight until her channel throbbed and she convulsed, sobbing out his name.

She came to in his arms with his fingertips lightly brushing over her skin. Like last night, he'd pulled the covers over them, creating a cocoon of heat and sexual musk for them to bask in.

Then he shocked her by doing what no other man before him had ever bothered to do—he complimented her. Nothing extravagant or unbelievable, just genuine and sweet words.

"I love your skin," he murmured at one point, comparing it to silk and letting her know how much he liked it plastered all over him. Then he praised her lips and hair, his hands plunging into the curly mass before he took her again, this time from behind.

Rainer's muscled body curved over her, his thick length penetrating her folds until she moaned and shattered once again. Throwing the blankets off them, he rubbed her back until she could catch her breath.

When she did, he simply took it away again with a series of scorching kisses that spoke of care mixed with hunger. "Just so you know, you don't have to finish me off when you take me in your mouth," he said when he let her come up for air. "That's not a hill I die on."

She giggled, stroking his chest because she couldn't stop touching him. "Very considerate. But I like it with you."

He frowned. "Was there someone you *didn't* like it with?"

Something in her expression must have given her away because he abruptly sat up, gaze serious. "Georgia?"

She tried averting her eyes, but there was nowhere to hide.

Rainer cupped her cheek. "I want to know everything about you. But if I'm overstepping my bounds, you tell me."

"I don't want to know about your girlfriends," she decided, not hiding the mulish twist of her lips.

He grinned suddenly. "Not what I would call most. I've only had one or two relationships of note. One in high school and the other in college.

"The high school one ended in the usual way," he continued. "Lots of drama. Got things thrown at my head. The college break-up was calmer in its way. Gut-wrenching, but calmer."

Her curiosity piqued, she couldn't help but ask. "How so?"

He lifted a shoulder. "We were very much in love. She was beautiful, free-spirited, and a little wild."

Georgia instantly hated her.

"She was also bisexual."

Startled, she blinked. "Really?"

"Yeah. I knew beforehand. That we both liked women didn't bother me." He chuckled softly, probably at Georgia's shocked expression. "We dated for a long while. Well, eight months, which felt like close to twenty years while in college. But she wasn't happy in a monogamous relationship. She wanted to open it up, explore polyamory. I knew that lifestyle wasn't for me, so we broke up."

After the following silence turned to expectation, Georgia blurted out, "I've only had one lover…but he died."

Rainer slid a soothing hand down her back. "I'm sorry, George—I mean, Georgia."

She cuddled closer. "You can call me George. Ephraim and Diamond always did. Most of my girlfriends do, too."

"Did your lover?"

"Not really. But you can use it if you feel like it."

Because it sounded different coming from his mouth. And it was what the people she felt closest to called her.

His lips skated over her forehead. "Thank you," he said. "And I'm sorry about your boyfriend."

"It was a complicated relationship."

"I get that. But to lose him and your foster brother—"

When she jerked violently at his comment, she felt him freeze. Knowing she'd given herself away, she averted her gaze.

"Georgia?" Rainer tipped her chin up.

Accurately reading the dismay in her expression, his lips parted in surprise when she didn't deny it. "*Oh.*"

CHAPTER SIXTEEN

Several hours passed as he held her, stroking her skin and murmuring assurances that she didn't have to tell him a damn thing. But it was clear he was dying to ask.

Georgia knew Rainer had secrets, too, ones he held onto tightly. She didn't know if he would ever confide in her, because trust like that needed a base in which to grow. So, she decided to tell him about her past, hoping her trust might be the first step to building that foundation. Even if he never shared in return, it didn't matter. Georgia realized she needed him to know her.

So late into the night, under a cover of darkness, she shared her secrets, starting at the beginning. "Mack never saw me as a sister, you know. He was in and out of the house too often to feel like we were his real family. His birth mother wanted him, you see—but she had a lot of problems. When those got bad, the state would step in. She'd lose custody, and they'd take him away from her."

Rainer never stopped touching her, but it was easier to face away from him while she talked. It didn't stop Rainer from wrapping himself around her, a six-foot-plus blanket of comfort. "But you *did* see him as a brother," he said.

"I shouldn't have," she admitted. "He went to great pains to make sure we knew that he didn't consider Diamond, Ephraim, or me family."

His hand tightened on her shoulder. "That must have made things tense."

"It did. Sometimes. But we all got used to it. After a while, he'd calm down. He was really only difficult for a short time after he returned. After a few weeks, it usually smoothed over."

"How did the more—'*em*—personal relationship start?"

She took a deep breath, staring at the ceiling. The reflection of the flames in the fireplace danced across the white surface. "You know, I don't even remember. It was like I woke up one day, and there were suddenly all these *expectations* on his side. Eventually, I started to believe I was in the wrong if I didn't fulfill them."

"So, he groomed you?" Rainer's voice held more than a little anger.

Georgia scowled. "I think I would rather you *not* make it sound like I was molested by someone's uncle. Because that happened to a girl I knew in junior high, and my situation was *not* like that. Mack and I were only three years apart."

"That doesn't mean he didn't pressure you."

"I try not to think about it like that." Georgia twisted around to face him. "At first, I liked being special to him…but some of what you are thinking is probably right. He didn't want to tell Diamond or Ephraim." She winced. "All the sneaking around made me feel bad, but he liked it."

Mack had found it exciting. Most of her girlfriends would have, too. But Georgia had hated every minute of it.

"I'm sorry." Rainer pressed a kiss to the nape of her neck.

"I should have done a better job of putting him off earlier," she admitted. "But it wasn't easy. Every time I tried to pull back, he'd get so upset."

"I'll bet it wasn't easy." There was that tone again, the one that told her if Mack were alive, he'd be eviscerated.

"He had already moved out by the time Diamond found out."

"Diamond knew? Did Ephraim?"

"No. Diamond asked me if the affair was going anywhere. When I couldn't say yes, she told me not to tell him." Georgia sighed heavily. "Ephraim and Mack's relationship had always been combative. Finding out about us would have killed Ephraim."

"I can imagine."

Georgia winced. She didn't like to think about how hurt her dad would be if he ever found out, but she planned to take the secret to the grave—because it *would* destroy Ephraim.

Fingers brushed her cheeks, and she realized Rainer was soothing her frown.

"You can see well in the dark," she murmured.

"Better than most people, I guess," he admitted, dropping a kiss on her forehead before urging her to 'get it all out'.

"When did it end?" he asked.

"Well, it sort of petered out when Diamond got sick. She had cancer for a long time, but when she had to check into the hospital, we knew the end was near. I spent all of my time with her. Even Mack came around, made nice with Ephraim for her sake."

"Were you both working at Elite by then?"

"Yes, him for years. I had been there for less than one when she passed."

"Did Mack just let you go?" Rainer managed to not sound skeptical.

"Not exactly." She shifted uncomfortably. "Mack seemed to think I was going to move in with him—that I was waiting for Diamond to pass to avoid hurting her. He was upset when I finally told him no, that it was me. That despite everything, I didn't want that kind of relationship with him."

"I don't suppose he took it gracefully?"

She sighed, a wealth of grief in the small sound. "He started drinking a lot more. A few months later, he took one of the Elite loaner vehicles overnight. He drove it up the coast, on the Pacific highway. It was raining, and the car hydroplaned. It went over the rails into the water. When they found the vehicle, it was empty. The police couldn't say whether he was swept out through the open window, or if he managed to get out of the car, only for the rough water to carry him out to sea." Georgia sank into the mattress. "We had a service...buried an empty box."

"And you blame yourself for his death." Rainer squeezed her. "George, you can't. He's the one who put all those unfair expectations on you. If he were still alive, I'd kick the crap out of him for the mess he made—what he put you through."

She groaned. "This is why I don't tell people. They think I'm damaged because of it. But that's not how it was."

"You loved him. Not the way he wanted, but you loved him and didn't want to hurt him." His tone sounded so understanding, not a bit of judgement.

"*Yes.*"

Rainer nuzzled his face into the crook of her neck. "I don't think you're damaged. I would prove it, but making love to you after those revelations would feel wrong—but make no mistake, I'm going to fuck your brains out come morning."

Georgia laughed aloud. "You're so fucking romantic."

Chuckling, he kissed her. "Don't you ever forget it, baby."

CHAPTER SEVENTEEN

Being deliriously happy while snowed in during a hellacious blizzard was probably a serious character flaw, but Georgia didn't care.

She was trapped with a gorgeous man with an even more gorgeous body. The only thing more beautiful might have been his soul.

Rainer was being so sweet, so understanding. Any other guy trapped in a cabin without electricity or running water would have been a complete grump, or worse. But Rainer kept a cool head, dealing with their problems with a rare patience she wasn't likely to find in another man. He liked figuring things out, but always asked for her input and even followed her advice when he thought it was better than whatever solution he'd come up with.

Rainer didn't even complain about the cold-as-hell water they washed up with. He just added an extra pot of snow to the fireplace to make sure it would be warm by the time she was ready to wash.

That right there, she told herself, *was a man who deserved a hundred blowjobs*. Maybe a thousand.

So, it was a little disturbing that he wouldn't sleep with her.

Oh, they had sex. A lot of it. But on the second night after her revelations, she woke up cold and alone. When she went looking for

Rainer, she found him in the nearest bedroom, sitting on the side of the bed—the bed that had clearly been slept in.

The look he gave her was a mix of guilt, frustration, and exhaustion.

"If you wanted to sleep alone, you could have said something," she said quietly.

Rainer put his head in his hands. "I don't—George, that's not it."

But he didn't explain. He just hung his head, closed his eyes, and sighed.

Get ahold of yourself. You knew this was coming. Someone like Rainer was bound to realize he could do better sooner rather than later.

"Hey, I get that you have second thoughts about getting involved," Georgia said, her voice a little huskier than she would have liked. "I know this isn't something you would have done—with me anyway—not under normal circumstances. But we can't afford for you to get sick. Sleeping in this cold room alone is not a good idea. We can just go back to sleeping platonically. Or I can sleep on the couch behind the mattress. I fit on it better anyway."

His head jerked up. "That's not what this is about. I *want* you."

Sure he did. That was why he was willing to freeze to death to avoid sleeping next to her. "You don't have to say that. I'm a big girl. I can deal with rejection."

"That's not what I'm doing," Rainer said, his tone sharpening.

Georgia pressed her lips into a tight line, taking a step back.

Sighing, Rainer stood. His face softened as he cupped her cheeks in his hands. "You're the first person who has made me feel normal in a *long* while."

She tilted her head up to search his face. "How long is long?"

"Over a year."

"It's been that long since you slept with anyone?" she asked in a low voice, a creeping suspicious building in the pit of her stomach. "But isn't that when your security thing happened?"

He didn't say anything for so long that she thought he wasn't going to speak. Then Rainer looked over her head and nodded as if coming to some decision. "You're not wrong—what you suspect. It's related."

Georgia reached out, squeezed his hands. "You don't have to tell me," she assured him. "Just because I shared doesn't mean you have to."

"I want to—I need you to understand."

He took her hand, tugging her to the couch. They sat together and she waited, her throat tight.

Rainer took a deep breath, blinked a few times. "Fuck, I don't know why this is so hard. I told my friends and my therapist all about it. And, compared to what happens to women all the time, my thing is nothing. *Nothing.*"

His body told her otherwise. A tremor passed over him. Her heart squeezed tight in her chest in sympathy.

Anxious to do anything she could to help, Georgia inched closer, but stopped before taking him into her arms. It didn't matter that they'd already had sex. She shouldn't touch him without permission just now.

But Rainer closed the distance, scooting over until his side was pressed against hers. He didn't take her hand, keeping his forearms resting on his thighs.

"I met a woman," he began.

Of course, it had been a woman. Nothing else would explain this reaction.

"Not going to lie—up until a few years ago, a lot of women came in and out of my life," he said, his smile self-deprecating. "I was young and rich, and I enjoyed my life. But this woman, she was something else. Eileen was mesmerizing. And I wasn't alone in my reaction to her. She affected everyone that way. Every room she walked into, conversations would stop or be derailed."

Georgia didn't move, silently cataloging the woman's attributes and comparing them to her own. She didn't rate, of course, but she didn't wheedle for his reassurance.

This wasn't about her.

"Eileen worked for the British Museum buying antiquities. I was an avid collector so, naturally, I thought it was a match made in heaven. But that was just a cover for her. Eileen's interest in me wasn't real. She just needed access to my computer records." He turned to look her in the eye. His were suspiciously red. "And she drugged me to get them."

"*Drugged*? Like she roofied you?"

He nodded. "Except I don't think she slipped something in my drink. My glass was never out of my hand that I recall. The drug must have been in her lipstick."

"Shit." Georgia's eyes widened, deciding it was stupid to be jealous over a poisoned kiss. "That's some serious Mata-Hari level, femme-fatale stuff."

"I know." He laughed, lifting a hand to wipe his eye. "I woke up the next day wondering what the hell had happened. It took me a while to figure out she'd broken into my laptop, accessing my financial records."

"Was she a corporate spy?"

His cheeks pulled up, and he shook his head. "Not according to the key-logger program I used—something Powell installed.

"Of course," she acknowledged. "What did she want?"

"She was after some broker in the art world. I thought it was weird because my information on the man said he was legit. At least I thought so until the broker ended up dead."

Holy crap! "She could have killed you." This time, Georgia did touch him, wrapping an arm around his waist. It was grossly inadequate. She wanted to wrap him in bubble wrap and put him where no one could hurt him.

"Actually, the police cleared her in that death," he said, shrugging. "A DEA agent investigating her came around. They interviewed me. Later, I found out that she teamed up with him, so, ultimately, Eileen must have been on the side of the angels."

Georgia scowled. "That does not excuse what she did to you. Even if she was some sort of undercover super-spy—there were ways to get that information without hurting you."

One broad shoulder lifted. "Maybe she thought I was one of the bad guys. And I wasn't hurt. Not really."

The sound she made was straight-up Diamond—when her foster mother decided it was time to stop bullshitting around.

"You're so clean that you damn near squeak," she snapped, her hand flexing with the urge to slap this Eileen woman silly. "And don't say you weren't hurt. It's no coincidence that this period is when you started living your hermit life or that you began to donate to women's and children's charities in large amounts. You did that because you identify with them—because you know what it's like to be vulnerable, to be violated."

Her hands and voice were shaking by the end of her speech.

Rainer sniffed, wiping a rogue tear away with the heel of his hand. "I know. My therapist and I have had this particular heart-to-heart a few times. I talked to Garrett, too, and took steps to train to get in better shape. I even learned some hand-to-hand fighting techniques so I wouldn't ever be that vulnerable. So, I'm not saying it didn't affect me. But I do think what I went through doesn't compare to the trauma of abuse survivors. I should have gotten over it by now. In most respects, I have, or at least I told myself I did. Until I tried to start dating again afterward."

His inability to sleep with her now made so much sense. "No more overnight guests?"

"No anything." He gave her a mirthless grin. "I told myself the reason those few dates went badly was that I simply wasn't into those women. That it would be different when I met someone I liked. But even though I do *really* like you, I couldn't sleep after we—"

Rainer broke off, scrubbing his face with his hands. "Well, you know.'

"I understand," she whispered. "It was fine when we were sleeping together for warmth, and nothing had happened between us. But now we've crossed that line into intimacy, so you can't be sure of me, not enough to leave yourself unprotected in sleep."

"I'm not exactly subtle, am I?" Rainer laughed self-deprecatingly. "And George—my issues aren't about the kidnapping attempt. I never agreed with Powell that you were involved. It's crystal fucking clear that you're not. Even Powell knows that now. Else you would have told the kidnappers where we were."

Frowning, Georgia closing her eyes when the obvious answer to his puzzling words bloomed in her mind.

"Powell bugged my phone, didn't he?"

Rainer's head pulled back. He grimaced. "I am not defending myself because I should have known, but I didn't ask until we were already here for a couple of days. Please know, I would never have authorized such a serious breach of your privacy. Had I really been worried about you, I would have tossed your phone away before we got on the plane."

She suppressed a snort. *At least he's honest.* And finding out the true reason behind his withdrawal tonight made her lenient. "Well, I hope you and Powell enjoyed my texts to Ephraim dissecting everything he ate and the ones to Judy from work on the man she's dating."

"I didn't read any," Rainer told her, holding up his hands. "Only Powell. He considers it part of his job."

Georgia leaned back, bracing her weight on the heels of her hands. "At least I know why he's so overprotective. He was your head of security when you were drugged."

Rainer nodded. A few more tears escaped, but even though he wiped them away, he didn't try to hide them.

Georgia could feel her heart cracking open, but not in heartbreak.

She wanted to travel in time to stop the event that had done this to him. But she also knew if she did, he wouldn't be the same Rainer. He wouldn't be the sensitive man who'd taken a good look at himself and decided to help *women,* the same sex as the person who'd hurt him, because he knew what it meant to be vulnerable. To be made powerless...

"I don't want this single shitty thing that happened to me to get in the way of my life, of whatever is going on between us," he breathed, looking down at his hands. "But it just keeps circling back."

He started to say something else, but stopped himself, closing his eyes. "I'm being stupid about this whole thing. I won't go to the other room to sleep. It's time I dealt with this."

Leaning over, he nudged her. "And there isn't anyone better to do this with than you—you're worth it. Also, it's not like you could strangle me in my sleep, even if you wanted to."

Mouth twitching, she acknowledged that. *Eileen must have been tall. And stacked,* she added morosely.

"I guess it pays to be a shrimp sometimes," she murmured.

"I didn't mean it like that," he apologized.

"I know…but I also think it's going to be harder than you think to just turn off that part of your brain that wants to protect itself." She reached over, squeezed his hand. "I mean, you could just stay awake until exhaustion finally drags you under, but that's doing it the hard way."

He raised one fine dark brow. "There's an easy way?"

She bit her lip, a tiny part of her flatteringly aware of how his eyes zoned in on that.

"Not easy, but less hard…if you let me help." Because she had an idea—or at least the beginnings of one.

Rainer took her hand in his, threading his fingers through hers. "What did you have in mind?"

CHAPTER EIGHTEEN

Rainer looked at the climbing ropes in Georgia's hands in disbelief. "You're kidding, right?"

This had to be a joke, but the look on her face was almost solemn. She handed him the colorful pile.

"I'm not. Look at them." She traced the red length of rope at the top. "These are fancy rock-climbing ropes, made out of some high-tech fiber. I'm sure they're strong, but, more importantly, they're soft. You can use them to tie my wrists. As long as we don't get too carried away, I should be fine."

But Rainer was still skeptical. "I'm not into BDSM, George. You don't have to do this to make me happy."

She pointed to a wall sconce on the right side of the mantelpiece. "The other end can go there, looping over the brass joint, that way I can reach the bathroom if I need to go in the middle of the night. More importantly, I can't get into the kitchen if we measure the length exactly right."

He frowned. "Why wouldn't I want you in the kitchen?"

Georgia showed him her teeth, sheepishly mugging in a way that surely made her look manic. "It's where we keep the knives."

He was still looking at her like she was crazy. "*Okay*. Err, I'm not sure I can tie a knot well enough that you couldn't get it undone."

She doubted that, but Georgia didn't argue. "So, it's more of a symbolic gesture. But maybe it's one that your subconscious will appreciate."

Rainer stared down at the red, green, and blue ropes in his hands. Then he set the two extra coils down and began to unwind the red one. "I can't believe I'm doing this."

But his skepticism didn't hold him back. He stretched the red rope out to its full length. Before she knew it, the rope was looped around the wall sconce. Rainer left equal lengths on either side so he could tie each end to her wrists, leaving her arms free to move. She might have been on a leash, but she had complete range of motion.

Georgia held up her hands, making a fist and imitating the stance of a boxer. "Are you sure you don't want to tie them together? I can still do some damage like this."

He laughed in her face. "Aw, George. You are adorable."

Scowling, she climbed into the bed. "By the way, there will be no nookie tonight. This is a test run."

He climbed in after her, cuddling against her back. "I understand."

"I can feel your hard-on, you big liar."

His laughter shook the bed. "All right. It's going to be a rough night, but I get it. No nookie."

Then he kissed her cheek and pretended to snore. Twisting, she poked him. He laughed again, cutting it out. But all too soon, the sleep deprivation caught up with him, and he dropped off, his even breathing signaling true sleep.

She could just make his features out in the faint firelight. Georgia pressed a kiss to one of his incredible cheekbones. "Sweet dreams, baby."

CHAPTER NINETEEN

Outside of the glass double doors, the level of snow had dropped enough to let the sunlight pour inside. It hit Rainer directly in the face.

Rousing he rolled over, untying Georgia's wrists before he got out of bed. He stood up, ready to bolt for his parka before realizing it wasn't necessary. The room was now at a bearable temperature. It was still cold, but he was no longer worried about his cock getting frostbite.

I hope this means no more snow. Then it struck him.

Hell. Georgia's plan had worked. He'd slept the entire night straight through without waking, no dreams. At least, none that he could recall in detail. He had a hazy memory of dreaming up a conversation with the mysterious Elaine, but halfway through, she morphed into Georgia and things got steamy.

Trying not to read too much into the unconscious products of his messed-up brain, Rainer got up and grabbed the buckets and bowls. He refilled them with snow from the bank just under the bedroom window, confirming that the sky overhead was clear and sunny. He saw with some satisfaction that the overall level of snow had dropped as well. It wasn't all that much, but as long as no more snow fell, they should be able to dig themselves out in a day or two.

His phone was out of juice, but he'd found a small battery-operated charger in Garrett's desk. He could snowshoe down the mountain far enough to get a signal and call in reinforcements. Except that didn't seem like much of a priority just now.

Despite burning an absurd amount of firewood, they still had around a third of the pile left. Also, no bears had discovered their outdoor refrigerator, so they were in no danger of starving.

Although getting fresh fruit and vegetables would be good. The canned stuff had gotten old fast. But when he suggested hiking down, Georgia wouldn't hear of it. "We can't be sure of the conditions down the road. I think we should wait a few more days."

He glanced at the snow out the windows skeptically. "Are you sure? What if it starts snowing again?"

Georgia sucked her bottom lip between her teeth as she mulled it over. He was immediately distracted. Damn, that should have been his mouth nipping at those lips.

"It looks so bright and sunny now, I think we can chance it," she said eventually. "But if it makes you feel any better, I saw an old radio in the garage. We can try to find a weather report. Or I can fiddle with that old generator and try to charge up our devices. Maybe the WIFI on your computer will work even if our phones don't."

Agreeing with her plan, because getting that generator up and running was useful regardless, Rainer spent the bulk of the morning helping her with the repairs.

Watching her work, those small dexterous hands taking things apart and deftly putting them back together was like watching a magician. He especially liked the way she would talk to the machinery, coaxingly with the occasional colorful threat thrown in.

"I think I finally figured out what's wrong," she said after examining the generator. "They pulled this fuel hose because it needs to be replaced, but I don't see any spares. I might be able to fashion one out of some spare tubing, but I think our best bet would be to borrow one from the snowmobiles. It's too big, but we can force it to fit with a few clamps."

Rainer was impressed. It had taken them more time to dig the generator out of the garage's clutter than it took for Georgia to diagnose the problem.

"Sounds good to me," he said, bowing down to her expertise with a grin.

She turned to him and grimaced. "Also, little problem. The generator's tank is empty."

"Ah." He glanced around. There were none of those red gas cans lying around. And because the house was solar-powered, and they'd already established the big fuel cylinder attached to the house was empty…

"Well, I guess we can forget the generator. At worst, we can always try smoke signals, right?"

Georgia held up her index finger. "Or we use that garden hose over there to siphon some gas from the snowmobiles. If they're empty, we might have to use the car, but I'd like to avoid that for now."

"Especially since I didn't store it in the garage." Like a noob, he had left the Jeep parked outside. If they wanted to access the gas tank, they would have to dig it out of deep snow first.

He scratched his head. "So how do we siphon? Don't we need a pump?"

"Nah, I'll show you." Hopping into action, Georgia fetched the hose. Jumping up to the trailer that held the vehicle, she turned the key in the ignition long enough to get a reading of the gas gauge. "We're in luck. It's full."

Shuffling back, she opened the tank and put one end of the hose inside, making sure it curled in deep. Then she hopped off the trailer and brought the other end to the generator.

"Now what?" he asked when the hose didn't start spilling gas immediately.

She wrinkled her nose. "Not going to lie. I don't love this part."

Georgia lifted the hose, put the opening in her mouth, and gave it a hard suck.

Horrified, he reached to stop her. "No! Don't do *that*."

Taking it out of her mouth, she shrugged. "It's the easiest and possibly the only way."

"*No*. What if you end up drinking gasoline?"

"I'm a mechanic," she said with a laugh. "It wouldn't be the first time."

That was the last thing he wanted to hear. "Oh, *George*. That's terrible."

"I'm kidding. I only got a mouthful once—the first time I tried it. I spit it out, then rinsed my mouth for like an hour."

The idea of her doing something so dangerous and potentially damaging deeply disturbed him. He waved his hands between them. "If there's no other way, I'll do it. More than one mouthful of gas is liable to give you cancer. I don't want you to have a repeat experience."

Georgia's amusement faded, and she stared at him for a moment.

He frowned. "What's wrong?"

"Sometimes, you're so sweet that I have a hard time believing you're for real." Then her lush mouth firmed. "At least let me do some. We can take turns."

He didn't like it, but she wouldn't back down. Finally grunting his agreement, he took the hose and gave it a hard pull before handing it back to her, his thumb carefully plugging the opening so the gas wouldn't drop back into the tank. "It's like Russian roulette, but with a possible mouthful of gas."

Her nose wrinkled adorably as she took the hose. "If that's you admitting to having ever played that game, I will beat your ass here and now."

A flash of heat coursed through him at her concern, but the words out of his mouth were a joke. "Kinky. I love it."

She shot him a look promising violence. He held up a hand. "I've never gambled with my life—only my money. Lost a bundle in Vegas before I realized I'm a shit gambler with a terrible poker face. I had to work on it. Improving it did wonders for me in the boardroom."

Relaxing, she giggled. She took her turn and handed it back. "I think we're almost there. Don't give it as hard a pull."

"Again, very kinky, baby."

Georgia's cheeks reddened, but she pointed to the hose imperiously. Rainer managed to avoid getting a mouthful of gas thanks to his quick reflexes. He put the end into the generator's tank with only a small splash spilled on the floor.

Rainer opened the side door to the garage. The snow packed on the other end was still waist-high, but it was simple enough to grab a fistful of snow to wash his mouth out.

"Did you touch some?" Georgia materialized by his side.

"No, I'm just washing away the idea of it. I may have mentioned before that I liked the smell of gasoline, but that was before I got a mouthful of fumes."

"You're sure you didn't get any liquid on you?"

"Absolutely sure," he said, wiping his hand on his pants.

Hands on her hips, the cocky mechanic emerged from her normally diffident shell. "Really? Because I'm going to test you for that."

He muscled the door closed, kicking the small bit of snow that had fallen inside. "How?"

Standing on her tiptoes, she reached up and pulled the collar of his shirt, drawing him down. Her kiss was soft and sensual. Then her little tongue licked at the seam of his lips.

Instantly aroused, he pulled her against him, his tongue stroking with hers to tease and taste. He lost a few minutes of rational thought, half wishing it weren't so damn cold in the garage so he could strip her down and take her then and there. Every cell in his body was screaming for it.

Long, searing moments passed before he came up for air, staring down at Georgia. That was when he knew, the quiet awareness filling his chest. His life had irrevocably changed.

Then she winked at him. "Yeah, just fumes."

Her eyes alight with deviltry, she turned around, rubbing her bottom against him suggestively before sauntering back to the generator. "Maybe we can run the heat for a short while tonight."

The exaggerated wiggle in her hips was meant to be funny, but it short-circuited his brain. Walking fast, he snatched her up from behind, swinging her up so quickly she squealed in shocked surprise.

"The fucking generator can wait. I'm hot enough."

CHAPTER TWENTY

Rainer stripped off her clothes with a brutal efficiency she didn't think he possessed. Once she was completely bare, he yanked off his clothes so fast that she heard a seam pop.

Georgia landed on her back on the bed, gasping when his hard, muscled length covered her. The coolness of the room was nothing compared to his heat.

One long, hot kiss and she was as turned-on as he was, moaning as her skin soaked up the feel of him. His touch, his skin, soft and hard at the same time, like a satin-covered stone that was warm and pliable. Arching like a cat to prolong the contact, she shuddered as his mouth moved down the side of her neck.

He pinned her arms against the bed, pressing the back of her hand against the mattress, right over one of the free ends of the climbing rope.

Rainer's head pulled back, giving the rope a considering glance.

"It's okay if you want to tie me up," she whispered, letting her body go lax. "I don't mind."

The length of the rope meant she was never really restricted to the bed. If he wanted, or needed, her to be restrained so he wouldn't ever doubt her, that was fine with her. Even in this, when she was literally at her most vulnerable, she would give him more. Georgia would give Rainer everything.

And it seemed he understood that. His grip tightened on her skin, his gaze so hot his eyes seemed lit from within. A shudder passed through him. Wordless, he began to tie her wrists, taking the same care to leave them comfortable but secure.

His hands passed over her, starting at her shoulders and stroking down the inside of her arms and waist as his mouth took one of the straining buds of her breasts and began to lick and suck.

Greedy for him, Georgia wrapped her legs around his waist, using them to push down the waistband of his sweatpants, which he was still wearing. She had worked them to his knees before he reared back and finished tearing them off himself.

He covered her, his already hard length seeking her softness, his heat a brand.

Georgia whimpered as he began to slide his cock over her wet folds. The teasing friction sent little shockwaves through her. But he didn't slide into her.

Rainer shifted down, his lips enclosing her clit. Georgia jerked, but she didn't try to move away. If she trusted him enough to let him bind her, to give herself so totally, then she could give him this intimacy as well. No more holding back.

Rainer put his hands under her thighs, pulling her closer so he could indulge. His lips moved over the delicate flesh, kissing and licking gently at first. But his tempo increased, drawing on her clit, his tongue penetrating her rhythmically until she was trembling, her legs shaking as she wrapped them around his back. Moaning aloud, she melted into the bed even as her mind splintered, all thought and reason burning away in the conflagration of her orgasm.

There was the sound of tearing before Rainer slid a condom on. She opened her eyes, reaching up to stroke the carved planes of his face. One of his hands gripped her thigh as he adjusted her lax legs, opening her fully.

"Do you want my cock inside you baby?" His voice was low and rough enough to send a frisson down her spine.

"Yes."

"Good." The tip of his sheathed cock pressed against her entrance. "Tell me how much," he ordered, continuing to tease her by sliding and rubbing, stoking the flames. It left her hungry, the muscles in her sheath clenching, aching for his possession.

"More than anything," she breathed, her heart hammering at the naked admission, the way he continued to strip her down to the heart. "I want you more than anything."

"Look at me."

Shakily, she looked up to meet his burning eyes. She didn't know what he saw, but Rainer made a sound that was almost a growl. And then his hips were surging, his length sliding into her ever so carefully. He was too thick to take easily, but she was ready, her need making her pulse around him.

Groaning, Rainer surged forward until he was buried to the hilt, swallowing her gasp with his mouth. "Oh, God, the feel of you," she whimpered.

Satisfaction transformed his features. "Like that, do you?" He withdrew before slowly inching back in. "Well you're going to love this."

Then he started to fuck her.

She held on to his shoulders as he started to thrust. He stroked deeply, sometimes slowly, teasingly, then hard and fast, stimulating that deep pleasure point in the very heart of her.

Trusting this new but powerful connection, Georgia let go, giving herself over to sensation in a way she had never been able to before. One tight twisting orgasm blended into the next until Georgia was boneless, her body sated and satisfied. But Rainer hadn't climaxed so when he flipped them, urging her to straddle him, she forced her lax muscles to work.

"I like this." Georgia reached down to run her fingers across his hairline where the vibrant red of his hair was starting to show beneath the brown. "With your roots starting to show, it's like fucking a burning ember."

Rainer snickered, but then his eyes lit on her wrists.

"Wait." Mouth firming, he pulled on the ropes, Winding the slack around her wrists, he bound them together. He held them in one hand, taking control despite the fact she was on top.

"Now ride me. Hard."

Breathing fast, her body thrumming with anticipation, Georgia gamely tried. But without the use of her hand, he had to help her balance. Gripping her wrists in both hands, he lifted them over her head as she rode him, gripping his cock with every stroke as she worked him over until he was groaning, his neck corded.

And then he broke, letting out a shout as he jerked his hips up, grinding into her as his cock throbbed, spilling into the condom. Georgia soaked in the dying pulses, climaxing a final time before letting herself fall forward.

Rainer wrapped his arms around her back, her bound hands between them.

CHAPTER TWENTY-ONE

When Georgia woke up next, the ropes had been unwound, but her wrists were still tied. She lifted her hands, examining the knots dispassionately.

She knew if she asked, Rainer would untie her. But she also knew he didn't want to.

That was fine with her. The fire was high enough and there was the smell of bacon in the air. Snuggling under the blanket, she lay on the bed, listening for him.

He appeared a few minutes later, a plate in hand. Rainer arranged the pillows behind her, helping her sit up. Then he began to feed her. A forkful of eggs, a piece of bacon. He didn't speak until he'd handed her the glass of orange juice. "I plugged my phone into the generator and managed to get a call out to the solar power manufacturer. The number was on the broken controller. They're coming out with a replacement today."

"Are the roads clear enough?"

His mouth quirked up. "I authorized payment for emergency service, and they said that wouldn't be a problem. They'll come up in a helicopter if they have to, to drop their technician. But I suspect it'll be a snowmobile."

The latter proved true. The technician came by in a rented vehicle with a partner. One climbed onto the roof with a snowblower, clearing the panels while the other replaced the controller.

But Georgia didn't oversee the repair. She was still tied up in the living room. Rainer dealt with the repairmen outside, dismissing them with promises of a bonus. The heat was just starting to pump into the room when he came back inside carrying a box.

"What's that?" she asked when he set it on the mattress next to her.

"I had the repair guys pick up a delivery at the post office in town, something I had shipped overnight mail."

Tearing off the tape, he discarded the shipping box and opened the smaller one inside. Georgia took in the thick leather cuffs inside, unblinking. His mouth twitched at her lack of surprise, but he grew serious when she held out her hands.

Rainer undid the ropes, tracing the skin of her wrists to make sure it was undamaged. When he was satisfied, she didn't have a mark on her, he wrapped the cuffs around each wrist. Padded and lined in soft fabric, he closed each one like a miniature belt before closing a special fastener over the top as well as a large metal ring. She didn't realize it was a lock until he took out the key. But she didn't object when he locked each cuff, then fastened the climbing ropes to the ring.

The knot wasn't elaborate. It was simple enough for her to undo with a little effort should the need arise. But it was her willingness to wear the cuffs that mattered.

When he was done, he took her in his arms. Already naked, Georgia climbed over his thighs, unzipping him. At his urging she freed his cock, taking it in both hands. She wanted to stroke the hot satin-covered steel against her cheek, to taste him, but her small ministrations were too much for him.

Hissing slightly, he pulled her over him, positioning her in place. They came together in one fluid motion, so in sync that she had no time to think, to second-guess her actions. In his arms, she was a creature of instinct, acting and reacting.

Georgia barely recognized herself. But she didn't want to turn her brain back on. Now wasn't the time to overanalyze what was happening between them. Thinking was overrated.

The next day passed in a blur. Rainer kept her bound in the living room, deciding it was warm enough with the heat on. They didn't have to retreat to the master bedroom. He took her there on the mattress, on the couch, as well as the floor, and once against the wall. He even had her on the kitchen counter, adding enough length to the rope so she could reach.

He bathed her in the closest guest bedroom, still bound. When she ate, it was because he fed her. Very few words were exchanged, aside from a few instructions and her murmurs of assent.

Georgia had given herself over to his total control.

That should have bothered her. She had never seen herself as a weak-willed person. All her life, she'd tried to be strong, to be ballsy and real, like Diamond. But here in this cabin, with no one to judge her, she was simply…his. Incongruously every move, meal, and sexual act felt oddly liberating. Surreal, but liberating.

As soon as the water heater had enough hot water, Rainer drew her a bath in the master bedroom. He took the rope and tied it to the base of the pedestal sink, working around the cuffs as he bathed her himself, taking special care to wash and condition her curly hair.

After he wrapped her in a huge fluffy towel, and she let him dry her, her mind quiescent.

Then he took her back into the living room, bent her over the armrest of the couch, and fucked her until she screamed his name.

"We have a small problem," Rainer murmured later that night, inclining his head to press a kiss to Georgia's forehead. They were sitting on the couch now, with her gamine form curled up next to him. Her head was resting on his chest as she watched the fire, her body naked under the blanket.

He was still dressed, which didn't seem to bother her. Nothing he did bothered her. Georgia's trust in him was absolute. It was the most precious gift, more valuable than anything he owned, worth more than all of the money he had in the bank.

"What's wrong?" she asked, tone still bland, unconcerned.

"We ran out of condoms."

That roused her. Georgia tilted her head up, a tiny smile playing on her lips. She lifted a wrist. "You didn't ask for more when you got these."

Chagrined, his mouth pulled back. "I forgot."

Her body shook with laugher. "Seriously?"

He lifted a shoulder, curling his arm around her more tightly. "I'm not the one who gets them. My assistant packs my bags, and he throws in a new box every time I go anywhere."

One fine black brow lifted as she gave him a mini scowl. "I thought you said you hadn't been sleeping around."

"I haven't been, but I didn't want to go into *why* with an employee. Every time he'd put one in, I'd leave it behind in my hotel room, or if I were in at one of my properties, I'd stick the box in a guest bathroom."

"You let your friends use your properties like Garrett let you use this one?"

"Yeah," he confirmed, although it wasn't a question.

Georgia moved her head from side to side, rubbing the back of it against his chest like a cat. She wrinkled her nose. "Leaving the condoms in your guest rooms works, I guess, but I don't think I'd use a box of condoms I found in a hotel room. I'd be convinced someone had tampered with them, even if the box looked new."

He hadn't thought of that. "Well, now I feel bad for being wasteful."

She put her hand over his heart. "Don't bother. I'm sure plenty of men just snatched them. There are plenty who don't worry about consequences."

Rainer frowned. "Notice how nice and quiet I'm being about Mack."

Georgia rolled her eyes. "He's not why I said that. Just a general observation about men."

"Well, I'm a planner. And I do think about the consequences," he assured her. "If the roads are not clear enough for the Jeep, I'll take the snowmobile down to the general store. We could use a few things."

"Given your love of winter sports, I have to ask, can you even drive one?"

He shrugged. "I've used plenty of jet skis. Can't be that different."

She was quiet for a long moment before she tugged his head down for a kiss. "Or you can stay here and fuck me without a condom," she whispered. "You were abstinent for a long time. So was I. We're both clean, right?"

"I am," he confirmed, thinking about all the tests his doctor had run after the Eileen incident. Except for the sedative, everything had come back negative. "But what about pregnancy? Do you know your cycle well enough to guess when it's safe?"

"Probably not, but we don't have to work that out. I have an IUD."

Unexpectedly, jealousy flared. "For him?" he asked, the possessiveness in his voice undisguised.

Georgia hesitated. She noticed but didn't comment. "No. It was my foster mother's idea. She took me to the clinic my junior year. I didn't even have a boyfriend at the time. But Diamond didn't want an unplanned pregnancy getting in the way of my future. She knew too many unwed mothers growing up."

"Okay," he said slowly, aware he was being given another precious gift. "No rushing out to buy condoms now.

The corner of her lip curled up as she noted the rapid swelling in his pants. She put her hand behind her back. "Do you want me right now?" she asked, eyes downcast. A soft blush burnished her cheeks, turning them copper.

His stomach muscles clenched. "I do," he breathed eagerly, unzipping his pants. He pushed his shorts down, pumping his cock a few times. Georgia's eyes fixed on his dick, her little tongue snaking out to lick her lips.

Rainer damn near lost it then and there.

"Come here." He tugged her by the arm. She flowed over him like a wave of heated silk. Encouraging her to arch her back, he dipped his head to take one pouting nipple between his lips. Shuddering against his mouth, she moaned as his fingers parted her delicate folds.

Her slick moisture gathered in his hand as he switched his attention to the other neglected nipple. George was small but her curves were lush, perfectly sized for his hands and mouth.

He gave her ass a final squeeze before urging her up with a firm hand. His dick had never felt so hard as it did against her wet heat. Then she was sliding down on him, a velvet vise that gripped him so faithfully he jerked up involuntarily, driving half his length inside.

"Look at me." Rainer put his hand on either side of George's face when she tried to hide her reaction by pressing her nose and mouth against his neck. But he wanted to watch as he drove into her bare for the first time.

Her cheeks were warm against his palms, but they grew hotter as he began to pour on the praise. "You're so sweet and tight around me. It's like you were fucking made for me, for my cock."

"*Rainer*," she gasped, Her lashes fluttered closed, her mouth gaping as he pressed her down all the way home. "Oh, God. You're so thick. I feel you everywhere."

His control in splinters, he took hold of her hips, guiding her until she was riding him. "That's it right. Take all of me," he panted as she squeezed him tight on the downstroke. "You fuck *me* this time. Fuck me *hard*."

Her eyes flared open, the look on her face almost fearful, but she didn't let him down. Picking up the gauntlet he'd thrown, she braced her hands on his shoulders, surging up and sinking her hips down as she greedily worked his cock.

On fire, Rainer tried to hold out, but the sweet burn of her was too much. He wrapped his arms around her, pulling her flush against him as her wet pussy slammed home one last time. Grinding up, he let go with a shout, pumping his hot seed inside her.

A keening cry escaped her lips as her muscles milked him dry. Sweaty and spent, he collapsed on his side, taking her with him.

When he could finally speak, he had only one request to make.

"*More*."

❧

Rainer woke early, his internal chronometer continuing to rouse him at seven. Staying in bed, he watched Georgia sleep before his patience ran out and he rolled her over, covering her body with his.

The ropes slid across his shoulders as she reached up to wrap her arms around his chest, welcoming his invasion with sleepy sexy murmur and soft kisses.

When he was sure she was ready, he thrust inside, her wet heat gripping his cock. Georgia was a velvet vise around him, soft and slick. She was sweeter than molten honey, and so tight it made him crazy.

And her love, her acceptance, her trust—she would never know the havoc it played in his head, the way she'd undone him and rearranged the puzzle pieces of him into a new and unexpected image.

Rainer was never going to be the same, and he would never forgive her for that. But he didn't have to. Georgia was his. She had given herself to him and he would never discard such a treasure.

So, he took her, trying to show her that with his body. Nearly feral in his possessiveness he consumed her, swallowing her breathy cries as she climaxed. A few more taut strokes and he exploding, pulsing hard until her pussy overran with his cream. Sticky and smelling of him all over, she unselfconsciously pressed him close, not letting go as those last precious spasms faded.

Until Georgia he hadn't climaxed inside a woman without protection in over a decade—the only other time with his high school girlfriend. As a man, he hadn't trusted any woman in his bed that much. But this was different.

Withdrawing, Rainer sat back on his haunches as Georgia lay spread open in front of him. He traced her folds as his glistening seed ran from the very core of her. The sight transfixed him. That and Georgia's faint but dreamy smile. Panting to catch her breath, she spread her limbs, her cuffed arms slack at her sides.

He watched her for a long time before getting up to fetch a warm washcloth. Georgia stayed in that drowsy relaxed state as he cleaned her up, opening her eyes only when he kissed her and told her he was going to be working in the office for a few hours.

"Want me to untie you?" he asked.

"I'm fine." She yawned adorably, closing her eyes.

Rainer let her sleep, not bothering to cover her naked body because the room was warm, and he appreciated looking at those glowing curves too much to cover them up willingly. If she were cold, Georgia could grab the blanket on her own. It was within reach. So was the fridge and the bathroom. He'd measured the length of rope twice to make sure.

He left his office door open, in case she called out, and settled at the desk to work. Feeling calmer and more focused than he had in a while, he dived into each task, catching up on the hundred or so emails that had accumulated in his absence.

And to think my assistant filtered these. His PA had only passed on the most important messages, the ones that required his personal attention. As far he could tell, they had followed his instructions to the letter—and still, he was barely a quarter done.

I need to fucking delegate more. Rainer's trust issues were bleeding into his business dealings.

Well, perhaps this was the push he needed to hire more people. Another analyst and perhaps an assistant for his assistant. Jotting down notes, he resumed tackling the inbox—determining to clear it before lunchtime.

He was so engrossed that he didn't notice the text alert from the silent alarm or the sound of the front door opening.

CHAPTER TWENTY-TWO

Georgia was a lazy lizard. That was what Diamond had always called her and Mack when they overslept and were in danger of missing their school bus.

She'd been lying in that half-sleep twilight state all morning, glorying in the fact she had nowhere to be. Given the fact Mitchell always stuck her with early shifts, she couldn't even remember the last time she'd gotten to sleep in.

Even on her days off, someone was waiting for her. Their neighbors would knock at their door, sometimes before they had to go to work, for a jump or to ask if she could 'take a peek' under the hood whenever their cars made weird noises. They knew she would always do it, regardless of the time. She was a pushover.

Except she didn't feel like one right now. And wasn't that ironic? She was naked, tied to a bed, and she felt fine. No misgivings. No guilt. And no shame.

So, when she opened her eyes and saw a big, dark-haired man carrying two grocery bags, she simply looked at him with mild interest.

It seemed the man was more surprised than she was. He dropped one of the paper sacks he was carrying when he saw her. Transfixed, the stranger stared at her, slack-jawed.

❧

"Holy fuck."

Rainer jerked his head up. That wasn't Georgia. It had been a man's voice. Grabbing the nearest weapon—a heavy geode paperweight—he bolted up and out to the living room where he'd left Georgia tied up.

It was lucky the man was carrying a grocery bag. It was an odd enough sight for Rainer to stop and look at the intruder.

"Garrett, you piece of shit, you just scared the crap out of me!"

His friend jerked, swiveling his head before jerking "*I* scared *you.* What the hell is that?" he asked, jerking his thumb at a motionless Georgia.

Rainer swore under his breath. His lover was lying there completely exposed. Rushing past Garrett, he snatched the blanket up, throwing it over her naked body.

"I'm sorry, Georgia," he whispered. Garett may have been his friend, but she had been lying out here defenseless and exposed to please Rainer. This was all his fault.

"It's okay," she mumbled before turning her head and closing her eyes.

Blinking, he took a step back.

"Is she drugged?" Garrett stage whispered.

"What? *No,*" Rainer hissed back. He stepped up to snatch the remaining sack in his friend's arms. The second one he'd let fall had spilled at his feet next to the coffee table, but that could wait until later.

Physically dragging Garrett, Rainer herded the other man into the office. Closing the door, he rounded on his friend. "Don't take this the wrong way, but what the hell are you doing here?"

Garrett burst out laughing. "That's what I want to know—what the fuck is going on? I thought you were in hiding, not hosting a sex orgy."

Rainer scowled. "I know you can count. One woman does not an orgy make."

Still smirking, Garrett sat back on the long leather couch set against the wall. "I thought you were coming up here alone, except for that mechanic who gave you the heads-up about the kidnapping. I would have never guessed you'd bring a woman. I mean, it's smart, but I had no idea you had it in you."

"I don't." Rainer couldn't quite look Garrett in the eye. "Georgia *is* the mechanic."

It didn't register the first time. Rainer had to repeat himself before Garrett understood.

"Your mechanic is a girl?"

"No, you ass. She's a full-grown woman."

Garrett whistled. "Oh, trust me, I noticed. And damn if I'm not jealous. My mechanic is male, balding, and has a paunch out to here." He held out a hand a few inches in front of his stomach. "If mine looked like that—"

Rainer held up a hand. "Do yourself a favor and don't finish that thought. I'm still not over the fact you saw her naked."

His friend snickered. "Is that supposed to be my fault? Because the last time I checked, this place has half-a-dozen bedrooms. There's no need to play your reindeer games in the living room."

Rainer scrubbed a hand over his face. "I know, I know. But it was necessary to sleep out here when the power went out. The guest rooms were frigidly cold, the gas lines frozen. The only wood-burning fireplace is that one in the living room."

"Oh, yeah. I had that one done the old-fashioned way for ambiance," Garrett said, crossing one leg over the other. "That's why I came out here. I heard from the power company—my office received the service notice for the solar panel repair. That's how I knew something had gone wrong up here, so I decided to drop by to make sure everything was all right."

He broke off, studying Rainer's face. "I did text you first."

Rainer covered his mouth, face hot. "I didn't get it. But thanks for coming to check on me," he muttered.

"You're welcome." The sardonic expression on his face was classic Garrett, but his eyes held a hint of concern.

"The cell tower must have gotten knocked out," Rainer added. "We haven't been able to get calls or send texts. Only the WIFI works. I organized the solar repair by email."

"Ah, well that explains it. I had fiberoptic installed a couple of years ago—the wires are buried underground."

Rainer pictured the long drive up the mountain. "Wasn't that expensive?"

"An arm and a leg, but a few of us who come up here went in on it together."

Rainer nodded, then hesitated. "Had I known you were coming, I would have…er…"

"You would have hidden your sex slave?" Garrett finished for him, laughing.

Rainer closed his eyes, praying for patience. "It's not like that. Georgia is special."

"You don't have to tell me *that*. There are not that many women who would willingly let you do that to them. Well, I suppose you could find some at a BDSM club, but even those might have a problem with being tied up while you went about your day."

Garrett cocked his head to the side, a move right out of his therapist's playbook. "But the way she's just lying there is a little unnerving. Are you sure she's okay?"

Dear God, Rainer didn't want to be having this discussion. "George is fine," he insisted.

"Really? Because I don't know whether to call a social worker for her or bow down to you—you put someone in a sex coma."

"Could you not?" Rainer snapped. "And it's not a sex coma. She just spoke. You heard her."

"Yeah, that's my point." Garret leaned forward. "I came in saw her buck naked, and she didn't even try to cover up."

"She's half-asleep. I woke her early."

His friend's face tightened. "Rainer, she talked to you. Yeah, she's out of it, but she was awake."

Where the hell was he going with this? "What are you implying? That she was coming on to you because she was naked and didn't rush to cover up?"

"Of course not. There was no invitation in her eyes." Garrett's face screwed up. "That's not what I'm saying. It's just that most women would have snatched that blanket to hide the goods. But your George barely batted an eyelash. Are you sure she's not on something? She didn't smell of booze, but what about drugs?"

"We just have the basic over-the-counter stuff, and she hasn't touched any of it. Hell, she didn't even get to pack her own bags before we came here. It's just been a very intense couple of days. George is not like your ex-wife," he added gently.

Garrett dipped his head. "Sorry, that's just where my brain goes. And it's obvious your little mechanic isn't another Katrina. Just chalk it up to me being a jealous bastard."

"I know that's not it," Rainer said, his mouth quirking up. "You're worried about me. And even though I'm coming off like an ungrateful SOB here, I do appreciate it."

Garrett studied him, his face uncharacteristically somber. "That thing last year messed you up. You shut down so completely, not dating, and barely going out if you didn't need to. And I'm not the only one who was concerned. I hoped all that paramilitary training we did with Auric would help you snap out of it, but it didn't seem to."

Rainer had stuck with Auric, training with Mason long after Garrett quit. He took solace in the newfound ability to defend himself. But it hadn't magically fixed all his issues, especially the ones he hadn't realized he had until coming here with Georgia.

Touched by his friend's concern, Rainer sat next to him. "It did help a little, but I guess there was more to work out."

Garrett snickered suddenly. "So, that's what the sex dungeon in my living room is? You working out your issues?"

He saw the look on Rainer's face, forestalling further argument by putting up his hands in pre-emptive surrender. "I get it. I do. That Eileen bitch swiped your legs out from under you, and now you need total surrender in the bedroom. I'm glad you found yourself a nice little sub."

"A submissive? That's what you think George is?"

"Yeah." Garrett widened his eyes for emphasis. "Make that a hell yeah."

Rainer looked down at his hands, considering that. It made a great deal of sense, now that he considered it.

Georgia was very capable and painfully bright when it came to all things mechanical. But it was almost as if that genius with metal and steel obscured the tender personality underneath.

He recalled the way she'd reacted when he visited her at her garage before the kidnapping. She hadn't been able to look him in the eye long, not until he'd focused his attention on the Talbot. Georgia had fully engaged after that, relaxing in his presence in a way he knew she wouldn't have been able to without the presence of a shiny car to act as a buffer.

Of course, shyness didn't automatically equate with a submissive personality. However, a good deal of Georgia's behavior over the last couple of days did point in that direction. Even when her safety had been at stake, she'd deferred to him, letting him decide when and where to hide.

That doesn't count. She had a head injury.

Maybe he was reading too much into her past behavior because it suited him. Because he wanted to believe Garrett right now. If George were a true submissive, then Rainer had a chance of moving this fragile but intense connection beyond the confines of this cabin.

"Although, she was the one who suggested the ropes," he mused, forgetting his audience.

"She did? Well, damn. Now I'm really fucking jealous."

Blinking, Rainer refocused on Garrett.

"Hey, you do whatever you need to do," the other man said. "I'll just be glad to have my friend back."

"Thanks," Rainer said, and he meant it. But he couldn't lie to his best friend. "But I'm not sure he's coming back. Not the same one you knew."

Garrett didn't give a fuck. "So you've discovered a kinky streak," he said, throwing up his hands. "Nothing wrong with that."

'There's not?" Because Garrett's initial reaction had been so shocked, it had made Rainer realize just how out of character he'd been acting.

He shrugged. "You're the last guy I would have pegged as a secret Dom, but if that's what gets your rocks off, go for it. There are plenty of girls who like that sort of thing."

Rainer knew it wasn't a simple as that. For one, the idea of doing anything similar to another woman was repugnant. It had to be Georgia. Only with her could he explore this side of him.

Uncertainty began to gnaw at him. Rainer didn't recognize himself anymore. This new need for control, to dominate, was a trait he had always associated with abusers.

This is where the monsters come from, the ones who hurt the women he had made it a mission in life to help.

You're not like them—not yet. He wasn't alone in this. George had consented on every level. But what if this hunger wasn't satisfied by what she'd given him? What if he ended up asking for more? For too much?

What would that make him then?

CHAPTER TWENTY-THREE

Georgia opened her eyes when Rainer put a hand on her wrist.

"Hey," she said, the sleepy lassitude burning away with the touch of his fingers on her bindings.

"Hi." He was sitting on the mattress next to her, his long legs splayed out in front of him. "Garrett left."

Garrett. The man who owned the lodge. That explained his sudden appearance. He'd been coming to check on Rainer.

Frowning, Georgia turned her head to check the floor. She must have fallen asleep while the two men were in the office because the groceries he'd spilled were gone.

"He sent texts to warn me he was coming, but I didn't get them. I'm sorry—it was my fault he saw you naked. I shouldn't have left you tied up so long."

She heard his words, but she puzzled over her own unnatural composure. "I should be embarrassed."

His gaze grew hot. "But you're not," he said.

Her brows drew together, her puzzlement genuine. But all the things she should be feeling after such an accident, the shame and embarrassment, were distant things. "No. It's weird. Had that happened anywhere else, I would spiral."

She shrugged. “Maybe it will hit me later.”

Like if she ever saw that man again. Yes, that made sense. But in the here and now, it wasn’t something to be concerned with.

Rainer scooted closer, his hand raised. The pad of his thumb traced her lower lip. Georgia parted her lips, licking it before drawing it into her mouth to suck.

He closed his eyes, shuddering.

A thought occurred to her, and she stopped. “You don’t expect me to have sex with your friends, do you?”

Rainer’s eyes flew open. “*No*! I told you, Garrett seeing you naked was unplanned. I swear.”

“I know. I was just wondering.”

He tilted his head to one side, the hand at her mouth moving to grip her neck. His hold was gentle but possessive.

“Is that something you’d be interested in? Being fucked by another man in front of me? Do you want to be shared?”

There was a dark and dangerously thread in his voice, but Georgia was in a place where she had no barriers, no capacity for prevarication.

“I’m not sure.” She frowned. “Would it make you happy?”

His fingers spasmed on her neck. It was just a touch, not enough to tighten his hold, but an involuntary and very telling gesture. “Not at the moment. Pretty sure it would make me homicidal.”

She smiled, incongruously pleased. “That’s all right, then.”

Georgia put both her hands over the one holding her by the neck. “Are you going to fuck me now?”

Fire sparked in the depths of those dark eyes. “No. You’re going to fuck me.”

His voice was guttural, rougher than she’d ever heard it. He took her hands, helping her out of bed and guiding her to the couch. But this time, he didn’t bend her over the arm.

He stripped down with fast, jerky movements. His shirt landed on the floor, his pants kicked farther away.

Rainer took her hands, picking up the slack and lopping it around to bring both wrists together the way he liked. Then he pushed down the waistband of his boxers and sat back on the couch, holding out his hands to help her climb onto his lap.

But Georgia didn't do that. She knelt in front of him, pushing between his legs. Using both hands, she took his heat in her hands and wrapped her lips around the head of his cock.

This was an act Mack had expected of her after he'd gone down on her. That was the main reason she'd decided she hated it. But now she was glad she'd never told Rainer that, because, as usual, everything was different when it was with him.

"*Fuck*," he swore as she inclined her head to take more of him into her mouth.

Peeking up from under her lashes, she noted the way his eyes squeezed shut. One hand stretched out to wrap around her neck as he let his head fall back.

Growing wet at the sight of his surrender, she licked the rim of the head, enjoying the way his entire body grew visibly tense. Then she turned off her brain, focusing only on the hard length in her mouth.

Granted, she didn't have an extensive basis for comparison, but Georgia thought he was beautiful. Smooth and hard, his pink member jutted proudly from the neatly trimmed fur at the base. Wrapping one hand there, she licked up the side, tracing one of those thick veins with her tongue before letting her teeth graze the rim.

Letting the rate of his breathing guide her, she sucked him in, taking as much as his length as she could. Georgia couldn't take all of him, but she wanted to. His taste, his groans, it all fed her greed. She wanted to consume him, to please him, so she fought to take him deeper because he loved it.

But Rainer didn't push for more when she hit her limit. A little too far and she gagged. "Come up here," he said, tugging her into his lap with implacable strength.

"I like how you taste," she confessed raggedly as his mouth flamed down the side of her neck. The dampness between her legs quickened and she opened her legs, arching against his cock, shiny with her saliva.

"I know. And you'll have me in your mouth again," he promised, putting his thumb against her lips to give her mouth something to suck. "But I don't want to come there. I'm going to finish in this sweet pussy, and you're going to take my cum and hold it deep inside, aren't you baby?"

Georgia whimpered.

He spanked her buttock, sudden and sharp. "That's not a yes."

"Yes, I promise." Georgia tried to climb him, desperate to get his cock inside. But with her hands bound, she was a little unbalanced and she ended up falling forward. She turned her head to the side just in time to avoid smashing her nose into his chest.

His chuckle shook her body. She could still feel the vibration when he lifted her, aligning her so she could slide down on his cock.

He hissed as her sheath closed around him. Eager and hungry, she started to rock, needing his help to balance.

Rainer put his hands on either side of her face. "You're never going to learn the feel of another man's cock in your pussy," he said, throwing his hips up to impale her with his full length. "This hot little cunt is mine," he whispered, gripping the back of her neck.

Then Rainer wrapped his arms around her, pulling her breasts flush against his chest as his cock thrust into her from beneath.

Holding her body against his pounding thrusts, Georgia focused on her sheath, telling him with every pull of those muscles that she was there with him, that she wanted that thick shaft deep and hard. And then she was crying out, trying to push inside his chest, her body tight as a spring before she broke. Then her vision went out, everything growing fuzzy at the edges before going dark.

When Georgia recovered, she was curled up in Rainer's lap, one leg splayed to the side as he played with her pussy. Tracing the folds with his finger, he dipped his finger in the cream running out of her and rubbed it around her clit.

The sparks ignited, but her body was wrung out, completely drained. "I don't think I can come again."

His grin was dark, predatory. "Challenge accepted."

CHAPTER TWENTY-FOUR

Rainer wanted to kick himself when he saw the slight tightening in Georgia's expression as she stepped down into the sunken living room. It wasn't obvious and she hadn't made a sound, but it was as if their connection had recalibrated his senses. He was attuned to her in *and* out of bed.

Scowling, he decided he'd have to strip her later to look for bruises. He didn't think he'd left any, her skin wasn't dark enough to camouflage them completely, but maybe he'd missed something.

Or it's not the outside that's sore. Even though they weren't using condoms, which could add to her irritation without sufficient lubricant, Rainer knew he'd been a little too demanding. Enough to leave his delicate lover tender despite his best efforts to take care of her. But the warm baths and baby oil massages couldn't undo the irritation his greed for her had caused.

Oh, she tried to hide it from him. When he caught her eye, Georgia would smooth out her walk, denying her aches when asked directly. But he knew in this at least, he couldn't trust her. She was like him—drunk on sensation, her hunger for him making her push her body past her limits. And she did want him so bad it hurt. George didn't have the sophistication to hide that from him.

We've overindulged. Even in his wild teens and early twenties, he hadn't been this bad. But this hedonistic pace couldn't be maintained. He'd have to pull back, resolving to start tonight. As for the future, he didn't foresee a problem. The isolation that had fostered their private sex-fest was about to end.

Powell had called.

He caught Georgia up during dinner that night where they sat at the table instead of the couch as had been their habit.

She blinked those big hazel eyes at him, lips parted. "They only got one kidnapper?"

"Yes," he admitted. It wasn't the best-case scenario, but he knew Powell had pulled off nothing short of a miracle tracking his assailants. "But in this case, knowing one means we can guess his co-conspirators with high confidence."

"Who are they?" Georgia leaned forward, her apprehension apparent.

Part of her had still doubted, he realized. She must have been wondering if she'd been mistaken in clearing her coworkers. Rainer had considered that possibility himself. The voice in her recording could have been an affectation—someone she knew could have been disguising their voice.

Of course, that assumed the man had been aware she was there, perhaps had even put on a show for her because they had planned to use Georgia to draw him out in some way—making her an unwitting accomplice.

It was a possibility Powell had considered but discarded as soon as he identified the actual kidnappers and established there was no connection to Rainer's mechanic.

"The one we traced is called Vasyl Kolesnik, a small-time Russian-born criminal of Ukrainian descent."

Kolesnik wasn't big in underground circles. He was a small-time hustler who was known to the police, but who had only been busted once after hijacking beer trucks in his early twenties. Since then, he'd stayed under the radar, although rumor connected him to several minor crimes. He was considered smart by the cops who knew him

—but not above getting involved in something as stupid as kidnapping.

"He might be arrogant enough to think he can pull it off," the lead detective had told Powell. "After all, he's managed to avoid being arrested a second time—until now."

Rainer told Georgia what little he knew about Kolesnik and showed her his picture.

She shook her head, but there was relief in her expression when she said. "I don't know his face. Does Mr. Powell have any idea what he was doing at Elite?"

"I believe he was there to pick up a vehicle."

Her nose scrunched up. "He's a customer?"

"No. He was picking up a car for a far more dangerous criminal—Maxim Novikoff. Rumor has it Novikoff is a lieutenant in a Russian mob outfit run by a family back East—the Komarov's. Novikoff does a lot of business on this coast for them, and he has the reputation of enjoying the finer things in life. He owns a few cars, including the Jaguar he sent Kolesnik to have serviced at your garage."

Georgia's hand clenched around her fork, her face going gray. "The Russian mob tried to kidnap you?"

He held up a hand. "No, I don't think so."

Her agitation remained. "But you said this man had mob connections."

"Yes, but he's on the periphery," Rainer clarified. "Kolesnik does work for the mid-level guys of the Komarov outfit on occasion, but he's not considered an insider. We've had FBI corroboration on that point. The agent Powell spoke to, Ethan Thomas, has connections inside that family. Thomas was able to confirm that Kolesnik wasn't acting on official family orders. Most likely, this was a side hustle for him."

Georgia scowled. "Kidnapping's a pretty big swing for a side hustle."

"True," he conceded. "But my point is that he was probably doing this on his own. And it's not his first get-rich-quick scheme. Kolesnik's name has come up in connection to some robberies—

successful, but not noticeably big money makers. But this was a conspiracy of opportunity. It was my bad luck to attract their attention."

"And you're sure you trust the FBI's opinion on this?"

"I do," he said, mentioning how highly decorated the agent was, leaving out the fact there was a surprising personal connection. *It's a smaller world than anyone realizes.*

Once Powell had been directed to Agent Thomas, he realized he'd met the man before. Ethan had grown up and remained good friends with Mason, the auric team leader who'd supervised Rainer's paramilitary training. That personal connection gave Rainer confidence in Thomas' take on the matter.

"The agent believed, and I agree, that Kolesnik's pulled in a few of his known associates once they learned I was a client at Elite. It's entirely possible they saw me there one day and recognize my face from some interview."

"Or they noticed how the salespeople and manager fawned all over you," Georgia suggested, a tiny glint of anger breaking through her obvious concern. "That alone would have tagged you as someone with deep pockets."

"Also a possibility," he said, lips twitching at her indignation, which he suspected was directed at her boss in particular.

"Anyway, Powell thinks Kolesnik cooked up the scheme after seeing me, then he pulled in some of his buddies to carry it out. The security team is tracking all of his known associates now, but the consensus is that they won't act on their own to make another attempt. Kolesnik was the brains, and he's in jail."

"Powell was able to connect him to the kidnapping?"

"Yeah. He got lucky. Kolesnik was caught by a traffic camera dumping the car—which my men had a partial plate on. With that, combined with their eyewitness reports and description of the car, they were able to compel a DNA sample."

She frowned. "What did they compare it to?"

Rainer hesitated. "To samples taken after the fight—I hit him with one of your crowbars. It had enough blood on it to run the test."

Her mouth was a round 'O'.

"I didn't realize you hit him that hard." She passed a hand over her eyes as if she could feel an echo of the head injury she'd sustained in that fight.

"It's likely you won't remember, given the blow to your head." He leaned over to cover her hand with his. "That also makes you an unreliable witness."

George put down the fork. "*Oh*. I didn't even think of that. I can't testify against them?"

It should have warmed him that she automatically thought of doing that for him. But the idea of her in the same room as Kolesnik made his muscles clench, his fight-or-flight switch firmly on *fight*.

"I don't think that will be necessary. They have the DNA evidence, my written testimony, and my security men as witnesses connecting him to the car."

Nodding, she looked down at her plate as if getting her bearings. "I guess that means we can go home now?"

"Yes," he said, picking up his fork and digging in with gusto, looking forward to getting home. "But we don't have to rush. Tomorrow morning is soon enough, now that the mountain road is passable."

"That's great." Georgia gave him a brilliant smile, then resumed eating.

Rainer studied her carefully averted face. He tilted his head, catching her eye. "Are you worried about what will happen when we go back?"

"I am," she admitted with a tiny shrug.

"Well, don't be," he assured her. "Until everyone involved is behind bars, I'm going to do everything in my power to make sure you and Ephraim are safe."

She stared at him for a beat before nodding jerkily. "I know. Thank you."

Then she turned her attention back to her plate, making little conversation for the rest of the meal.

CHAPTER TWENTY-FIVE

Georgia picked up her suitcase, frowning at their surroundings. They had just landed on the tarmac and disembarked from the jet, but this was not the same airport they had flown out of.

Standing on her tiptoes, she searched for a central hub. But there was only the air tower and the hangers to store the planes.

"Is something wrong?" She turned to find Rainer's attention fixed on her.

The impact of those eyes hit her even harder today because he'd been so distracted last night, his mind on the kidnappers and what he needed to do to finish their ordeal.

It had seemed too selfish to bring up their situation in the midst of that. But the question still burned in her mind. *What happens to us when we go back?*

Georgia hadn't had the guts to ask, because she was afraid that she already knew.

Rainer hadn't touched her last night. After dinner, he'd gotten a few phone calls. Excusing himself with flawless politeness, he'd taken the calls in the office. When he came out, it had been edging toward midnight. He'd gotten into bed with her, pulling her into his arms, but he hadn't touched her intimately.

She had stayed awake, silently waiting for him to strip off her clothes, but he dropped off to sleep almost immediately. Georgia had fallen asleep, telling herself the fact he hadn't wanted to have sex didn't mean anything. He was still holding her there in bed, his chest pressed to her back.

When they woke up, some of Powell's men had arrived. One set the house to rights, putting back the mattress, while the other prepared their departure. She had been embarrassed, waited for them to smirk about the one bed, but the two men were distantly polite and professional. After breakfast, the pair escorted them down the mountain and onto the plane, sitting at the other end to give them privacy. Now one took Rainer's bag and they disappeared, presumably to fetch a vehicle.

She took the fact that he didn't offer to take her bag as a sign. "I know I was kind of out of it, but I'm fairly sure we flew out of a major airport. I thought we would fly back into one as well."

"Ah, I see. Well, flying out of a major airport is atypical for me," Rainer said. "The wait times for a runway can get crazy there, which is why I normally fly out of smaller places like this. I only flew out of a major when we left because the jet service I use had just landed there. It was faster for them to refuel and tap a fresh pilot for us than get someone out here. But smaller airfields are faster as a rule. Why do you ask?"

"I, uh, was going to go look for a taxi stand. They're sometimes cheaper than an Uber."

There was a moment of silence when all she heard was the wind.

She was looking at the ground, so she only saw the polished leather of his shoes stepping closer. "George, can you look at me?"

Reluctantly, she obeyed. Eye to eye, it was impossible to conceal the doubt and indecision she'd been hiding from him all day.

His hand moved up to splay over her nape. Instantly relaxing under his hold, she melted against him with a sigh.

"Did you really think things were over between us?" he asked, stroking down her back.

"The thought crossed my mind," she admitted, mouth pursed.

He grew very still. "Is that because you want it to be over?"

"*No.*" Georgia clutched his arm. "I don't...but I thought you might. That last night was your way of telling me we were winding down."

He scowled. "Why would you think that?"

Reddening, she shrugged and looked down, her eyes fixed on his chest. He was wearing a polo shirt and khaki pants, dressed more preppy than she'd ever seen him.

"Because we didn't have sex. I thought maybe you were trying to prepare me for the fact it was over—that it was a 'what happens in the mountains stays in the mountains' kind of thing."

Rainer groaned. He bent until his forehead touched hers as his hand moved down to cup her ass. "That's not why I didn't fuck you last night," he whispered, the bad language transformed into a husky caress.

He paused to take her mouth, a short, sipping kiss. "I was just trying to give you a break. I haven't been taking it easy on you, and I know you're a bit sore."

Her hands closed on his shirt reflexively, wanting him even now in this public place. "I'm *fine*."

"Baby, you were starting to walk funny." He laughed before the smile fell away. "I'm not about to let any harm come to you, especially not through my own hands or actions."

He took her wrists, holding them against his chest. "That's a part of us now, all right? I want you to understand—everything that happens from now started there. That's our foundation."

His grip tightened a fraction. "If I hurt you in any way, know that it was unintentional. Not that matters between us should ever get to that point—I expect you to call me on any shit you're uncomfortable with *as* it happens."

Georgia met his gaze, the minor bustle of their surroundings fading until she was alone with Rainer, the only two people in the world.

"I understand," she agreed, throat tight. "And expect the same from me—I will never intentionally hurt you."

The corners of his mouth pulled up. "Somehow, I never doubted that."

Wrapping an arm around her, he turned them to face the approaching vehicle, a Mercedes town car. One of his security men got out of the passenger seat, coming around to open the door to the back before taking her suitcase to the trunk.

Rainer bent his head until his mouth was just next to her ear. "And for future reference, always assume I want sex."

Flushing wildly because she was fairly sure the security man had caught that, she ducked into the backseat.

"Are you going to drop me at the apartment with Ephraim?" she asked as the car left the airfield.

Reassured that her new and intense connection to this man wasn't going to disappear now that they were home, she was eager to see her foster father. "Because he's expecting me. I spoke to him this morning. He said he likes the place but won't tell me much about it."

She thought that might be because he was missing the house too much, but when she asked, he'd told her that wall and floors were not what made a home.

"Our old house is not where Diamond's heart rests," he'd told her. "That will move with us and will go wherever we call home.

That had made Georgia cry, but she had been comforted by the words in the end because he was right.

Rainer raised a brow, seemingly satisfied by the uptick in her mood. "He didn't send you any pictures?"

"He can barely text," she sighed.

His nose wrinkled. "But he runs a business."

"And he had his staff set up his website. His secretary would check his emails and reply to them. He can use a computer, of course, but the model he uses to run his accounting software is a stripped-down one that is at least five years old." She smiled. "He fights against upgrading it, but he's careful to make regular backups in case it dies."

"That sounds like him—old-fashioned but not so much that he sticks his head in the sand. He's careful."

"Exactly." She was glad he understood because it was more than likely Ephraim was going to kick up a fuss about staying rent-free in one of Rainer's places, sooner rather than later.

Georgia nestled against him in the backseat. "It's his way. Except for the tax code. That's the one thing he keeps up with fanboy devotion, all the while pretending to be put out whenever they add a new codicil to some obscure payroll regulation."

Amused, Rainer peppered her with questions about her foster parents and her childhood, not stopping until they had driven into the subterranean parking lot of a tall, sleek building with blue reflective glass windows.

"This is an apartment building?" she asked. "Because I always thought it was offices."

"Nope." Rainer smiled as he ushered her into the elevator. He held her suitcase, the leather messenger bag he used as a briefcase strapped across his chest. "Strictly residential."

Feeling jittery for no reason, she bobbed up and down on her toes until they stepped off the elevator on the twenty-second floor.

She pounced on her father as soon as he opened the door.

It was a measure of how much Ephraim had missed her that he didn't chide her for nearly knocking him down. Instead, he squeezed her tight, patting her on the head as if he couldn't quite believe she was back.

Rainer tapped her on the shoulder. "I'm going to check in with the security office while you two have your reunion."

He was gone before she could tell him to stay.

"So, has that boy been treating you right?"

Ephraim was watching her with that knowing look in his eye. "Of course, Rainer's been great. He made sure nothing happened to me."

"I may be an old fart, but I'm not senile yet. I know something happened."

Pursing her lips, she started to shake her head. Ephraim was a good dad, but he shouldn't have been able to tell she'd taken a lover. Diamond would have known just by looking at her, but not him.

"*Hamuda*, he didn't even bother to move your things in here."

Georgia took a step back. "He didn't?"

Ephraim gestured to a hallway. "Your things were in the second bedroom, but no sooner had I started to unpack them than Mr. Bigshot's men came and took them away."

His tone was gruff, but the twinkle in his eye told her he was amused—up to a point.

Georgia didn't know what to say. "Where did they take them?"

Her father pointed to the ceiling.

She frowned, cocking her head to the side. "Am I supposed to ask God?"

"No, I mean ask your Mr. Moneybags. He lives upstairs." Underneath the bluster, Ephraim was close to laughing.

Her mouth dropped open. "Excuse me, *what*?"

"I suspect that's where your things are, too. On the twenty-fourth floor."

"Did you give her the tour, Ephraim?"

She whirled to see Rainer had returned.

Ephraim held out his hands. "This is the living room, and that's the kitchen," he said, pointing to the end of the room. Like the lodge, the shiny chrome facilities were at one end of the large, open room.

He jerked his thumb at the hallway on the right of the door. "Bedrooms are that way. But I suspect George won't be sleeping here, will she?"

Rainer didn't bat an eyelash. He nodded at Ephraim, softening the carved planes of his face with a slight smile. He held out his hand to Georgia. "Want to continue the tour?"

Her wide eyes flicked to Ephraim, but her father smirked and waved her on. "Go."

Sucking in a deep breath, she walked over to Rainer and took his hand.

"Dinner's at seven," he called over his shoulder as he led her out the door.

CHAPTER TWENTY-SIX

Rainer kept a careful eye on Georgia's face as she entered his apartment. One of two available penthouses, his home was a three-thousand-plus square foot suite spanning two levels and four bedrooms as well as an office and a gym.

But Georgia hadn't noticed any of that yet. Her attention was fixed on the stack of boxes piled in the foyer. One item, a battered stuffed cow, perched on top.

Georgia snatched the cow, hugging it to her chest. "So, is there not enough storage downstairs?"

His heart was suddenly pounding so hard she could probably hear it. "I know it's presumptuous, which is why I didn't have these unpacked. But I was hoping, given how close we've become, that you'd consider moving in here with me."

His voice was hoarse by the time he was done. It didn't help that Georgia was just staring at him. Then she looked down at the cow as if she were having a silent, one-way conversation with it.

Damn it. "You know what? This was a bad idea. It's too soon. I can have these taken downstairs right away. My people can have your bedroom set up in less than two hours—three tops."

It was going to be very awkward facing Ephraim every time

Georgia didn't go back downstairs to sleep in her bedroom—and he wasn't willing to back down on this point. She could go through the motions of living with her foster father, but her nights would be spent with him.

Then Georgia stumbled toward him, wrapping her hands around his waist. She buried her face in his chest, still holding the cow.

Rainer had his answer.

"I'd like you to sleep with me, but you can still have your own bedroom for whenever you need a break," he said, wrapping his arms around her.

His lips twitched as she tightened her hug, driving the plastic eyes of her stuffed animal into his back.

"If you don't mind, maybe the cow can stay in your room. He's cute and all, but I think having an audience might put a damper on things."

Her snicker was muffled against his chest. She looked up at him, lush lips fighting a grin. "Mr. Mooney will be staying in another room. What we do is not appropriate for his innocent eyes."

Body relaxing, Rainer hugged her to him, letting his head fall back. As long as she was willing, he wasn't taking advantage of her. He simply needed to make sure he had her consent. *Which is why you should show her the changes to the bedroom before you do anything else.*

But Georgia had plans of her own. Her hands moved to tug his shirt collar. Obeying her wordless directive, he snatched her up instead of bending, guiding her legs around him as he took her mouth.

She parted her lips for him obediently, whimpering as he covered her ass with his hand, cupping and kneading.

"Okay, tour later," he muttered, tearing his mouth off hers. Hoisting her higher, he walked straight past the living area to his room down the hall.

He dropped her lightly on the bed, belatedly noting she was still holding the stuffed cow.

Georgia turned her head all around, taking in the spacious master suite, but stopped short when she saw the California king's wrought-iron headboard.

Two adjustable ropes were tied to the decorative rings. They stretched over the pillows, ending in a pair of padded cuffs.

"I just added this," he confessed, patting the recently installed headboard. "My old one wouldn't have accommodated them—no place to tie the bindings."

Georgia blushed, butting his arm with her head. "Did the installation guys lay those out for you?"

"I did that myself, thank you," he said primly before adding slyly. "There are leg restraints this time, too."

Lips parting, Georgia took a shuddering breath. "Where are they?"

Rising, he walked to the foot of the bed, pulling out the ankle cuffs he'd attached to each leg of the frame.

Satisfaction flooded through him when her legs crossed, thighs clenching together.

"Strip," he ordered, voice hoarse.

Standing in a fluid move, Georgia started to unfasten her pants, then hesitated. "Mr. Mooney," she said, snatching him up.

Pivoting on her heel, she opened the nearest door, which happened to be the walk-in closet.

A squeak escaped her. "This is bigger than my whole damn garage."

"Former garage," he corrected.

Winding up, it looked as if she were going to toss the cow inside, but she corrected and placed him gently on the nearest shelf, on top of his sweaters. Closing the door, she ducked her head sheepishly.

Chuckling, he shook his head. "Get naked, woman," he ordered, stripping off his shirt.

She obeyed with alacrity, but he was still faster. Kneeling at her feet, he stopped her hands when she was about to push down her panties.

Pressing his mouth to the cotton-covered mound, he did it for her, sliding the briefs down in a molasses-slow movement.

His hungry gaze met her desire-drugged one. "Welcome home, baby."

Staying on his knees he crowded her against the closed closet door, taking one of her legs and hitching it over his shoulder. The musky smell of her arousal made his mouth water, her folds glossy with it. Making a pleased sound in the back of his throat, he used his tongue to lap her clit, his teeth grazing the delicate nub.

Gasping, Georgia clutched his head, her fingers burying in his hair as he began to eat her out in earnest. Rainer set a relentless rhythm that had her moaning and whimpering until she clenched around him, throbbing against his lips.

He caught her when she would have fallen over, carrying her to the bed.

Her body was lax, her hips still twitching as he fastened the cuffs to her ankles and wrists. *Admit it.* He'd ruthlessly orchestrated her climax to get her this way, yielding and utterly defenseless.

Except Georgia had no defenses against him on a good day. Had he asked she would have lay on the bed, and waited for the restraints but Rainer liked doing it this way better. This was her first night in their home after all.

"Open your eyes, baby," he instructed as he settled on the bed, hovering over her.

Lashes fluttering, she obeyed, the hazel shade closer to molten gold as she ran her eyes over his chest and then down. Her lips parted as she saw how hard he was. Her breath sped up. She slid her feet out, opening her legs wider in silent invitation.

Then her tongue flicked out to lick her lower lip.

Shit. "You shouldn't have done that, baby." Crawling up, he braced himself on his hands and knees, his dick level with her mouth.

He didn't even have to ask. Georgia opened her mouth, wrapping those luscious lips around the head of his shaft and sucking.

"*Hell,* that feels so good," he muttered, letting her have more of him.

He knew from experience that she couldn't take all of him, but she still tried, drawing him into her mouth. But with her hands bound, the rhythm was his to set. Giving himself over, he began to fuck her mouth.

"That's it, baby," he hissed as his dick disappeared deeper until it must have been tickling her throat. "Just there, no more. Don't hurt yourself."

But Georgia wasn't in the mood to be careful. Sucking and nibbling, she made a 'nom-nom' noise in her throat. Bursting out laughing, he withdrew before he came. His minx tried to follow him, straining against her bonds and sucking harder to try to keep him.

Pulling her leg up a fraction, he smacked the side of her ass cheek. "Bad girl," he said before kissing her, their tongues tangling until he withdrew and turned his attention to her breast. Suckling each pert globe in turn, he nipped at her nipples before settling between her legs.

Sliding his cock over her pussy to spread her nectar where he needed it, he put his hands on either side of her head. Growing impatient Georgia squirmed, trying to push him over the edge.

"This is our first time in our new bed," he informed her. "I intend to take my time."

Her lashes fluttered. "The whole bed is new? Not just the headboard?"

"I bought it when I moved in, but no one but me has slept in it. But now you're here so it's ours." Pressing a kiss to her forehead he claimed her in a long, slow thrust.

Neck cording, he stayed in place, letting her get used to him. Georgia tried to reach for him, but came up short, the length of the rope too short to let her hold him.

Clutching the comforter, she tilted her hips and jerked, trying to get him to move. Teasing her, he refused to budge, until she started using her strong sheath muscles, clamping around his cock and releasing until he broke.

"You win baby," he laughed as he began to thrust in earnest, rocking in and out of her slick, hot channel with deep strokes, which she accepted with keening little noises.

Rainer swallowed those up, taking her mouth as he took her body in a long slow dance to Nirvana.

"Oh God, *Rainer*." Her orgasm nearly did him in, his vision swamping out as she shuddered underneath him. But he held on until she was climbing a second peak before he grasped her thighs, spreading her for a series of rough, grinding drives.

Crying out, she strained against the bonds as he pushed in a final time, muscles tense as iron as he filled her with his seed.

She was still spasming around him when he undid the cuffs, freeing her before turning them around so she landed on top. He didn't want to crush her, but he liked being close afterward.

Her sweat-slicked body was cooling before she could speak. "I think I'm a nympho now."

An inelegant snort escaped him. "I love fucking you, too."

Georgia raised her head, light dancing in her eyes. "Have I ever told you how romantic you are?"

"Hmm. Let me try again…you have the sweetest, tightest pussy in the world." He grinned, his hand passing over the silken skin to settle on the luscious globe of her ass. "And the most delicious ass I've ever had the pleasure of squeezing. How's that?"

Her laughter vibrated in his chest. "Better. A girl likes to know she's special, or that her pussy is at least."

He gave her a minute before flipping them so fast she squealed in alarm. He thrust his rapidly hardening cock back inside her. "Correction. It's my pussy."

Georgia's face softened, the muscles growing lax as he began to surge, riding her with increasingly greedy strokes.

He pinned her wrists down with his hands. "Every inch of you is mine," he said, punctuating his words with thrusts deep enough to make an audible slap. "Your mouth, that sweet pussy, the glorious ass, your soft skin—all mine."

Georgia absorbed his aggressive declaration with a gasping moan, growing impossible wetter. "I am, I'm yours," she breathed, using the freedom he allowed her to wrap her legs around him, pulling him tight as if she were trying to meld their bodies together. "And you're mine too."

"Yes." *I love you.* The words were on the tip of his tongue, but the hunger dug its claws in, burning away all speech and rational thought.

CHAPTER TWENTY-SEVEN

Georgia opened her eyes with a start, realizing she had passed out after her last body-wracking orgasm.

Panic fluttered in her chest as she recalled all the things she said, the way she had ceded all control to Rainer in bed. Whatever he wanted, she did, giving him her body with no reservations, no rules. Their connection was blistering, burning so hot that she didn't even think about what she was doing when they were together.

Reason was rearing its ugly head now. Her infatuation at first sight had officially exploded into reckless full-blown love.

The potential to get hurt was very real here.

The worst part was that she knew she wasn't even going to try to pull back. She couldn't, even if she wanted to. Rainer wouldn't let her. Yes, he was willing to give her some breathing room, always presenting her with a choice. Except it was anything but. Her clawing need had rewired her brain. Georgia didn't even hesitate, blithely giving away her freedom in exchange for that blistering connection.

It's a two-way street, she assured her pounding heart. Rainer was in this as deeply as she was. And if any man was worth this headlong obsession, it was this fascinating one.

He was sleeping quietly now, his arm flung out toward her as if he were reaching for her even in sleep. And just like that, she could feel him inside her, his taste flooding her mouth.

Closing her eyes, she shook her head, getting out of bed before she could press against him, rubbing her breasts against him to wake him up.

Instead, she forced herself to get up and examine her surroundings.

The master bedroom was stunning. Sleek contemporary furniture was widely spaced out with the massive bed against one wall and a big, mirrored bureau against the other. Next to it were two plush armchairs with a table in between to make a little reading nook. Beyond it, was a wide balcony bare of furniture. This was separated by a pair of sliding glass doors that framed a picture-perfect sunset over the Pacific.

That view more than anything else drove home one undeniable fact. "He's too rich."

Hands closed over her shoulders, making her start. "I hope you won't hold that against me."

His voice was a little rough, still touched with sleep. But his hands were warm on her skin.

"It's unnerving," she admitted. But that didn't stop her from leaning against him.

His arms wrapped around her, tucking her under his chin. "It didn't seem to bother you at the lodge."

Titled her head up until she met his eyes, she murmured, "Maybe because I knew it was your friend's house. But this is all you."

He turned her to face him completely when she winced. "Hey, one of those rooms is yours now. Two if you want your own office."

"I don't have much use for an office."

"How about a garage?"

Startled, she looked up. "But it's one big parking lot downstairs."

"With storage units that are basically several fenced-off parking spaces. I have a pretty big one downstairs. And it's mostly empty. If we push everything in it to the side, it will make for a rather good workspace. I don't think the other owners would mind if you turned it into a garage."

"Are you sure?"

"They don't live on-site." He sucked his lip into his mouth, letting it escape with a pop. "Also, I happen to be the majority shareholder, so it's not likely they'd fuss."

Rolling her eyes, Georgia fought a grin. "All right, Richie Rich. Shower first, then tour."

After they cleaned up Georgia borrowed one of his shirts and a pair of his boxers so he could show her the apartment without feeling exposed.

Despite her continued reservations about her surroundings, she remained collected, going through each spacious room on the first floor with affected nonchalance. She even poked fun at the harsh lines of his modern furniture and sparse decorations.

"Such a male apartment," she teased, waving at a bare glass bookshelf in one of the spare bedrooms. "Are you allergic to clutter?"

"I used to have more pieces on display," he informed her, putting his hands in his pockets. "But I haven't gotten around to taking them out of storage after the move."

A tiny pucker appeared between her brows. "I thought you said you lived here for a few years."

"Just over one. I spent most of my life on the East coast."

She tilted her head questioningly. "And these pieces—is that like an art collection?"

He nodded. "Yes, although it leans more to antiquities than paintings, although I do have a few of those."

"By antiquities, you mean museum-type statues and ceramics?"

"As well as ancient coins. I went through a big coin collecting phase at one point. It's how I caught the bug initially."

She turned, her hand running up the inside of his arm. "But you've lost your taste for it because of Eileen."

Georgia did cut right to the heart of the matter. She saw through his excuses down to the hurts that had never quite healed.

"Well, I guess we've established I'm not as over that as I believed," he admitted with a mirthless grin.

"Because you proudly showed off your collection to her and she stabbed you in the back?"

Grunting, he stared at his shoes. "Something like that."

Georgia's hand shifted, pressing against his chest. "You shouldn't let what that *woman* did ruin your enjoyment of the things you love."

His lips twitched. Only Georgia could make 'woman' sound like a swear word. But she had a point.

"You're right, of course. I hadn't stopped to think about it, but I suppose it's time to reclaim my collection." Slinging an arm around her shoulders, he walked her out of the guest room. "Maybe we should go to the storage place this weekend, so we can go over the things I have. You can pick whatever you want to bring back or choose new stuff from the piles of catalogs I still get."

He gestured to their minimalist surroundings. "Put your own stamp on this place. It could use some softening up."

Georgia snorted. "Soft? I don't think I can do soft. If you left it up to me, I'd put up Bugatti W16 on display in here." She kissed her fingertips with a loud smacking sound. "Because that engine is a work of art."

His mouth dropped open, caught by the idea. "Shit, baby, that sounds cool. Let's do it!"

Georgia giggled and turned around, shock making her do a double-take. "Wha—where are all my boxes?"

She looked back over her shoulder. "Do you have a bunch of freaking house elves on the payroll? Because I know your security is too good for them to have been stolen."

He covered his face, shoulders shaking. Georgia could make him laugh without trying. "I texted my people the green light before we jumped into the shower. They put the boxes in the spare room closest to the master bedroom."

A fine black brow raised in mocking awareness. "The one you skipped over?"

He held up his hands. "I didn't have them unpack them. They were just moved. I still want you in my room with me, but you can use the spare bedroom as a staging point—unpack your boxes, bring in whatever you want to the master suite."

"And you're going to make space in that huge honking closet for me? Because I demand half."

"That won't be a problem."

She nudged him with her hip. "I'm kidding. The section that's still clear is more than enough for me."

He shook his head. "You say that now, but I have some definite plans for your wardrobe."

Georgia wrinkled her nose. "You're going to make me wear dresses, aren't you?"

He ran his palms down her back. "I have some fantasies that involve lifting your skirt and having my way with you, so maybe you'll indulge me on special occasions. But I'm a fan of a sharp sexy pantsuit, too. Maybe with some heels?" he asked hopefully. "You're so tiny, I'm going to get a crick in my neck kissing you."

"Very well." Georgia waved airily, a queen addressing her loyal subject. "If I must. But I get to pick them. No stilettos. Those are murder on the feet."

Rainer perked up. "So, you've worn stilettos before? Because one of my fantasies has you standing on that coffee table over there in nothing but heels…with my mouth buried between your legs."

Georgia inspected the glass-topped coffee table with a skeptical eye, but it turned to fascination when she realized the base was iron that held a massive amethyst geode.

"I'll do it," she breathed, touching the glass over the shimmering purple crystals with a reverence he hadn't expected.

Mental note, cover Georgia in colorful gemstones. Preferably when she was otherwise naked.

That gave him another excellent idea. "I want you to stand there after we fuck, so I can watch my cream run down your silky thighs."

Shocked eyes flew to meet his. "You want me to *what?*"

Cupping her nape, he pulled her close for a brief but possessive kiss. "If you have trouble on the heels, you can sit there and spread those gorgeous legs so I can admire your beautiful pussy like the work of art that it is—pre or post fucking. I'm good with either."

She covered her flaming cheeks with your hands. "You better give the house elves the day off when we do that," she scolded.

His eyes widened. "But you'll do it?"

"Of course I'll fucking do it," she said, lowering her hands. "It sounds super-hot."

Rainer was reaching for her when he caught a glimpse of the wall clock behind her. He groaned. "We have exactly ten minutes before your father gets here for dinner."

Panic flared. Georgia let go of his hand, then ran down the hall. "Damn it, Rainer, he can't see me like this! I need clothes."

"I think you're perfectly presentable," he called, grinning when she swore at him.

He turned to find his part-time chef exiting the kitchen. "I think we'll have dinner in the formal dining room," he told him.

Wordlessly, Massoud nodded, returning to his domain to prepare.

CHAPTER TWENTY-EIGHT

Georgia exited the spare room two minutes late. Considering that all her things were packed, she had done a remarkable job of getting ready. A record for one of his female guests.

Except she wasn't a guest. She lived there now.

Rainer gave her a slow smile as Georgia checked her reflection in the hall mirror.

She wasn't wearing a dress, but a silky-looking green romper with three-quarter sleeves. It was paired with flat beaded sandals that highlighted how small her cute little feet were.

The romper wasn't tight, but it skimmed her curves faithfully enough to make his member stiffen. Vowing to buy her at least two green dresses in the same shade, he gritted his teeth and counted to ten. Fortunately, the timely arrival of her father was enough to kill his arousal.

Ephraim greeted him with reserved politeness. Rainer had the distinct impression the man wanted to like him, but felt he had to give him a hard time on principle.

Since he was the reason Georgia had been hurt and had been forced to go into hiding, Rainer decided the man was entitled to his opinion. As long as Ephraim didn't talk Georgia out of moving in with him—and he'd kept quiet on this matter so far—then he could afford to give her father time to make up his mind.

Plus, he could tell Ephraim was trying not to show how impressed he was with the apartment. Which was why he waited until he and Georgia were nicely lubricated with a little wine to present them with the penthouse's showstopper—the upstairs dining room.

Occupying half of the second story, the sumptuous room held a sixteen-seat mahogany table under a row of three tasteful crystal chandeliers. One-third of the semicircular wall was made of glass panels, with a set of double doors. Beyond was a balcony with the same view as the bedroom—the sapphire blue Pacific.

Georgia turned to him, laughter in her voice. "Does it revolve, too?"

"Ha, ha," he said, motioning her to refill her glass of wine. Once they were all topped up, they went outside on the balcony, letting him point out highlights of downtown San Diego and the bay beyond.

Behind him, one of Massoud's assistants materialized and began to unload the dumbwaiter of the dinner trays sent up from the kitchen.

"You have to admit it looks like one of those revolving rooftop bars," Georgia teased after taking a sip. "Not that I'm complaining. This view is perfect as any of those."

"It's why I chose this place," he admitted. "This circular top floor is divided among the penthouse suites. The previous owner had his bedroom in the neighboring room, but I turned it into an office instead. But this space has always been a dining room."

Georgia turned to watch the kitchen staff put out the meal. She whistled. "I was starting to think they were real house elves—all your domestic staff are so low-key."

"My fault," he said softly, catching her eye. "When I moved in, I was in a place where protecting my privacy was the most important thing to me. All the new staff was selected for their discretion and ability to operate independently without needing me to direct them."

Ephraim pursed his lips in disapproval, but Georgia moved closer, her hand curling around his upper arm.

"None of the staff is live-in," Rainer elaborated. "Although,

Massoud lives on the first floor, for easy access. I text him when I'm going to have guests and he comes in to prepare the meals, stock the fridge, etcetera. The cleaning staff is a team that services all the penthouses and the three floors below them."

"Dad, you have maids now?" Georgia asked, brightening.

"Yes, a nice lady named Magdalena came by to clean the bathroom and straighten up," Ephraim said, heightened color brandishing his cheeks. "I didn't know to expect her the first time, and she saw me in my underwear."

Georgia giggled before clapping a hand on her mouth. "Sorry, Pops."

When Ephraim sighed and turned away, she mouthed 'tighty-whiteys' at him. Choking back a laugh, Rainer directed them to the table, where Ephraim got his revenge.

"So, Rainer, tell us about your family."

It was a good thing he'd already told Georgia the worst bits during their late-night pillow talk.

"Well, my dad was a lot older than my mother," he began, trying to make a long story short. "He was in his mid-sixties when I was born—she was twenty-six."

"Oh," Ephraim said, startled.

Rainer lifted a shoulder. "His family still refers to her as the 'little gold digger that could' or worse."

Georgia winced, but Rainer was used to telling his story to his friends. "After he passed, I pretty much cut ties with them. It wasn't difficult. Most are in Europe."

Ephraim nodded awkwardly, clearly sorry he'd asked.

"As for Mom, she's on husband number four now," Rainer said with a resigned wave. "I have a half-sister somewhere, but after my mom divorced her father, the ex got custody—by mutual agreement—and they don't stay in touch. I met her once or twice, but they don't want a relationship with me either, or at least the dad doesn't. The end of the marriage was acrimonious, to put it mildly."

There was a long silence. "I'm sorry," Georgia said. "Maybe when she's older, she'll get in touch on her own."

Rainer shrugged. "She knows I'm open to contact, but she has her own life and I have mine. But I did okay familywise. My dad didn't die until I finished college, and he was all there until the end," he said, tapping his temple. "I consider myself lucky. He was pretty sharp and a decent-enough dad, given the circumstances."

They didn't roughhouse or play catch like other fathers and sons did, but his dad had taught him other things—how to appreciate art and music. He'd also taken great pleasure introducing Rainer to gourmet foods from around the world.

More importantly, his father had shown Rainer how to take care of himself. And he'd taken pride in his son's accomplishments.

Yes, Rainer been fortunate in fate's choice of fathers. He'd had been given a solid foundation. Now he had his friends, Garrett and Mason, and a few others Georgia hadn't met yet.

Ephraim cleared his throat. "Err...Georgia, why don't you say grace?"

Georgia shot Rainer an apologetic look before folding her hands together and closing her eyes. Rainer followed suit, but his eyes flew open when a string of completely unintelligible words came out of her mouth.

Oh, of course.

"I didn't know you spoke Hebrew," he said when she finished.

"Just some of the prayers," she said, smiling sheepishly. "Diamond didn't care what language we said grace in, so long as we did."

"That's sweet," he said, his eyes lingering on the delicate lines of her face. Her hair was down today, the texture like dense silk. He made a mental note to run his hands through it the first chance he got—she very seldom left it down.

He caught Ephraim staring at him. The man inclined his head as if acknowledging his good taste. Rainer nodded back, digging into the fine meal his chef had made—a duck tajine with rice and raisins.

The rest of the meal passed quickly. Ephraim didn't speak much, but when he did, he displayed a quick wit and a quiet, sly humor. The only hiccup arose when he shared that he wouldn't be allowed to see clients in his apartment.

"Your Mr. Powell had reservations about letting in strangers when you're in residence."

"Oh." Georgia's face fell in understanding. "It's too bad, because that apartment would certainly impress new clients."

She turned to him with a pleading expression. "But what about the more established ones? Some of his clients have been with him for years and years."

"I'm sure Powell wouldn't have a problem with your repeat customers," Rainer offered. "But it's not a sustainable long-term plan —not much walk-in clientele up here. But there's a ton of office space in the adjoining buildings…including the one across the street, which I also have a stake in. I'm sure we can find something there."

"I don't intend to take charity," Ephraim said repressively. "I know what office space goes for downtown."

"But it would be so convenient," Georgia enthused.

Ephraim tsked. It was enough to shut her down. Disappointed, she took a sip of wine to cover her pout.

"Speaking of work," Rainer began. "I was thinking that maybe George would also be interested in a little career upgrade."

Her scowl was immediate. "Say what?"

He lifted a shoulder. "I do have a fair number of cars, enough to make hiring a full-time mechanic for maintenance a smart move. It would save time, too. I wouldn't have to trek out to places like Elite. Plus, there's enough room in the warehouse that you could continue projects like the Talbot."

"You keep a warehouse of cars?" she asked, looking a little green around the gills.

"Yes, and if you started doing some restoration work there, I am pretty sure I can drum up enough clientele to keep you in business— provided I don't buy all the cars off you myself."

Georgia bit her lip. "I don't know…"

Ephraim snickered. "Not so funny when the shoe is on the other foot, is it?"

Georgia glared at her father, but crumpled immediately when Rainer reached out to touch her arm.

"It would be nice to set your own hours, wouldn't it? I can guarantee that none of the car guys I know would complain that you don't see clients before ten AM..."

Ephraim's eyes darted back and forth between him and Georgia as if he were a spectator at a tennis match, but he wisely kept his mouth shut.

"That would be nice," she admitted. "But there's more to running a business than the actual mechanical and restoration work."

"Ephraim can do the books," Rainer suggested with a wiggle of his brows.

The older man smiled, eating a forkful of his dish before replying.

"That would be a very nice way to bring our interests together," Ephraim said, his eyes soft as he faced his daughter.

Rainer hid a grin. The man was shameless, but since he was an ally at the moment, Rainer wasn't about to call him on it.

Unable to withstand the force of that look, Georgia crumbled like a cookie. "I'll think about it," she murmured, resuming her meal with a mulish expression.

"Sorry if Ephraim gave you a hard time," she told Rainer after the man had gone, dinner long over. "I should have realized he would ask about your family. We've spent so much time together that I forget that he hasn't had a chance to know you."

"It's not a big deal," he assured her, throwing an arm around her shoulders to guide her to the bedroom. "I'm not embarrassed about my background. Plus, I'm not above using pity to get him on my side."

"Yeah, I noticed." She poked him below the ribs. "For future reference, we team up to gang up on Ephraim, not the other way around."

He stopped at the threshold of their room. "Are you sure about going back to work tomorrow?"

She sighed. "I know you want me to jump on your offer, but mixing business with pleasure is a bad idea."

Rainer grunted, glad she didn't bring up Mack. "You don't have to work on my cars at all," he pointed out. "You can focus on restorations and sell your wares to my contacts. Trust me, Ephraim showed me the before and afters on the Talbot, and I've seen the others on your

Instagram. With quality work like that, I can find you plenty of clients."

She frowned. "When did he show you pictures?"

"When you went to the bathroom—I was desperate for small talk," he confessed. "But I'm glad I was. I had no idea how badly smashed up the car had been before you started the restoration."

"It was in bad shape," she acknowledged. "But I hate leaving everybody at Elite in the lurch. I should go back for a little while at least, give them a couple of weeks' notice."

"Mitch doesn't deserve your loyalty. He's too much of a misogynist to appreciate your skills. Now is the perfect time to quit—they've already gotten used to working without you."

Georgia scowled.

Rainer grimaced, but this was a harsh truth she needed to hear. "It's a pretty rare business that values dedication like yours—believe me, I would know. To a place like Elite, you're an interchangeable cog."

She looked down at the floor. "I know that."

He wrapped his arms around her. "Bankrolling talent like yours is what I do. Let me worry about the overhead and the setup. You can focus on what you do best—making old cars beautiful again."

"So, I wouldn't just be using you for your money? This would be a real investment?"

"Of course it would. And if things were to go wrong with us—not that I think they will—you'll have your own business in your name, all the profits yours after I recoup my investment capital...with interest."

Her eyes narrowed. "How much?"

"Oh, something reasonable," he assured, then grinned. "What kind of a businessman would I be if I didn't make a little something off talent like yours?"

The mercenary words seemed to please her. "I'll give my notice tomorrow, but I do want to give them a few weeks to find my replacement."

Hands in his pockets, Rainer rocked back on his heels. "That's the best I'm going to get, isn't it?"

She nodded. "I have to break the news to Judy carefully."

"Who is that?" He frowned, trying to remember a saleswoman named Judy.

"My work-wife, the receptionist."

"Ah. Well, if business takes off, you can afford to bring her with you."

"Let's not get ahead of ourselves. I'm not as confident as you are that I can run a business."

"Do you honestly think I'd set you up to fail? Just consider me your personal business advisor. Your *very personal* consultant."

Georgia giggled. "Fine. I will keep that in mind."

CHAPTER TWENTY-NINE

Georgia had known telling everyone at Elite that she was giving her two weeks' notice was going to be difficult, but she had no idea what she was in for.

What is it they say? No one expected the Spanish Inquisition.

Mitch took it pretty well considering. "Well, aren't you an opportunistic little bitch?" he said with a sneer when Georgia explained her work on the Talbot had led to Rainer Torsten bankrolling a car restoration business.

"It was his idea," she mumbled defensively, all the eyes on her making her shrink in on herself.

They were in the break room, Georgia having decided to tell Mitch during a rare lull in the workday in front of witnesses, including Judy, Sam, and Fredo.

"I think it's great," Judy said loyally. She came to sit next to Georgia at the table, a supportive hand on her shoulder.

Mitch sniffed dismissively. "Yeah, the car is nice, but we all know Mack is the one who got the ball rolling on that. All you had to do was continue what he started."

"That's bullshit," Georgia snapped in a rare moment of anger so great that it moved her to defend herself. How dare he impugn her skills? She was a better mechanic than him with one hand tied behind her back.

"Mack didn't want to touch that car, because he knew it would make Ephraim happy. His beef with our dad was that big and that petty. I did all the work. Anyone who follows my Insta knows it—I was posting updates at every step."

"Whatever," Mitch muttered. "You and I both know a big shot like Torsten wouldn't drop a wad of cash after seeing one car—not unless he was getting something extra to sweeten the deal."

"Hey!" The indignant exclamations that came from both Samantha and Judy simultaneously should have been a balm to her soul, but Georgia hunched over as if she'd been struck.

"Don't be an asshole, Mitch," Samantha snapped. "If Torsten wants to invest in Georgia, it's because she's talented."

The unspoken implication that he wouldn't want her for anything else was clear in Samantha's tone. And yes, it stung despite the fact she knew Sam wasn't trying to be cruel. It simply didn't register to the stylish blonde that a man like Rainer would ever desire someone like Georgia.

Aware he was setting himself up for a reprimand from HR, Mitch rolled his eyes, leaving the break room.

"He's just jealous," Judy said, patting Georgia's hand. "It's better that you're moving on. You don't want to stay working under that sexist pig. He just can't imagine a world where a woman would get a chance like this unless she was sleeping with someone."

Flushing, Georgia nodded, looking down at the table. She felt about two inches tall.

Fredo pushed in his chair next to Judy. "Do you think Brantman will be pissed off that you're poaching one of his big clients and starting your own business?"

"Maybe," Georgia confessed. "But we're not going to be in competition—not really. It's not as if Elite sells many classic cars. Most of the inventory is new. We mainly just service them. And I'm not going to be in a position to do much of that in the beginning. I was thinking of shunting the service back here if I can't fit in a tune-up or oil change."

"You never said how Torsten heard about the Talbot in the first place," Fredo said.

Georgia shrugged. "I honestly don't know. I was approached by one of his people," she lied.

"And you didn't ask?" Judy frowned.

Georgia lifted a shoulder. "I assumed he heard someone here mention it."

"Or he came across your Instagram," Judy suggested.

"It doesn't make much of a difference now. But it's cool," Fredo said, pointing a finger at her as he stood. "Don't forget I said that when you start making the big bucks. I may need another job if Mitch the bitch keeps on being such an asshole."

Making a mock shudder, he rinsed his cup at the sink, saluting them before leaving.

Alone with Judy, Georgia took a sip from her mug, avoiding her friend's eyes.

Judy leaned forward, eyes narrowed. "I can't believe you slept with my imaginary boyfriend," she scolded.

Choking on her coffee, Georgia spit French vanilla goodness all over herself. She grabbed a paper napkin from the dispenser in the middle of the table, a deep, wracking cough making her shoulders shake.

"It serves you right." Judy scowled. "Now spill or I will never speak to you again."

Bewildered, Georgia stared at her friend. "How did you know?"

"Please, woman. I know that guilty look on your face—it was the same when you accidentally threw my kimchi away."

"I thought it had gone bad," Georgia protested. "I didn't know that's what it was supposed to smell like."

"Enough about my lunch," Judy snapped. "Tell me about Rainer. How did you really meet?"

"I…"

"Georgia!"

She bit her lip. "I can't tell you everything because he asked me not to share."

Judy's lip curled, then her eyes bugged out of her head as a thought occurred to her. "Did he make you sign a Christian Grey-style contract?"

"*No,*" Georgia hissed. "And please, lower your voice."

Georgia felt like crap, but she couldn't tell the truth—not all of it. Rainer was ninety-five percent sure the rest of the Elite staff was clear, but he didn't want to take any chances.

"Does it have anything to do with your dad losing his business?"

Taking the lifeline, Georgia nodded. "Ephraim had to close the office and downsize all the staff…and we sold the house."

"Oh George, that was where you grew up." Judy's lip stuck out in a sympathetic pout. "I'm sorry. I totally forgive you for stealing my imaginary boyfriend."

"If it makes any difference, I had no idea he was into Dominicans when I went to offer him the car."

"He is?" Judy slapped her palm on the table. "Damn it, why couldn't he like Korean girls?"

Georgia shook her head. "Gotta have the melanin."

"I wouldn't have guessed." Judy smacked her lips. "Does he have any hot friends at least?"

"His friend Garrett just got divorced."

Perking up, Judy put her mug down. "And?"

"Yes, he's attractive."

And he was, Georgia realized with some surprise. *But that's what happens when you're so into someone else.* You didn't notice another man's hotness—not even when you're passed out naked in front of them.

"The idea to bankroll a car restoration did come after the start of the personal stuff," she admitted in a small voice, shoulders slumped.

"You know what," Judy said, slapping the table. "Who the fuck cares? Nobody gets anywhere without some connections or giving up the nookie. I haven't, which is why I'm still stuck at the reception instead of getting promoted to sales."

Crestfallen, Georgia scooted her chair over to hug her. "You didn't get the promotion because you didn't sleep with Mr. Brantman?"

"No." Judy twisted her lips morosely. "He didn't proposition me. What he said is that men want to buy from other men—and if they do buy from a woman, she has to look like Sam." Blinking rapidly, Judy stared at the ceiling and swallowed. "Except that last part is me being bitchy. Honest, but bitchy."

Pushing back her chair, she got to her feet, patting Georgia on the back. "Take this opportunity and make it a big success so you can give me a job. Because I would be a hell of a salesperson."

Sitting up, Georgia straightened her shoulders. "Rainer suggested I do just that."

"Did he?" Judy brightened.

"Yeah. Give me three months and then you can start selling my cars," Georgia promised.

Making a rumbling noise that sounded like a small diesel car engine, Judy hugged her. "I lied. I'm still not over you stealing my fake boyfriend," she said, rocking Georgia in her seat.

"I know." Georgia caught her hand. "But please don't tell anyone. A lot is going on behind the scenes, and I don't want to muddy the waters."

Judy went to the sink to wash her mug. "I have no idea what that means, but yes, I promise I won't mention Rainer chains you up in a sex dungeon every night."

"*Judy*." Her friend was kidding, but if Georgia wasn't careful, her wild blushes would give her away.

She held up a hand. "Or anything else that might lead people to get the wrong idea that is actually the right one."

Waving her arms dramatically, she exited, leaving her alone. Groaning, Georgia let her head fall on the break room table, only for it to stick to the surface. Fredo never wiped properly when he spilled on the table, just like in the garage after an oil change.

"Perfect, just perfect," she mumbled.

CHAPTER THIRTY

Rainer took a good look at himself in the bathroom mirror, examining his hairline. His roots had grown to the point where he was starting to look bizarre, brown hair with red roots.

"Like Swiss chard that has spoiled," he muttered, resolving to take care of the matter by calling in his hairstylist for a home visit.

Maybe I'll try green this time. That way when his roots began to show, he would look Christmassy.

But when the stylist came by a few hours later, he surprised them both by telling him to go back to the original red. The final result ended up a bit darker than he remembered his hair being, but his stylist assured him that it would blend in seamlessly when it began to grow out.

Feeling rather good, he checked in with Ephraim and discovered the older man was meeting a friend for dinner. Whistling, he ordered a private meal for two from Massoud.

He didn't mind sharing meals with Georgia's dad, aware that they were accustomed to spending every dinner together. But he was hoping it wouldn't be every night.

Rainer was whipping up a welcome-home cocktail when Georgia

came through the door, shoulders slumped. Dropping her bag on the floor, she stumbled into his arms like a dejected puppy.

"Aw, baby. What happened?" he asked, his arms wrapping around her in a firm hug.

"Aside from the fact I'm whoring myself out to start a business?" she mumbled into his chest.

"*Hey.*" Rainer gave her a warning squeeze. "None of that. I am the one who shanghaied your entire life and turned it upside down. For fuck's sake, I tie you to my bed every night. If anyone is taking advantage, it's me."

"It's not taking advantage…not if the other person lets you tie them up," she pointed out, letting her head fall back so she could look up at him. Her eyes flared. "Your hair is red again."

He dropped a kiss on her forehead. "Yup. I was going to go for another crazy color, but decided it was too much work."

Her hand flattened over her heart, the warmth of it permeating to his core. "I think you look amazing."

Cheeks heating, he ducked his head.

Georgia grinned. "Are you blushing? That's so adorable!"

"A redhead's curse." He tapped her behind in warning. "But don't think you can distract me with compliments. I want the name of every person who called you a whore, and I want them now."

Her eyes widened. "Nobody called me that. Not to my face."

She was a terrible liar. "It was the shithead Mitch, wasn't it?"

"No, it's just the way I felt…cause Mitch strongly implied it," she admitted in a small voice.

Red rage tightened his muscles. "I'm going to fucking *kill* him."

She threw her arms around his neck. "Mitch is and always has been an asshole. I didn't tell you so you would confront him. What he said—which wasn't as bad as calling me a whore—wouldn't have bothered me if I didn't feel that way already. After all, I wouldn't have this opportunity if we weren't together."

"Don't be too sure of that," he said. "You are incredibly talented. I'm just the lucky bastard who realized it before anyone else and snapped you up. Regardless, you'll feel differently once you see the contract you're signing."

She frowned. "Why?"

"Because the terms of what I get out of it are explicitly laid out. They're fair, but it's not a free pass. You're going to be earning your shot—never think otherwise."

Georgia melted into him like wax. "Thank you. I needed to hear that."

"It wasn't just Mitch giving you shit." A statement of fact. Rainer knew human nature and not everyone would be happy someone from the bottom of the power structure was getting an opportunity like this.

Georgia shook her head. "Judy knows me so well that she sort of guessed we were involved...and she was a little mad at me."

His head drew back. "Why?"

Her expression became sheepish. "She'll kill me for telling you, but I think I might have mentioned it earlier—she's a fan of yours. You're her imaginary boyfriend."

"Ah." He pursed his lips. "And in her eyes, you stole me."

"Yes. She was a little annoyed, but it also came at a bad time—Mr. Brantman turned down her request to become a salesperson. So, I told her she can start working with me in a few months, once I get a few cars finished."

"Do you think she'd be good at it?"

"I do. She knows how to talk to people—a little too well maybe. I'm fairly sure she ended up telling Samantha about us. Sam gave me a pretty weird look when I was leaving."

He pushed a stray lock of hair off her forehead. "All the more reason to stop working there as soon as possible. As for Judy, Brantman's loss will be our gain." He braced himself to tell her about his afternoon phone call. "Speaking of Brantman, he contacted me. Someone had informed him of our venture, and he wanted to talk about it."

"Oh. I bet Mitch ran right out of the break room to snitch on me."

She frowned. "He must have called him because Mr. Brantman wasn't in today. He's on vacation."

"Yeah, he contacted me from his hotel room in Sydney. He wants in on our deal."

"What?" She scowled. "Does he expect me to keep working for Mitch?"

The horror in her voice was undisguised now. *I really need to kick that guy's ass.* Too bad it would just get him sued.

"Your operation would still be independent, but he wants to be able to have first dibs on your product. The ones he likes will go on display on the Elite showroom."

"Oh…I guess that would be good for business." Her tone held all of the enthusiasm of a child faced with a plate of broccoli.

"It would be at first. But don't worry about him taking over," he assured her. "Even if we gave him right of refusal, which I don't intend to do, not every vehicle you work on is going to fit the Elite mold. And I'm not about to hamstring your growth by taking the deal he proposed as is. *You* will be the one who decides which cars you want to offer Elite. If you subcontract with them, you can earmark a limited number of cars in advance, while keeping yourself free to build your clientele the rest of the time."

He squeezed her tight. "I'll make sure Brantman won't stiff you on the commission either."

"Good."

Satisfied she was feeling better, he glanced down at himself.

"Oh no!" Georgia gasped. "I got grease all over you."

"I'm fine, babe." He was wearing jeans and a t-shirt today—his uniform for working from home. "My dry cleaner gets to earn his fee this way."

"You dry clean your t-shirts?" She snickered.

Hands on her shoulders, he propelled her in the direction of the shower. "Laundry service, whatever, smart aleck."

When they reached the bathroom, he stripped them down in front of the power shower before examining her critically.

"What is it?" she asked as she toed off her socks.

He snickered, kicking off his boxers. "I think I'm going to like welcoming a dirty girl home every night."

She grabbed his cock in retaliation. Always highly responsive to her touch, he got her even dirtier before washing them both clean.

CHAPTER THIRTY-ONE

Panting and covered in sweat, George let her head fall back on the surface of Rainer's desk. Her hands were limp, legs dangling over the side.

The unplanned bout of desk sex had started after dinner when Rainer had gotten a call from one of his subordinates. The issue had been a minor one, but it had allowed Georgia to watch Rainer in work mode.

Curling up in one of the chairs opposite the desk, Georgia drank in the sight of him. It slowly dawned on her that he was a little pissed over whatever the call was about. Unlike so many employers who would rant and rave, Rainer kept his cool. But he was *firm*.

When his speech grew downright clipped, her female parts clenched.

Shit. It's true. Power was an aphrodisiac. Except it wasn't his position as the boss that was getting her wet, more like the take-charge, no-nonsense attitude that had gotten him there.

Deciding that being a female stereotype was something she could live with as long as it was Rainer, she waited until he was off the phone, his work problem solved. Then she jumped him.

What followed ticked off some major boxes on their sexual to-do list.

"It's not the geode coffee table, but this is good, too," he murmured afterward, sweaty and incredibly pleased with himself. He slid his hands down the inside of her legs, stroking the silk of her inner thighs.

Too sexually sated to move, Georgia watched the lights of the city beyond the windows when Rainer went to the bathroom to clean up.

He returned a minute later with a wet washcloth. Humming a nonsensical version of 'Camp down races' he made her giggle as he cleaned her up. She was starting to regain her strength when he disappeared a second time, presumably to toss the washcloth in the laundry chute downstairs.

She had just discovered the chute day before—and it was already her favorite feature of the apartment. Georgia had been excited for her dad to have one, too, but it turned out to be a feature exclusive to the penthouse suites. Rainer told her the entire apartment had the option to use the same laundry service at a discount—and he'd signed Ephraim up.

That sort of high handedness would have annoyed her in another person, but she really liked that Rainer took care of Ephraim. And if Ephraim believed that the service was included as an amenity all the better...

Mostly recovered, Georgia was starting to worry about the paperwork beneath her. She forced herself to sit up, knocking a manila folder onto the floor in the process. Wincing, she hopped off the desk and bent to pick up the spilled documents—freezing when she saw the picture underneath the stapled message.

The woman in the photograph was drop-dead gorgeous, an amazon goddess with the most perfect afro she had ever seen.

Dressed in blue jeans and a black leather jacket, the woman was standing on a busy street, talking to a man in aviator glasses who was almost as imposing and perfect as she was. This paragon had his hand on her lower back. The black-and-white shot was a still from a surveillance camera, but it was in high definition and close enough that she could see every perfect detail of the woman's face.

Georgia didn't need to read the note attached to the picture to know this was the mysterious Elaine, the woman who had hurt Rainer.

Her beauty is a weapon, she reminded herself, her stomach flip-flopping and tying itself into knots. But it was impossible not to compare herself to the stunning woman in the picture. Unable to stop, she flipped through the rest of the folder, which included more pictures of varying quality as well as reports on when and where the woman had been sighted.

There were other photographs as well—all men who were bruised and battered, including one who had to be dead.

Her blood iced over.

"The dead guy is a murderer." Rainer's voice came from just beside her. "He was part of a white supremacist gang that's left a trail of bodies behind them. Rumor had it he was responsible for ninety percent."

Startled, she glanced at him. He held out his hands. Smoothing down her dress, she closed the folder, avoiding his eyes as she handed it back to him.

"No, Georgia." She looked up to find him still holding his hand out to her.

"*Oh.*" Taking it, she let him guide her to the couch against the wall.

"I wasn't trying to shut you out," he explained, tapping the folder in his lap. When he wrapped his arms around her, something in her broke. Suddenly, she was clinging to him.

"She could have killed you."

He leaned back on the couch, taking her with him. "Had I been what these men were—criminals and degenerates—then yes, I might have ended up dead."

"Are all her other victims bad guys?" she asked, gesturing to the folder.

"Most, yes. Although, I have a few reports of people like me who had information she needed. None of those people were seriously injured. In most instances, she managed to get what she needed without incident. I have a feeling she rarely has to resort to drugging anyone. But I had excellent security *before* I landed on her radar, corporate espionage being a real concern for someone in my line of work."

He opened the folder, then angled the picture at the top of the pile in her direction.

"Most of those came from this man," he said, tapping the woman's impressive companion. "He was a DEA agent who came to see me when he was tracking her. He even arrested her briefly, but he was forced to let her go for lack of evidence."

Startled, she scowled. "And now he runs around with her?"

The couple in the picture looked like exactly that. The man was touching her intimately, the gesture protective. As if she needed any sort of protection. The woman was toned and muscular, her body sleek, giving Georgia the impression of a blade in motion, even though it was a still image.

"According to the agent's former partner, Daniel Romero was recruited to the CIA."

Her confusion sharpened into shock. "So, she's a spy, not some sort of vigilante?"

He lifted a shoulder. "I'm not sure. I'd like to think so for personal reasons—it's much more palatable to have been roofied as part of some covert operation than by a run-of-the-mill thief after one of my connections."

Georgia scowled. "I don't care if she's double-o-seven herself! There was no reason to hurt you at all."

"Maybe in her mind, she wasn't," he pointed out. "Compared to what she's suspected of doing to these other guys, I got off pretty easy. And the presence of Daniel Romero at her side means there is a deeper thing going on. I don't have the whole picture."

Georgia snapped. Grabbing his hand, she shook her head. "Don't do that. You are a good person who didn't deserve to be made collateral damage."

Sighing, Rainer pulled her into him tighter, burying his face in her hair. "Thank you for being mad on my behalf. Most of the other people I told—my guy friends—laughed it off or just said it was bad luck and to pick my dates more carefully."

Blistering words on the tip of her tongue, Georgia opened her mouth to go off—but he forestalled her by tapping her on the nose. "That doesn't include Garrett. He may have been angrier than me. I told you earlier, I didn't realize how badly messed up I was for a long time."

"Oh," she mumbled. "I like him a little better now. Not that I disliked him or anything—but I feel better about him seeing me naked now."

His gruff growl made her smile. "Well, I *don't*. That is not happening again."

She laughed, her hand flattening on his chest possessively.

Setting the folder aside, he covered her fingers with his. "I am grateful you care enough about me to get mad, but I think I'm ready to move on."

He gestured to the images. "I started to investigate Eileen because I believed I would feel better if I understood what she wanted that night. I still don't know, but judging from what I discovered, it's more complicated than I initially thought."

"But your gut tells you she's on the side of the angels. That's why you're letting this go."

"No. I had those suspicions before. But when we got home, that last picture was waiting for me, the one confirming the rumors that she had joined forces with the DEA agent I met. And I realized it doesn't matter anymore. Whatever dark underbelly Eileen is moving around in, Romero is a grown man. He has the training to deal with it. And it's time I stopped wasting time and resources on something that is out of my hands."

Georgia's lips parted. "So, this is why you dyed your hair back to its original color?"

Rainer studied her before snorting. "You know what, it probably is. I started doing the weird colors to feel different, to shake things up. But I don't need to do that anymore. Since you came into my life, I feel more settled—which is pretty damn weird given what we get up to."

Snickering, Georgia laid her head on his chest. "You know, I had grand plans for revenge against this Eileen woman. If I ever ran into her in a dark alley, I was going to kick her ass. But after seeing her looking all 'Mission Impossible,' I'm sorry to say—and this genuinely hurts to admit—that I don't think I can take her."

Rainer's laughter shook her upper body.

"Which is why," she continued indignantly, "I would hot-wire the nearest car and run her over with it instead."

His hand cupped her nape the way he'd recently started doing, his hold possessive as hell. "That's my smart girl. Always play to your strengths."

Wrapping her arms around his waist, she tilted her head back in expectation of the kiss she knew was coming. Rainer didn't let her down.

Shelving her plans for bloody retribution, Georgia vowed to focus on the here and now. That was what Rainer deserved. And so did she.

CHAPTER THIRTY-TWO

"Do you think you're going to need a sign?" Judy asked over the phone.

Georgia stared critically at the space around her. The warehouse where Rainer stored his cars had plenty of room for her future business—too much perhaps.

"I'm not sure. This place is so big that I wouldn't know where to put it. Also, I'm sharing the space with Rainer's existing collection. I need to figure out some way to divide the room that won't cost an arm and a leg. I wouldn't want people to think his cars are for sale."

She had stopped here as a sort of celebration. Today had been her last day of work at Elite. Samantha and Judy had bought cupcakes. The atmosphere had been festive, if a little forced. But Mitch managed to get through it without being a total ass. Someone must have been whispering in his ears about not burning bridges.

"Oh, I don't think that's necessary," her friend said, the sound of chewing telling her Judy was still on her lunch break. "Once Rainer spreads the chum among his rich friends, most of your early clients will be word of mouth. They'll come in knowing only specific vehicles are up for grabs. Granted, that whole half of the warehouse is serious eye-candy, so we will likely have some looky-loos who just want a peek, but that's to be expected."

Georgia groaned aloud. "I didn't even think of that. That sounds *terrible*."

She couldn't think of anything worse than having a stream of strangers come in for no other reason than to browse. She could talk cars to them, of course, but what if they decided they wanted to buy a car that wasn't for sale? Georgia pictured the average Elite client—aggressive businessmen who enjoyed haggling with their salespeople like it was a sport.

This was why she desperately needed Judy.

"Don't worry, not-curious George," her friend said. "I know you'd rather get a root canal than make small talk with strangers. By the time you're open for business, I'll be there to run point with the money men. Maybe I'll even snag one for myself this time."

Snorting, Georgia rolled her eyes. "As long as I don't have to talk to them, you can do what you want. Well, within reason. We'll have our own reputation to cultivate and protect, just like Elite does theirs."

Judy blew a raspberry over the line. "Woman, I will be professional with a capital P. Unless flirting seals the deal—but nothing hinky. Not that I think the spirit is going to move me in that direction. Rich guys who look like yours aren't exactly thick on the ground."

"True," Georgia admitted. "Rainer is one of a kind."

This time, Judy made a gagging noise. "All right, so tell me, did Mr. Moneybags win the argument about the pit?"

"Not yet." It was a small point of contention; however, Rainer had been tenacious about it. "But given the layout of the space, I think I'm better off with a car lift. If we dig a pit for undercarriage work and oil changes, it will always be in that one spot."

"Plus, you'd have to get permission from the warehouse owner," Judy added, plastic crinkling indicating her meal was ending.

"Well, turns out Rainer owns it," Georgia added in a small voice.

Judy laughed. "All right, that's it. Your first-world problems have taken up my entire lunch hour. But before I go, I want to say one thing—if the reason you feel safer with a car lift is because you can sell it if this whole thing falls apart, then go for the pit."

"But—"

"No buts," Judy admonished. "You need to be all in. If you're worried about the commitment a pit represents, then you're holding back because you're not convinced that you're going to succeed. And you need to believe that, for both our sakes."

"You sound like Rainer now," Georgia grumbled.

"Great minds," Judy said lightly. "Okay, I do have to run now. Kiss, kiss."

Georgia hung up, pulling a face that would have made Diamond scold her.

It's not going to stick that way, she told herself. But the reminder of her tough and cheerful foster mother did the trick. Judy was right. Georgia had to go into this believing she was going to succeed. There was no room for doubt.

And she *was* going to get a lift, but not because it was the safer choice. At this point, she didn't know how many cars she was going to be handling at a time, nor did she know their makes and models. She was working on a few leads, of course, but nothing was set in stone.

Georgia used to be the type of person who would second guess herself until she talked herself out of things. But she was trying to listen to her instincts now, and they were telling her she had to stay flexible. New businesses had to be nimble, and the fact was she didn't know how to use this space efficiently yet. If she needed a pit at some point, then she'd have one dug out then.

Feeling good about her decision, she jotted a few notes down. Georgia spent another hour making lists and placing calls to suppliers before texting Rainer that she was coming home. But she didn't leave for another fifteen minutes because she couldn't resist crossing the warehouse to admire the double row of cars owned by her man.

It was an embarrassment of riches. In addition to the requisite Porches, Ferraris, and Bentleys, there was a McLaren Elva so sleek she got wet just looking at it. Fanning herself, she decided not to look under the hood of the Batmobile-like vehicle. She still had to drive herself home, and that would not help her stay cool and calm behind the wheel.

However, if Rainer were here, she'd pull him into one of these cars and go to town on him. Which one, though, would require careful consideration. Most of these sweet rides did not have a backseat. She'd have to check each model out, see if the front seats reclined back far enough.

Fanning her hot cheeks, she crossed back to her side of the garage, waving to the security camera over the door. Mr. Powell had several installed to safeguard Rainer's collection.

Georgia also knew he had some trained on her side of the warehouse. For the time being, that was fine. She was going to add walls for an office somewhere down the line, next to the existing restroom. No cameras would be allowed inside the office, so she and Judy would have a space where they could drink coffee and work on their computers without feeling the eye of big brother upon them.

Realizing she had forgotten her phone, she practically skipped across the warehouse, tossing the handset in her bag before opening the door to the back lot with her hip.

Her Crown Vic was only a few steps from the door. She'd parked it there, aware the light was fading earlier and earlier each evening. There was also a nip in the air, but Georgia had always loved autumn, or what passed for it in San Diego.

She was halfway to her car when she realized it was darker than it should have been. Her parking spot should have been illuminated by the light attached to the warehouse wall. For some reason, the bulb was out. Making a mental note to have it replaced, she unlocked her car and slid into the driver's seat.

The minute she touched the steering wheel, she realized she'd made a mistake. Freezing, she clutched the leather tightly as the sound of breathing behind her made the little hairs on the nape of her neck stand on end.

CHAPTER THIRTY-THREE

"Georgia."

Swallowing hard, Georgia closed her eyes and shook her head. The death grip she had on the steering wheel was making her fingers ache. But her brain told her that this was real. She wasn't imagining it. Because that wasn't some crazy man determined to assault her.

That was Mack's voice.

"Georgia, please look at me."

A hand reached out, touching her shoulders.

"*No*," she yelled, her voice shrill. "You are not here. You're *dead*."

The touch came again. It broke something in her head. Suddenly, she wasn't there anymore. Georgia's only clear thought was to get away.

But the man with Mack's voice was restraining her. He had hold of her shirt and though she was pulling away, scrabbling for the door handle, she couldn't break free.

"Georgia, stop," he said. "And damn it, look at me."

Her breath was coming fast and ragged. Georgia's body was wracked by tremors, but, at the same time, she was so stiff that it hurt her neck to turn around.

Mack's hair was shorter, buzzed close to his head. It made his face look broader and harder; the sharp planes of his face unsoftened by the floppy, boyish haircuts he used to wear.

Bile rose in her throat. Swallowing hard, she took a shaky breath and pointed at him. "D-do you have any idea what you did to Ephraim, to *me*? How could you let us think you were dead? *What the hell is going on?*"

Her voice shook almost as badly as her hands.

Mack pursed his lips. Guilt flared in his eyes, but it was doused quickly. "Things are going on that you don't know about. I needed to leave. I shouldn't be here now—but you fucked up, and I had to warn you. Because I still care about you."

Georgia blinked, her mind struggling to process his words. "I don't understand."

"Yeah, I know." Mack snorted, shaking his head. "But it will be okay. You still trust me, right?"

A little bit of her soul shriveled. It was a familiar question. When he'd been pressuring her into a romantic relationship, he'd asked her that often, subtly implying that he was older and wiser without actually saying it.

Stomach twisting, she shook her head.

Mack's face darkened, but she could see the shock in his expression. Despite breaking off their relationship, he hadn't expected her to deny him. Not over something this fundamental and long-standing.

That was because he blamed Diamond and Ephraim for their break-up, her mind supplied. It was why he had railed so viciously against them, especially Ephraim. All this time and he still didn't believe that it was Georgia who had wanted out. Her love was for her brother, not the man who wanted them to be lovers.

His fingers on her shoulder tightened, pressing and giving her a single sharp shake. "Fuck, Georgia, you need to listen to me. I don't know how you got mixed up with him, but you need to stay away from Rainer Torsten—get away from him now."

"Why?"

"It doesn't matter," he snapped, and she could feel his anger now.

It was a tangible force, beating at her. Georgia flinched, the reeling sensation sending her back to the scared teenager she'd been. But the desire to fix it for him—that was gone.

Mack swore. "Just get out of his house. Don't see him. Don't take his calls."

"You're part of it—the kidnapping plot." The words were choked out, but it wasn't just fear. Her anger was there too.

"Damn it, Georgia, you're not supposed to know anything about that."

"Then maybe you shouldn't have had your partners in crime plan it in the bathroom at work!" she shouted.

Mack cocked his head to the side as if processing that. But he didn't respond. Narrowing his eyes, he gave her a firm look.

"I'm going to go now. If you tell anyone you saw me, even Ephraim—especially Ephraim—there is going to be trouble. So just do what I said. Go to Torsten. Tell him it's over. Pack a bag and get out."

He opened the door before pausing.

"That shouldn't be hard," he threw out, unable to resist. "You've done it before."

Then he was gone.

CHAPTER THIRTY-FOUR

Georgia had no idea she got herself home. One minute, she was sitting in her car, struggling to keep from throwing up in the parking lot, and, the next, she was blinking in the bright lights of the penthouse foyer.

When a hand touched her cheek, she startled. Blinking, she focused on Rainer's concerned face.

"Baby, I asked if you were okay?"

Taking a shaky breath, she shook her head. "I don't feel very well."

Rainer's handsome face creased into concern. "Do you want me to call a doctor?"

Georgia stared at him blankly. Her ears had started ringing, and she was having a hard time processing his words. Rainer turned to say something to someone behind him, his voice sharp.

He was worried about her.

Oh, God. Swamped with guilt, she pulled away from him. "I'll be fine. I just have a headache. I'm going to wash up and lie down for a while."

"Okay." Rainer rubbed her back, his sympathy little daggers to her heart. "I'll come and check on you in a bit."

Nodding mechanically, she stumbled away, stripping her clothes off for a steaming hot shower. It wasn't until her second scrub down that she realized she was focusing on her right shoulder as if trying to scour off the impression of Mack's fingers.

Sobbing, Georgia pressed her forehead to the tiled wall. What the hell was going on? Why had her brother faked his death?

Idiot, she berated herself. It had something to do with the kidnapping. But for the life of her, she couldn't figure out what. She could barely think at all.

"Georgia, you're turning into a lobster." Rainer materialized out of the steam, opening the door to the shower. He turned the dial back to a cooler temperature. He disappeared for a second before returning with two white pills and a perspiring bottle of Gatorade.

Too drained to resist, she let him pull her out of the shower. He wrapped her in a huge terrycloth towel, urging her to take the pills with soft words and gentle caresses. He said something about dinner and disappeared again.

Burying her face in her hands, Georgia crumpled onto the bed next to the nightgown Rainer had laid out for her.

Faced with yet another example of his kindness and consideration, she pulled the sheath over her head and stumbled across the hall to the spare bedroom he'd given her when she moved in. Not bothering to flip the light switch, she laid down on the bed, facing away from the door. When the door opened, she pretended to be asleep, ignoring Rainer's soft questions until he went away.

Certain that George was suffering from a migraine, Rainer texted Ephraim to let him know dinner was off.

The best thing you can do for her is let her sleep it off.

She'd done the right thing going straight to bed in a dark room. With luck, she'd sleep through the worst of it. However, if she was still in pain when she awoke, he had his doctor on speed-dial.

My poor baby. She'd looked so ill, her golden-brown skin almost grey. He made mental note to ask his physician if she could have a cat scan. Perhaps George needed a prescription for migraine medication.

He was texting his doctor when Powell appeared at the door.

"You're not answering your phone."

"Sorry," Rainer said, eyes on his phone. "But Georgia isn't feeling well. I'm going to get Dr. Green out here to see her in the morning."

"She's not ill."

Scowling, Rainer looked up to find Powell watching him, the man's flat expression even more closed down than usual.

"We need to talk."

❧

Rainer stared at the video of the man climbing out of Georgia's backseat, his blood ice-cold.

One of the other kidnappers. It had to be. One of the men they hadn't apprehended had gone to threaten Georgia. But the camera wasn't placed near the back of the warehouse, but at the parking lot entrance. There wasn't enough resolution to make out his face, just his general size and height.

Less than a minute later, Georgia almost fell out of the car, staggering to the thin border of shrubbery that separated the building from the black asphalt of the lot. She fell to her knees, retching in the bushes.

Fuck. "Do you have any photos of the man?"

A hard copy of the photograph was set in front of him. It was blown up and slightly grainy, but the image of the man's face was clear enough.

Why the hell did he look familiar? Had Rainer seen him before? Perhaps at Elite?

"Tell me you're running facial recognition with your CIA buddies," he said, scowling at the picture on his desk, racking his brain to place the man.

"We didn't need to. He's been identified."

Rainer looked up, waiting.

Powell grimaced. "His name is Shane Mackenzie."

Rainer's head drew back. "Wait. Isn't that..."

His voice trailed off when the head of security nodded grimly. "Mack. The other long-term foster child of Ephraim Levi and Diamond Jones, Georgia's foster brother. I recognized him from the pictures Ephraim keeps of the family downstairs in his office."

Rubbing his face, Rainer swore. "Fucking hell. No wonder Georgia looks like that. She literally saw a ghost."

But why the hell had her brother suddenly risen from the dead? And what had he said to her to make her react like that?

"Her shock does appear genuine."

Groaning, Rainer met Powell's eyes. "You think this has something to do with the kidnapping? Don't tell me you still suspect George of being involved?"

Powell lifted his shoulders. "As I said, her shock appears to be genuine. But it seems too coincidental that Mr. Mackenzie has resurfaced just after Georgia quit Elite motors to come work for you."

Rainer hated it, but Powell was right. "Fuck, Elite is still at the center of this shitshow. Mack used to work there—he was the one who got George that crap job."

He hadn't done her any favors, letting her work under that asshole Mitchell. *But Mack had been above Mitch,* he remembered. He'd been able to keep Georgia from being mistreated, up until he disappeared.

"She said he was in a car accident."

"Yes. That's the official cause of death," Powell confirmed before reacting all the details. "We've begun a deep dive into Ephraim and Georgia's phone records to see if Mackenzie has been in touch since his presumed death. So far there are no smoking guns."

Rainer swore for a whole other reason. "She's not involved."

Georgia had been shattered by what happened tonight.

Powell winced, an unusual gesture for him. "Let me make sure of that...but also it's a little telling that she didn't immediately confess that her foster brother is alive."

"So, she might need to work up to it," Rainer muttered, stung. "God knows what he told her. Perhaps he threatened her."

Powell sighed. "I just want you to be ready for the worst-case scenario. Even if she didn't know he was alive and he is involved, she might choose to protect him instead of telling you the truth."

Rainer closed his eyes. Of course, Powell would believe the worst, but George was not about to betray him. He had to believe that.

He cleared his throat, but it was like someone was squeezing it shut from the outside, strangling his words. "I am not going there. Not yet."

"Well, let's hope Ms. Hines wakes up in a talkative mood," Powell added. "In the meantime, I'll find out where Mr. Mackenzie has been this past year."

Powell's deliberate use of George's last name wasn't lost on him. Rainer grabbed his phone, gripping it so tight he was surprised he didn't crack the glass screen.

"While you're at it, find out who else Mack was close to at Elite. There's a reason those second-class gangsters went there to hash out the details of their plot. Someone else is involved."

Kolesnik and the unidentified man—who couldn't have been Mack, else he would have given away the fact he was still alive—had been there to meet another conspirator. They had to identify that person ASAP.

And no matter what Powell implied, Rainer knew that the other accomplice wasn't Georgia. It couldn't be.

Ignoring the sinking feeling in his stomach, he stood and poured himself an exceptionally large glass of bourbon.

CHAPTER THIRTY-FIVE

Georgia didn't know if she'd slept at all. It felt as if she'd been lying awake in this bed for hours, her eyes so dry they ached.

When the sky behind the blinds began to lighten with the promise of dawn, she struggled to sit up. It felt as if her body had turned to stone. Her limbs were so heavy that each of her movements was sluggish and painful.

Panic rose, quick and sharp. Her head spun as she swung her legs over the side of the bed. Grabbing fistfuls of the comforter, she sucked in big lungful of air to try to calm her racing heart. Oxygen returned to her starved muscles with a stinging force.

It had taken her most of the night, but she had figured out why Mack might have faked his death.

Somehow, Mack had teamed up with Kolesnik. They had probably met at Elite. Mack had been a gregarious mechanic—he'd been far more politic and popular than Mitchell. Many of the customers had liked shooting the breeze with him. Charming and self-possessed, he'd been a particular favorite with the dealership's few female clients as well, although he had always maintained a strict line between business and pleasure, even when they weren't together.

Somehow, Georgia doubted that a criminal like Kolesnik would team up with a mechanic to kidnap a millionaire. Why would he? Unless he wasn't the mastermind.

Which could only mean one thing. Mack had been the one to come up with the idea to kidnap Rainer. Somehow, he'd talked Kolesnik and his henchman into carrying it out and then had faked his death. Which didn't make any sense until she realized that professional criminals likely wouldn't share the ransom with a mechanic.

Georgia had never thought of her brother as cunning, but he had always been very smart.

So, Mack had pretended to die so they could conduct the crime on their own. He must have had some plan in place to get a cut after the fact. How exactly Mack had thought he was going to pull that off, she had no clue.

Her brain was too exhausted to figure it out. She could feel it in her skull—sensitive and raw from lack of sleep and too much guilt.

No matter how much she wanted to absolve herself of responsibility for Mack's actions, she couldn't. He was her family. And he was going to hurt Rainer.

Pushing off the bed, she took a few shaky steps toward the pile of boxes she hadn't gotten around to unpacking. She couldn't go into the master bedroom without waking Rainer, and she needed clothes. With luck, she'd find something suitable to wear in one of these boxes.

It was tearing her apart, but she had to stop Mack. She could only hope the police would listen and take her seriously.

❧

Rainer woke up with a headache. Downing a cold bottle of water from the mini-fridge, he showered and dressed in his sharpest Etro suit before going to check on Georgia.

She's going to tell me everything this morning.

It might take a little prodding, but she was obviously crushed by what her brother had done.

Georgia won't protect him. She loves you. No, she hadn't said the words, but he knew she did. A woman like Georgia couldn't fake that emotion, give herself so totally and without boundaries the way she did unless she was in love.

She will choose me.

But then Rainer found the spare bedroom empty. He threw out an arm as he lost his balance, his knees cut out from under him. Catching himself against the doorframe, he braced himself until the wave of dizziness and pain passed over him.

Layer by layer, he rebuilt his composure. The bathroom was empty, but he was ready for the blow this time. Methodically clearing the rooms, he made his way to the living room. He didn't have to check the kitchen to know it would also be empty. Rainer could feel the solitude of the other rooms, a whispery visceral knowledge.

For a second, he considered going upstairs. After all, hadn't Eileen been after his office records? Perhaps Georgia was rifling through his desk right now. But he dismissed the snide thought as soon as he had it.

The memory of those shattered hazel eyes was too powerful. Wherever Georgia was, she needed him. Mack was clearly coercing her somehow—maybe even blackmailing her.

Another thought occurred to him, and he nearly slapped his own face.

If Mack had tried to force Georgia to help him, he would fail. But expecting her to take Rainer's side over the man she had loved as a brother her entire life might also be a bridge too far. Which left only one other viable possibility.

Stuck between two terrible choices, Georgia would run.

Fuck. Rational thought flew as anger took over. Where the hell had George gotten the idea that she could run away from him?

Chest heaving, he almost tore his jacket removing his phone from the inner pocket.

"Powell, it's me," he growled, his throat too tight to sound normal. "Where is she?"

CHAPTER THIRTY-SIX

Rainer stared straight ahead as Waters drove them through the nearly empty streets. In half an hour or so, the morning traffic would pick up. Another twenty and these streets would be packed almost to the point of gridlock.

But it didn't look as if Georgia were making a break for the airport. The train station was still a possibility. Perhaps his misguided lover thought she could hide in L.A. Or San Francisco.

Well, if she were foolish enough to believe that, he'd soon teach her otherwise. Rainer wasn't about to let Georgia go.

They turned a corner a bit sharply, jostling Rainer against the door of the town car. Next to him, Powell turned to check that his men were still following along behind them. His head of security was still convinced Georgia was leading them to the kidnapper's den. Rainer knew better, but he wasn't about to send the other men home. He might need them in case Georgia managed to board a train like a brokenhearted little hobo.

At least I'm retaining my sense of whimsy. And George had better be prepared to be tied up to his bed again—this time permanently.

Well, if she were exceptionally good, he might parole her in a few months. She did have a new business to start. But for the near future, she'd be running it from the basement garage of their secure building.

Powell stirred. "The tracker on Georgia's phone has stopped."

The use of her first name should have been a clue. "Is she at the train station?"

His head of security shook his head. "No. And she's not at the airport either, but we need to stop her now before she turns this into a clusterfuck."

❧

Rainer could hear the sound of Georgia weeping from ten feet away. His sweet girl was crying her heart out as quietly as possible, but the force of her emotions was too much to do it in silence.

Several uniformed police officers were eyeballing her as they passed the bench she sat on. But most were young men who didn't stop to ask her what was wrong.

Or the sight of a woman sobbing in front of a police station is a common one. Which was a fucking depressing thought, but probably a correct one.

Standing a few feet behind her, Rainer fought the urge to sweep her up in his arms and carry her off. The cops inside the building might think he was abducting the weeping girl, and he had no desire to be shot by a trigger-happy rookie.

To that end, Powell and his men waited an unobtrusive distance away. Since he was out in the open, they weren't about to stand down, not completely.

His head of security had just shown him the garbled text Georgia had sent him telling him about her brother Mack and his suspected involvement in Rainer's kidnapping.

The confession had broken whatever was left of the barrier he had built around his heart after the Eileen fiasco.

He loved her...and he was going to take her home and tie her to his bed until she agreed to never scare him like this again.

Then he watched Georgia fumble through her pockets for her

phone. She pressed the screen a few times before putting it to her ear with shaky hands.

"Rainer…it's me. I have to do something important right now. I don't know how long it will take—well, Mr. Powell will tell you all about it."

She shuddered, wiping a few stray tears off her face. Her voice was husky, and a touch ragged after all the crying. "We can talk about it later," she added in a whisper.

"Or we could talk about it now." Rainer didn't remember moving, but he was pressed against her now, his hands covering her shoulders.

Startled, she twisted, her eyes swollen, cheeks streaked with tears. She took one look at him and crumpled. Rainer came around the bench, sitting before wrapping her in his arms.

Georgia pressed her face into his shirt front, weeping openly.

"Shh," he soothed, grateful that she wasn't trying to push him away. "It's going to be okay. You're safe now."

Her little hand fisted against his chest. "But you're the one in danger. Mack—"

"I know," he interrupted. "We caught him on the warehouse security cams. We knew his face from Ephraim's pictures."

She looked up at him, a little pucker between her brows. "You have cameras outside, too?"

"Some," he admitted.

They would be adding a hell of a lot more, too. He didn't tell her that, but he would eventually. Rainer and Georgia were a team. He wasn't going to hide anything from her.

"We can continue this conversation at the apartment," he told her after another uniformed cop—a woman this time—paused at the stairs of the entrance to give him the hairy eyeball.

"But I came to turn Mack in for faking his death," she said, wiping her cheeks with both hands.

"And you have no idea what that means to me."

Rainer squeezed her tighter until she was almost another layer he was wearing. "But Powell tells me that it will start a pissing match between the local cops and the FBI agents that he has helping with his investigation."

"Oh." Georgia passed a hand over her mildly puffy face. "I should have thought of that."

He rubbed her back. "It's okay. You've had a shock. Why don't we go home and talk some more? We'll come up with some sort of game plan."

Her lips parted, and she sucked in an audible breath. "Oh, shit. Ephraim is going to have an aneurysm when he hears the news. How the hell am I going to tell him?"

Rainer winced. "Very carefully?"

He deserved the incredulous glare she shot him. "Sorry," he apologized. "We'll figure something out."

Pulling her into his arms, he led her to the car, soothing her the entire ride back.

But it turned out they didn't have to break the news to Ephraim after all. One of Powell's men had taken care of it for them, or so they were informed in front of Ephraim's apartment.

They had gone there instead of summoning the older man upstairs, deciding he needed to know about Mack immediately.

Rainer covered Georgia's ears when the junior security man told them what he'd done. "Damn it, you could have given the man a heart attack. You should have let us break the news."

"It's okay." Georgia tugged his hand away, clearly having heard him. "I wouldn't even know where to start."

A grunt his only answer, he ushered George inside to see how her father was taking the news.

As expected, Ephraim wasn't handling it well, or at all. Despite the photographic evidence laid out on his coffee table, George's father refused to accept that his son was alive.

"These can't be him," he insisted, offering alternate explanations that ranged from the video being doctored or spliced with old footage, to Mack having a doppelgänger who had decided to impersonate him.

"It *is* Mack. He talked to me, told me to stay away from Rainer,"

Georgia said gently, sitting next to him so she could wrap her arm around his stooped shoulders. "He lied dad."

But Ephraim was hard to convince. Georgia shut down his irrational arguments with a gentleness and grace he hadn't expected from someone still reeling from the same devastating blow.

Rainer had cradled her distraught form against him the entire car ride back. But here she was, comforting another, being his rock. His little love was one of those people capable of digging deep, maneuvering past her own pain to do what was needed.

She probably had no idea how rare that was.

His brain fast-forwarded a few years, and he could see Georgia with their kids, soothing them after they skinned their knees or had a fight with their friends at school.

I am going to marry her. The realization didn't feel new. He wasn't shocked—just annoyed with himself. He should have known it would be George. More importantly, he should have done something about it by now.

They finally left when Ephraim, worn out by the day's revelation, asked them to go.

Deciding they'd all had quite enough, Rainer bundled Georgia against him and hustled her upstairs. He didn't care that it was only ten AM, putting them both straight to bed.

CHAPTER THIRTY-SEVEN

Rainer refused to cut and run a second time. "We are not going into hiding again," he told Powell sternly when his head of security suggested a second trip out of town, this time with Ephraim in tow.

Stewart held up his hands in surrender. "I figured as much. But I only ask for the old man. He could use a change of scenery."

"Yeah. I know. The poor guy has aged five years these last couple of days." Rainer leaned back in his office chair, scrubbing his face with one hand.

"He feels responsible for what Mack did, but to hear Georgia tell it, those two have always butted heads." Powell smacked his lips. "Fathers and sons, man."

"Yeah." Rainer sighed. There was a silver lining now. At least he and Powell finally understood why Elite was the center for this damn conspiracy. And his head of security had truly accepted that Georgia had never been part of it.

Mack was in the wind, despite Powell's bulldog-like efforts to track him down. All of the man's old phone numbers or credit cards were defunct, and none of his friends had admitted to hearing from him.

Since it was harder to live off the grid than most people realized, their best guess was that Mack had bought himself a new identity, complete with IDs, before going under.

Just my luck. I had to be targeted by a smart and patient planner. The only flaw in Mack's plan had been committed years before—when he lobbied to get Georgia a job at his place of work.

"By now, Mack has to know George didn't abandon me. How likely is it that these assholes will make another attempt without Kolesnik to do the dirty work?"

Powell ran a finger over one of his eyebrows. It was so finely shaped that Rainer wondered if he had them waxed, but he would never ask. He understood Powell had an image of cool perfection to maintain.

"If they're smart, they'll give it up, but it seems like Shane Mackenzie went to a hell of a lot of trouble to disguise his involvement to give up without some sort of payoff."

"No shit. Unless there's some other compelling reason he would go to that extreme. There isn't, right?"

Powell shook his head.

"Yeah, that's what I thought."

Without the kidnapping ransom, faking his death was both stupidly extreme and pointless. Not only that, but according to Powell, the only way to put Mack in jail was to catch him in the act of a *second* kidnapping attempt. This was barring some sort of miracle where they stumbled on a lair littered with evidence of Mack's involvement in the first kidnapping, which didn't seem likely.

"I still can't believe faking your death isn't illegal," Rainer muttered.

Powell shrugged. "As long as you don't commit fraud in the process—if, for example, a loved one tried to cash in a life insurance policy on you. But baring that, there are no legal ramifications if you want to drop everything and walk away from your own life."

Rainer grunted. "Mack deserves jail and more for hurting Georgia and Ephraim the way he did."

"Except ruining your relatives' lives isn't illegal."

Powell sniffed, but wasn't unsympathetic to Georgia and

Ephraim's plight. "If you intend on staying put, I'll need to hire a few more men. Ephraim doesn't get out much, but both he and Georgia will need their own security details."

"Hire whoever you need," Rainer said, waving away the added expense. "We'll hunker down here until you have everything in place."

Staying in the penthouse was hardly a hardship, particularly since he had his own office space. Georgia, on the other hand, was going to need some help in that regard. Rainer didn't want her to lose momentum on her new business.

"Where are we on my plan to convert our storage area into a workspace for George?"

Powell glanced down at his phone, pulling up some notes. "The other owners didn't have a problem with it as long as it wouldn't increase foot traffic in and out."

Rainer nodded in acknowledgment. "Shouldn't be an issue."

The garage was reasonably safe. The only way inside was through the elevator, which required a key fob for access, and the main garage door leading to the street. The latter opened only for tenant vehicles with a non-cloneable sensor in their car, but it remained a security vulnerability because a pedestrian could slip in behind them.

To prevent that, they had added a discreet camera at the garage gate and routed the feed to both Powell's people and the main security office. The elevator already had a camera. Not that they were going to leave George vulnerable during the time it took his people to get down the stairs. One of the security guys would be assigned to stay with her while she worked.

A few of the existing security men had pre-volunteered for the job. Not that Rainer blamed them. Guarding the cute girl who could talk cars was a superior detail to babysitting a very depressed Ephraim. Of course, if he suspected any of actually flirting with her, he'd have Powell switch them to the sad accountant so fast their heads would spin.

"Any idea on what she's going to work on first?" Powell's normally neutral tone held more than a hint of interest. Yes, it was going to be interesting having an in-house mechanic.

"I think she's narrowed it down to a '58 Corvette, but there was also a 1900 Super Berlina in the running."

Powell whistled. "Nice."

He left with a nod, promising to get the new security team in place as quickly as possible. Trusting his man to do his job, Rainer put in a few hours of work before going to find Georgia.

He found her in the spare bedroom, which she was using as an office. She was sitting cross-legged on the floor in a tank top and a pair of his boxers, surrounded by papers and printed photographs of classic vehicles in various states of disrepair. It was a common sight.

Rainer knew she was using work to distract herself from the Mack situation, but it appeared to be working, so he wasn't about to point it out.

Becoming aware of his presence, she looked up at him, a flash of guilt crossing her face. "Hi. I'm sorry I used a lot of your ink. I thought printing pictures of the cars would help me decide which ones to work on first, but it didn't."

Damn, she was adorable. "You know, you could just buy them all."

Most of the vehicles she was looking at were being auctioned off in the seven-to-fourteen-thousand-dollar range. At those prices, it wasn't unreasonable to get well-stocked.

Georgia got to her feet, wagging her finger. "Nu-uh. No biting off more than I can chew. Also, the best way to crash a new company is to overspend before we get a bead on demand."

Hands in his pockets, he shrugged philosophically. "I just don't want you to miss something cool. Most of your inventory is going to be sourced from auctions, right?"

"Mostly," she admitted, sucking in her lower lip and biting it.

"Hey, that's my job." Taking her chin in his hand, he used the pad of his thumb to pry her luscious lower lip from between her teeth. Her soft breath fanned his finger, and, just like that, he was hard as a rock.

Reading his intent, Georgia started breathing faster, shuffling and clenching her thighs together. He was seconds away from stripping off the boxers she was wearing and pushing her back on the bed when her phone began to buzz.

Her hands flew to cover her mouth for a second before she grabbed her phone and turned off the jingle. "I forgot I set an alarm for the last five minutes of the auction for my first choice."

She pointed to the open laptop at the edge of the scattered paperwork. A counter was flashing over the picture of the Corvette. "Excellent choice."

"I'm sorry, I have to make sure no one outbids me at the last minute."

He held up his hands and backed away. "I understand."

Georgia blushed. "I'll be there as soon as I'm done."

"Good, because I want that naked pussy in my mouth in…" He checked the timer, tacking on time so she could send her details to the seller. "Seven minutes—ten tops."

Her whimper shot straight through him, making the bulge in his pants swell. But she tore her eyes away, crouching by the laptop. "Not nice. Very not nice."

Rainer snickered. "I would say sorry, but I'm starting to hurt here. I'm going to jump in the shower, a cold one. Try not to take too long…"

Georgia cupped her eyes, giving herself blinders to focus on the screen. Rainer retreated, stripping and showering in record time. He was toweling himself off, intending to go back to the bedroom to drag Georgia out the second she was done, when he saw her.

She was naked, kneeling on the bed with her hands bound in the restraints.

Rainer dropped his towel. The cold shower had helped ease his erection, but Georgia had just blasted his efforts to hell.

He leaned against the doorjamb. "Did you win, baby?"

Her luminous eyes flicked up to meet his before bashfully turning back to the coverlet. "I did."

His grin was slow. "Well, I think this calls for a celebration."

Georgia's breathing was ragged when Rainer pushed away from the doorway. His proud length was hard, a detail that sent a flood of warmth to the slick flesh between her legs.

She squeezed her eyes shut, trying to calm her breathing. They had been together for months, but Georgia was no closer to controlling her reaction to Rainer. All he had to do was look at her with those dark eyes that were lit from within as if they contained a banked fire. The heat in them would melt her, every single damn time.

Sometimes, it was easier not to look at him.

Of course, Rainer liked that. He touched her ankles, running his hands up her leg to stroke her inner thigh. Then he took hold of her hips and pulled her to him.

Georgia peeked at him from under her lashes.

His broad muscular shoulders nudged her thighs a little wider. "Still feeling shy with me, baby?"

Predictably, her breathing came a little faster and Rainer grinned before dipping his head. His breath fanned her intimate flesh before his tongue flicked out to take a long, slow lick. He smiled against her heat when she whimpered. Long moments passed. Straining against the bindings she began to rock into his mouth as her desperation began to climb. The tight claw of need had her in its grip, but Rainer seemed determined to torture her.

Not above begging, she whispered to him, promising him anything if he would just let her come.

"Anything?" he asked, pushing two fingers inside her.

"*Yes.*"

He gave her a naked body a thoughtful and distinctly proprietary appraisal. "When do you have to change your IUD?"

Startled she twisted to look at him, blinking. "What?"

"I know they last a long time," he said, stroking in and out her with his hand, seemingly focused on bringing her to the bring but not letting her go over. "But they don't usually stay in forever."

"Uh, I have to ask my doctor for sure. I think it's fine for another year. Maybe two."

"Two?" One of his brows raised, a calculating expression on his face as he methodically worked her clit. "I like the timing of that. Two years."

She shuddered, the light in his eyes making her breath hitch. "You don't want me to replace it?" she asked when she could breathe again.

"No, I don't." His hand moved over her abdomen, spreading his fingers over it possessively.

"Okay," she agreed in a small voice. "I won't."

Primitive satisfaction flared his expression. "*Good.*"

Bending his head he used his tongue and teeth to bring her to a shuddering climax.

Arching her back she sobbed in release, half wishing her birth control were out now.

Later. They had time. Georgia wasn't ready to share him yet.

She was still trying to recover when he flipped her over, arranging her on her hands and knees, her ass at the edge of the bed. His hot hands covered her hips, stroking her clit as his cock rubbed against her cleft, teasing and rubbing until she was ready again. Aching, she pushed back to try and make him bury himself inside her.

His chest pressed against her back. "Still so hungry." A finger traced her rim before penetrating her. She clamped down on it, throwing her hips back at him. "I love that, you know. I can go down on you for hours, make you come over and over, but you'll still want my cock after. Like it's the only thing that can truly satisfy you."

Georgia's answering whimper made him chuckle darkly.

His deep voice rumbled in her ear. "Ask me nicely and I'll fuck you. It'll be a long, hard ride and I won't stop until your pretty pink pussy is sore and satisfied—and drenched in my cum."

His voice was dark, velvet temptation. All the while, he continued to work his fingers in and out, teasing her.

She tried to hold him inside, but his fingers weren't enough. She needed his thick length inside her.

"Please," she whispered, not above begging. Georgia rubbed her ass against him. "Please, *fuck me.*"

A tremor passed through her, but she wasn't the source. The shudder had been passed on from him.

Georgia yelped as Rainer grabbed her hips, entering her with one slow thrust. Then he withdrew and slammed back in, burying his shaft to the hilt.

Helpless in his hold, Georgia turned her head, one cheek flat on the coverlet, her hands fisting as Rainer began to stroke in and out. Closing her eyes, she focused on the hot brand invading her, clamping down every time the steely shaft thrust home.

She got a warning tap on her behind for her trouble, but Georgia didn't stop, and it snapped what little restraint Rainer had left. He began to pound into her, the sounds of hips slapping against her ass drowned out by her helpless cries.

Splintering, Georgia throbbed around him, falling forward on the bed because her arms couldn't support her. Rainer snaked an arm around her, a hand squeezing her breast while the other wrapped around her neck. Grinding and thrusting, he swore under his breath until his whole body tensed, his cock jerked, and she was flooded with liquid fire.

When Georgia came to she was lying in the middle of the bed, her bonds undone. Rainer was wrapped around her like the big spoon, his cock softer but still substantial inside her.

Taking one of his big hands in both of hers, she brought it to her mouth, pressing a kiss to the back before cuddling it against her chest.

"I need my hand for a sec."

Humming in displeasure, Georgia reluctantly released his arm. Rainer did something behind her, then he set something in front of her on the mattress.

Georgia frowned at the navy-blue velvet jeweler's box.

"When our kids ask later, this is not how I did this," he informed her in a matter-of-fact voice. "I did not propose to you after some extremely hot and dirty sex where you were tied to my bed. For future reference, I did this in some glamorous European city, maybe at the top of the Eiffel tower or during a romantic gondola ride."

Startled, she twisted to face him. Rainer looked down at her, but he wasn't smiling. His expression was deadly serious.

"I love you, George."

Gasping, she reached out for him reflexively, pressing her face into his chest.

"George?" His fingertips tapped her behind.

"I love you, too." Her voice was muffled against his chest—which was vibrating with his laughter.

"Good." He pressed his chest against the top of her head. "Although I have to admit I kind of knew you did, else I wouldn't have had the courage to ask you to marry me."

Raising her eyes to his face, Georgia worked a hand between them to wipe away the rogue tear that had just escaped.

"Yeah, you were pretty safe." She hadn't exactly hidden how she felt, even when it would have been better—her painfully obvious crush leaving her exposed and vulnerable. Except Georgia didn't have the tools to do that. Not with this man. One look and she'd lost whatever barriers she'd had, leaving her defenseless. "I didn't know how."

A corner of his mouth turned up, the warmth in Rainer's face making him impossibly more handsome. "Which is why you are my favorite person in the world."

His finger moved to stroke her lip. "I've seen you with other people enough to know it's only me you look at like…like…"

"Like a pathetic star-struck teenager?" she finished.

His kiss soothed whatever lingering embarrassment she might have felt. "What you are is perfect. And if you hadn't been so shy, you would have seen that I looked at you the same way you did me. The way you love me is a gift, which is why I'm putting a ring on it…so do you want to see it?"

Laughing, she opened the box. "Holy mother—"

Rainer slipped the gorgeous thing out of the little slit in the cushion. The round yellow stone was breathtaking. On the band was delicately formed striations vaguely reminiscent of stylized wings, giving the piece an art deco flair.

"I took some liberties with the design, altering it a bit so it would suit," he said, his eyes flicking to hers to check her reaction.

"It's beautiful," she said, stars in her eyes. "It reminds me of something."

His smile widened, and she knew he had chosen something special to her for his inspiration. Her hands cupped the one holding the ring.

"What is it?" she asked. An image was hovering at the edge of her consciousness, but it kept slipping away.

The light in his eyes sparkled. "Okay, so picture a gold plate with a touch of red in place of the rose-cut canary diamond."

"That's a diamond?" She gasped. Georgia had believed the stone to be a bright citrine, her birthstone. "It's *huge*."

Rainer nudged her. "Forget the diamond, look at the band."

Taking it from his hand, Georgia sat up, his finger tracing the winglike design imprinted into the metal—which was likely platinum and not silver or white gold like she thought. Then it came to her. She had seen this design many times.

"Oh my *God*. It's the 1936 Chrysler logo!"

Squealing, Georgia threw herself at Rainer, pressing ecstatic kisses all over his face. "Thank you, thank you, thank you," she said, climbing on top of him to kiss him some more.

Chuckling, Rainer wrapped his arms around her. "Give me five more minutes to recover and you can thank me properly."

Rolling her over so he was back on top, he took the ring and slipped it on her finger. "From here on out, it's you and me. Whatever happens next, or at any time in the future, we do together."

Georgia pulled his head down, kissing him with open-mouthed possession. "Together," she promised.

CHAPTER THIRTY-EIGHT

Georgia rolled the new creeper up and down over the concrete under her with her legs like a child. But she couldn't help it—it was so damn comfortable.

The creepers at Elite, the wheeled platforms they lay on while working under cars, had been hard plastic molded for larger male bodies. An hour into using them and her lower back would be killing her because her tush was too round for her body to lie flat.

But this creeper was top of the line. The padding cradled her body—and tush—so well she suspected Rainer had the thing custom made. How he'd gotten her butt print was a mystery for the ages.

A little over six weeks had passed since Rainer proposed. They had spent most of that in the penthouse while Powell and company continued their investigation. But despite their diligent efforts, nothing new had been discovered.

They hadn't been able to track down Mack's new identity. Georgia had been relieved by that at first, torn by her lingering loyalty to him, but the more time passed, the less sympathy she had for her former foster brother.

Whatever guilt she'd had for rejecting him was gone. Mack hadn't just hurt her when he'd faked his death—he had destroyed Ephraim.

Her father had suffered enough. The first blow had been losing the love of his life. Then he'd been betrayed by his oldest friend, losing his business and his house. These things were more than enough.

But the blow inflicted by Mack? Georgia would never forgive him for that. Ephraim was a shell of his former self, but he was trying to function for her sake.

Without Rainer, Georgia would have spiraled under the combined impact of those hits.

"Focus on our future," he told her a week ago when he'd found her dejected and morose after unpacking her boxes, an old family photo in her hand.

He wiped her tears, before surprising her by whipping out a length of black satin to blindfold her.

"Are we adding blindfolds to the ropes?" she asked, expecting to be led to the bedroom. But Rainer had other plans.

He guided her to the elevator, whisking her down the recently cleared storage area, which he had converted into a temporary workspace for her.

The creeper had been wrapped in a big bow. There had also been rolling tool cabinets, fully stocked, sturdy metals tables, an engine pulley system, and the car lift she'd earmarked for her garage.

He'd even created a break area with a full-size fridge, coffee table, and not one but two brand-new, stain-resistant couches set in one corner of the fenced-off space.

Georgia had been stunned by his generosity, accepting the gift of the space in the spirit they had been given, with one exception.

"New couches?" she asked, pulling away after hugging him and pressing a thousand kisses to his face.

"For me and Ephraim and whoever else wants to hang out and watch you work," he said, bouncing on the balls of his feet like a little boy.

"Don't you mean for the security guys that you'll have babysitting me down here?" she asked, one corner of her mouth turned up.

"Them, too," he added, pulling her down to straddle him on the couch. "Not planning on fighting me on that?"

Georgia rested her head on his shoulder. "Nah. I just hope they won't be bored."

"Trust me, they'll be lining up for this duty," he said with a resigned sigh. "But this area will also come in handy for other reasons," he added, giving her ass a little squeeze.

"*Rainer*," Georgia protested. "I know it's fenced off—but everyone can still see us."

The guards were upstairs, but the fencing was chain-link with some fabric mesh added for privacy, but the tenants with nearby parking spaces could still come around to the sliding gate for an unobstructed view.

"Not that." Rainer tweaked her nipple over her clothes. "I just meant that it's only a matter of time before your old neighbors track you down for help on their family vehicles. A good mechanic is hard to find, especially one who works for parts and brownies."

Since she'd gotten several texts to that effect in the last week, she didn't argue with him, except to point at him.

"It's cake and casserole," she corrected. "But *new* couches aren't necessary. They are only going to get covered in grease."

"We scotch-guarded them," he said, patting the backrest next to him. "Besides, didn't your garage at Ephraim's old house have a couch?"

"Yes, but not a nice one," she said. "I found that old one in the dumpster near Ephraim's old office."

His look of shock and horror had been so profound she'd had time to take her phone out and snap a picture. *For our kids,* she told herself.

"*Bedbugs,* George," Rainer scolded when he recovered. "That's how you get bed bugs."

And so, she lost that argument. As it turned out, the only items Rainer bought used were vintage cars, antiques, and antiquities. Not that she'd gotten a good look at the latter. But they had plans to visit the high-end storage unit this weekend where Rainer kept his collection so they could choose the pieces they wanted to move into the penthouse.

Georgia was excited to pick through his collection, but, for the moment, that anticipation might have been eclipsed by the excitement over the delivery of the Corvette she'd bought at auction. It had arrived yesterday morning, right before Rainer had left for the office.

"What color are you going to paint it?" Dylan Waters asked over the music playing softly from the phone dock she'd found waiting on the coffee table.

The junior security guard sat on the couch, alternating between flipping through magazines and playing a game on his phone.

Rolling out from under the vet on the creeper, Georgia raised her head. "I'm not sure. Red and white would be the safe choice, but I'd think I'd like to shake it up. Maybe I'll do it in teal."

The junior security man nodded. "That could be nice," he said, mouth pursing contemplatively before turning back to his phone.

Technically, he wasn't supposed to be doing that, but Georgia didn't mind. It wasn't as if he could miss an ambush down here. The space echoed enough that they could hear someone approaching, even with the radio on. It was fortunate the garage was pretty dead during the day, with most of the activity happening early in the morning or evening as people left and returned from school or work.

It was also better ventilated than most parking garages, so she wouldn't be sucking in exhaust fumes all day.

But Rainer assured her this arrangement was temporary. Once the threat had passed, she'd be working in the warehouse. In the meantime, enough time had passed for her and Rainer to establish a routine.

Every morning he would nudge her awake for some morning sex because he, 'wouldn't last the day without it'. Since neither could Georgia, she was happy to oblige. After they showered, they'd share a leisurely breakfast, eating in the living room before she slipped a pair of coveralls over her clothes. Rainer had ordered half a dozen, each embroidered with her name over the breast.

After they would ride the elevator down together, parting in the garage with a kiss long enough to make their respective security details uncomfortable. Then Rainer would head off to work in a chauffeured town car, and she'd walk to her sectioned-off area of the garage to get to work.

The Corvette's engine was in surprisingly good shape. It needed a few parts and an extensive tune-up, but Georgia soon had the thing purring like a kitten—a quiet one. She had never been a fan of modding the muffler and exhaust system of a car to make an engine louder.

She was knee-deep in paint swatches when she got a surprise visitor. Samantha waved at her from the gate entrance.

"Hey girl, I hope you don't mind me dropping in!" Wearing one of her trademark wrap dresses and holding a cardboard coffee cup, she walked over, heels cracking on the concrete like little gun shots.

"I was in the neighborhood to deliver a car to one of my regulars," the glamorous blonde explained. "And after hearing all about your new operation from Judy, I thought I'd stop by and take a peek."

"It's not a problem, but this is just our temporary space," Georgia explained when Sam looked around as if expecting to see all the shiny cars Rainer had bought from Elite over the years.

"Of course, you're just getting going." Sam pulled up a chair and launched into an impromptu speech about the sales side of the car business. Since she didn't appear to be angling for a new job—Sam did very well at Elite—Georgia assumed she was taking a mercenary interest in case she managed to make a success out of her little venture.

Also, cultivating a deeper connection to Rainer wouldn't hurt her any Georgia thought cynically. Whether it was for future sales or to meet similarly wealthy young bachelors, Sam knew the advantage of networking.

Even though she and the leggy blonde had never been close, Georgia appreciated the effort the saleswoman was making, despite the slightly condescending tone she was using to give her advice.

With that in mind, Georgia listened politely as she worked, occasionally chiming in despite the fact she was still planning to have Judy handle all of their customers whenever possible.

You didn't burn bridges when you were starting a new business.

Rainer got the visitor's notification from Waters when he was on his way home. *Samantha Jones.* Wasn't that a television character? Why the hell was a television character visiting Georgia?

After he opened the hyperlink on the name, he recognized the photograph. He vaguely remembered the blonde who had sold him one of his Ferraris.

Hmm. He knew Powell liked Mitch as Mack's accomplice, but as far as he knew, they hadn't found anything definitive on the man.

Rainer texted Powell back.

Has she been cleared?

So far, she's clean, but the search is only 90% done.

Ah. Well, that was good enough for him. Powell's background checks were better than the CIA, or so Waters had told him more than once.

But when he got home, there was something off in Sam's smile. He noticed the brittle edge in her expression as he approached the gate, having parked his car a few spots down from Georgia's workspace.

Rainer slowed his steps, wondering if he should call back his security detail. Per the routine they had established in the last month, his bodyguards had gone upstairs on arrival, while he lingered with Georgia down here. Waters, the man assigned to her today, would stay with them until she was done and ready to go upstairs.

It wasn't the first time they'd had company either. Judy, Ephraim, and a few other friends from their old neighborhood had cleared Powell's background check gauntlet. As he'd planned, they came and sat in the conversation area, chatting with Georgia as she worked on a restoration, or in one case, a former neighbor's car.

He really shouldn't have been surprised to see Samantha here. The saleswoman was sitting on a rolling stool between the couch where Waters was watching her with a dreamy expression, and the 'Vette, which was on the car ramp. Georgia was underneath on the creeper, working and talking like nothing was wrong.

And she's right. Everything is fine.

Samantha raised a manicured hand to hail him. "Hello Mr. Torsten —or can I call you Rainer now?" she asked, switching to his first name without waiting for an answer.

Grabbing a soft drink from the fridge he sat down. Samantha smoothly included him in the conversation she and Georgia were having about a new restaurant she'd tried, located a few blocks from them.

She was perfectly charming. For some reason, though, Rainer's hackles didn't lower. Maybe it was the subtle tension carving a shallow groove around her mouth, or the way she kept glancing at Waters. Rainer retreated a few steps to the edge of the work zone, toward the hood end of the Corvette, wondering if he should nudge Georgia into knocking off sooner rather than later so they could excuse themselves.

I hope she doesn't invite Sam to dinner.

He was chiding himself for the ungenerous thought, when Waters suddenly slumped over, dropping his phone on the concrete with a clatter.

Rainer scrambled to his feet "Waters? What's wrong?"

He'd taken a few steps in the guard's direction when Sam leapt out of her seat, the hand she'd had in her bag snapping up. His brain registered the strange outline of the oversized pistol a split second before he reacted.

Rainer threw himself onto the hard floor. Rolling automatically, he opened his mouth to shout a warning as something whistled past him.

He jerked his head, realizing that the object shot at him wasn't a bullet, but a tranquilizer dart.

What the fuck?

"George, stay down," he yelled when he heard the distinctive sound of the creeper's wheels on the concrete.

He crawled around the front of the Corvette, intending to pull her out from the other side, but Sam was on him. Between one blink and the next, she'd switched guns, swapping out the tranquilizer for a sleek Berretta. And she was pointing it at his head.

Time slowed down. Samantha was yelling at him, but he couldn't make out the words. But he got the gist when a dark van shot into the garage, tires squealing.

And then shit got confusing. The headlights of the Corvette flared, the engine turning over.

"*Get back,*" Georgia shouted. He turned his head just in time to see her behind the wheel of the Corvette as she floored it. The car shot forward.

Rainer jumped, his back slamming against the chain links as the 'Vette pinned him against one corner. Georgia had managed to get the vehicle wedged so that the open door was forced against the side panel of the car on the right, effectively trapping him between it and the back of the fence.

Georgia had just created a tiny fenced-in prison just for him. The kidnappers couldn't get to him. And he couldn't get to her.

"George!"

He wanted to yell at her to run, but she was already moving. She clambered out of the driver's side, right into Sam's waiting arms.

But Samantha didn't shoot her. She slapped her across the face before turning her nails into claws and lunging. He thought she was going to blind her, but Sam was going for her hands, trying to pry the Corvette keys from her grip.

Georgia curled into a ball, protecting the keys underneath her.

"Get the fuck away from her, you *bitch,*" he shouted, rattling his cage with helpless fury.

But Sam had come too far to give up. She backed up and picked up the Beretta, which she must have dropped earlier.

"Don't you touch her you *bitch.*" Rainer started to climb, intending to go over the top of the fence, despite the spikes studding the top.

But Sam didn't shoot Georgia. Two men wearing balaclavas materialized at her side, and she stopped. Somewhere in the distance, a door slammed, and then they were running—not alone. One masked man had picked up Georgia.

"Let go!" Twisting and kicking, she struggled against his hold, but compared to the muscled behemoth, she was tiny. The masked man hauled her up with one arm, before sprinting to the open van door just outside the door.

Something flashed silver in the light before disappearing under the Corvette—Georgia had thrown the keys underneath the car, protecting him to the bitter end.

Rainer was still screaming himself hoarse when he sailed over the top of the gate, tearing his shirt and scraping his abs on the sharp points.

But it was too late. Georgia had been thrown into the back of the van. He was more than a dozen yards away when the door slammed shut behind her.

The van peeled out of the garage before he could get to it.

CHAPTER THIRTY-NINE

Georgia's ears were ringing. Dazed, she belatedly registered the blow as the arm retreated. One of the men had hit her this time—a strong man capable of inflicting way more damage than Sam. Whimpering, she curled up against the wall panel, crying out when a quick jolt slammed her aching body into the side.

The driver behind the wheel was treating the van like a race car.

"He's going to flip us," she cried, throwing out an arm to brace herself as the van careened around another curve, the right-side wheels clearing the ground ominously

"Shut up." Cold steel pressed against her forehead. Georgia blinked up at Sam. The woman didn't look pretty now. Her hair was a mess, and she had a crazed look in her eyes.

But her makeup was still perfect, even as she was pressing a gun to Georgia's head. *That is so fucked up.* In a fair world, her mascara would have run, giving her raccoon eyes. Or better yet, blinding her.

"You should have minded your own fucking business, Georgia," Sam spat, pushing the barrel hard enough to bruise. "If you hadn't gone to Torsten, this wouldn't be happening."

"Stop it," one of the men snapped in a thickly accented voice. "We need her alive for the ransom video."

"What?" Georgia's voice broke. "Are you ransoming me now?"

"You're marrying the son of a bitch, aren't you?" Samantha snapped, waving the gun.

Georgia groaned. Of course. Judy must have told Sam. They hadn't come for Rainer at all.

Well, shit. She pressed against the wall of the van as it took another sharp turn. Samantha swayed violently with the motion, and Georgia expected a bullet to shatter her skull at any moment.

It will be painless, she told herself, hoping it were true. No sooner did she have the thought than Georgia realized she wasn't going to go without a fight. She had too much to live for now. Rainer was *hers.* Their life was a dream, and, damn it, she would *fight* for it.

But another hissed complaint from one of the masked men made Sam put the gun away.

The van was speeding down the streets before it abruptly slowed. Less than a minute later, it came to a shuddering stop.

Bright light hit her horizontally as the sliding door was yanked open. No one was holding her down. Propelled by a burst of adrenaline, she jumped up, leaping past her assailants, only to crash into a new pair of arms.

Shock held her immobile as she stared into Mack's face.

"Mack, I told you to mind your fucking business!" Samantha screamed over her head.

The shrill words broke the layer of ice that held her immobile.

"No! I'm not going." Georgia squirmed and kicked out, but the vice of his arms tightened. Someone was screaming. She registered that it was Sam just before Mack twisted, holding her as he pivoted one hundred and eighty degrees. He staggered, letting go of her. Weak from shock, she stared blankly at the rosette of blood that had suddenly bloomed on his abdomen.

"*Georgia.*" His hand reached out for her.

Finally registering that he'd been shot, she stretched out her arms to try to catch him, but he was too heavy. Mack slid down her front, taking her with him as he went.

Georgia hit the dirty asphalt with a grunt. Mack's bulk was suffocating, and her side was burning. She was going to push him off, but a movement out of the corner of her eye told her the kidnappers were moving, so, instead, she clung to him until she was too weak to maintain her grip.

The realization she'd also been shot came too late. She was covered in hot metal, the taste of it in her mouth. The world was going dark. Her eyes closed to the sound of distant cannons.

CHAPTER FORTY

Rainer paced the hallways in front of the OR where Georgia was being operated on. Technically, he wasn't supposed to be back here, but Powell had a quiet word with the head of administration. Rainer was waved through. But this hospital wasn't one of those fancy teaching institutions with big picture windows for observers. Built at least two decades ago, the operating room was a windowless chamber.

The only good news was that the surgeon on call was very experienced with gunshot wounds.

He closed his eyes, thrown back in time a mere hour—and a flash flood of nightmare images threatened to crush his brain.

One heartbeat and Rainer was struggling to undo his seatbelt. Powell didn't try to stop him. He knew Rainer's life was worthless if Georgia died. And Rainer hadn't forgotten his training—all those hours running drills under Mason had made him fast, honed his reflexes. In the next heartbeat, Powell was shoving a gun into Rainer's hand and pushing him behind his two other men.

Another beat, a snapshot of the alley. It was getting dark, the shadows coming together to hide. But he could see the abandoned van, the door open. His mind didn't register the two crumpled bodies in front of it until he was halfway there.

After that, the beats came hard and fast, blurring together. Rainer couldn't distinguish one from the next because Powell was pushing Mack to the side, revealing a bloody Georgia, pale and lifeless on the floor.

That was the moment he stopped feeling his heartbeat. It froze in his chest as if refusing to work until Georgia opened her eyes and looked up at him.

But she didn't. Unresponsive until they swept her away from him, the operating room door a threshold even he couldn't cross.

Staggering to the wall, Rainer slid down into an empty plastic chair. Powell must have secured it for him because it wasn't there earlier.

Rainer was still sitting there staring at the OR door when Garrett arrived, towing an unexpected guest.

Mason Lang knelt in front of him. "Hey, I heard things went *fubar,* but the doctor said your girl is going to be okay. The bullet didn't hit her organs."

"That's what they said," Rainer repeated hollowly.

But Georgia had lost a lot of blood. The pool under her body had been so big. Intellectually, he knew some of that had to be Mack's. Powell had said something about angles, trajectories. Enough for Rainer to get the gist.

The bullet that hit Georgia had passed through Mack first. He'd had his arms around her, had been shot in the back…as if he'd been trying to protect her.

The hospital staff had been giving him regular updates Rainer barely registered because they had not yet said the words he needed to hear. *She's going to be fine.*

Rainer buried his face in his hands. "She kept them from getting to me."

Mason's hand landed on his shoulder. It stayed there, trying to steady him. "I know. Powell says she sacrificed the car she was restoring to do it."

Rainer hadn't even known the engine was running. It hadn't been working yesterday.

He raised his head. Mason flinched at his expression. It was subtle, but Rainer still caught it.

"She can fix it," he said, throat so tight he sounded as if he were strangling. "George can fix anything."

Except herself. His heart squeezed so tight it felt like he might be dying. But he forced himself to take a labored breath, and then another. He wouldn't stop until George woke up.

❧

Georgia's lashes fluttered, and she gasped. It was a mistake. Taking a deep breath hurt like a son of bitch. The words echoed in the air, a garbled mess. "*Sonubithh.*"

A flurry of movement out of the corner of her eye, and then Rainer was there. "Hey, sleepyhead."

Georgia relaxed, sinking into the bed. Rainer was all right. They hadn't gotten him. She felt his hand move over her hair, over her cheeks, and she pulsed with joy. It was duller, her entire body aching and sluggish, but she didn't care. Her love was here. Nothing else mattered.

"I love you, too." A drop of saltwater on her lips. His tear. "And if you ever do anything like that ever again, I will never forgive you."

She tried to move her arms. Rainer was hurting and she need to comfort him, but her stubborn limbs wouldn't move. They were too heavy. But he quickly found a solution. Rainer climbed into the bed with her, careful to stay on her uninjured side.

"What do you remember?"

Georgia tensed, the distant sound of cannons echoing in her ears. "I got shot." The words came out indignant. But the memories were hazy. Filling in the pieces was starting to make her dizzy.

"Don't try," Rainer whispered when she confessed as much, her eyes already starting to close. "For now, the only thing you think about is recovering. We'll fill in the blanks later."

Too tired to argue, she leaned against him. All too soon she slipped back down under.

Georgia didn't feel it when Rainer got up and left the room.

The doctors told Rainer that Mack's convalescence would be much longer than Georgia's. Given the way he'd been holding her when shot, the bullet had angled in such a way that his liver had been lacerated and his gallbladder perforated. But a person could live without a gallbladder, and Mack was big and physically fit. The doctors were cautiously projecting a complete recovery.

Rainer spent the night at the hospital, stretched out on a cot next to Georgia so he wouldn't jostle her in his sleep. But he slept poorly, tossing and turning as he tried to find the cleanest path out of the shit storm Sam and Mack had thrust them into.

Except it wasn't all bad. You would have never met George had it not been for them.

Groaning, he got up, washing in the narrow shower in the bathroom before changing into the fresh clothes one of his people had brought last night. He had a choice between jeans and a t-shirt and a suit, but he didn't need the armor of formal clothes. Not for this.

The nurses had kept him apprised of Mack's condition. A few hours after the surgical anesthesia wore off, the man finally began to stir.

Rainer slipped into the room as the hospital began its early morning bustle. He wasn't quiet, but it still took a few minutes for Mack to rise to full consciousness.

The younger man stared at him. "Is Georgia okay?"

And there it is. The reason Rainer hadn't been able to sleep. No matter what his faults, Mack loved Georgia. When push came to shove, he'd proved he'd lay down his life for her. And despite everything, deep down, she still loved Mack. Just not the way Mack wanted.

"She will be."

Mack's eyes narrowed. "Then why are you here?"

Rainer crossed one leg over the other, leaning back in a gesture calculated to irritate. "We have Samantha Jones in custody, along with two of Vasil Kolesnik's known associates. Everyone is going down."

The ghost of a smirk crossed Mack's face. "You don't have anything on me."

Yes, Mack was smart. He'd done his homework, and he knew faking his death hadn't broken any crimes. "I'm aware. Which is why you're going to confess and tell us everything before Samantha has a chance to twist the detectives to her side."

He settled his hands in front of him, weaving his fingers together loosely. "I'm sure you know how persuasive she can be."

Mack's features tightened. For a second, Rainer thought he had him, but then the other man shook his head, his lips set mulishly. "Nothing I did for Sam was illegal."

Rainer doubted that, but he knew the best legal scenario was for Mack to confess. "I'm not sure you'll be able to convince a jury of that."

"Why?" A sneer. "Because I'm black, and Sam is white?"

"I was going to say because you're a man and she's a woman," Rainer said, raising a brow. "And then there's the fact you did play dead, which isn't going to go over well with the authorities...but I know people. Tell us everything, cooperate with the investigation, and I can push for the minimum sentence."

Mack scoffed. His mouth opened, but Rainer leaned forward. "Do it...and for every year you spend in prison, I will compensate you."

The man's head jerked. "You're going to pay me to confess?"

Rainer's smile was so sharp it could draw blood. "Think of it as the plea deal of the century."

"You're a cold-blooded bastard, aren't you?" Mack's eyes closed. "Poor Georgia has no idea what she's getting herself into."

Rainer ignored that. Georgia knew exactly who he was. She might not approve, but she would eventually understand he'd done what he thought was best, for everyone.

"A million dollars for every year you spend in jail. Five sounds like a nice round number, doesn't it?"

Mack's breath caught. "You can do that—get me five years?"

"I can strongly suggest," Rainer said honestly. "But if you get paroled after twelve months, you get two million. That's our minimum."

"I can do five," Mack said quickly.

"Up to you." Rainer shrugged. "But don't get ideas about misbehaving to pad your sentence. Being a model prisoner is part of the deal."

He stood, pouring a glass of water from the jug at the bedside table. He handed it to the younger man. "And there are other strings. These rules apply before, during, and after you serve your sentence. Violate the terms of our agreement, and it all goes away."

Mack's brow creased. "After? You mean meeting with my parole officer and all that shit?"

"I mean you stay away from me and Georgia and whatever kids we have—unless she wants to see you."

Mack's face curdled. "You're really going to marry her? That wasn't a joke?"

"No, it wasn't a fucking joke." Rainer scowled. "And stop fucking interrupting me. Once you get out of jail, you won't come around. You're going to be the uncle who sends cards on birthdays and Christmas, but who does not come around to Sunday dinner—*ever*."

Rainer waved a hand in front of his face. "And whatever the hell went down between you and Ephraim, you fix it sooner than later—even if you have to do it from the other side of one of those plastic visitor's windows at your prison."

"Fuck, you are a control freak," Mack muttered, avoiding his eyes. But then he sighed and feigned nonchalance. "But you may as well tell him where I am. Maybe he can come see me before the cops take me away."

Rainer got to his feet. "I'll do that. In the meantime, don't speak to the cops. My lawyer will be by soon, along with Stewart Powell, my head of security. You'll tell them both all you know, and they'll prepare your statement, which we'll hand over to the authorities. I'll be contacting the district attorney's office later this morning to work out your deal."

CHAPTER FORTY-ONE

The pieces of the puzzle finally began to come together after Mack began to cooperate.

Somehow, Rainer stayed on top of the fast-developing story while managing to fuss over Georgia enough for her to complain that he was driving her crazy. But she said it with a smile, holding onto his arm as she drifted off to sleep for the fifth time that day.

The idea to kidnap Rainer for ransom had come from Mack. He'd said it as a joke, told in passing to Mitch and Samantha on the day Rainer bought an electric blue Ferrari from Elite nearly two years ago.

Samantha had been the one to sell him that car. She'd closed the deal, subtly offering herself as a bonus when Rainer signed along the dotted line. But he hadn't taken her up on the offer.

But before the Elaine incident, being hit on had been a near-daily occurrence. And Sam wasn't his type. So, he'd passed on her offer as politely as he could. It wasn't personal.

"I don't even remember that," Rainer later confessed when he filled George in on the details.

She scoffed. "I'm not surprised. According to the tabloids, you were ass deep in random pussy back then."

"Ew. Phrasing," he said, defending himself. "I may have tried to do the 'work hard, play hard' thing, but I wasn't indiscriminate. I'll have you know I was always very choosy when it came to the female company I kept."

"Hmm," she sniffed. "Well, apparently, Samantha took your rejection personally."

That was an understatement. Sam treated her client roster like a personal dating service and experience phenomenal success doing so.

One of the married ones had even offered to leave his wife for her, so when Rainer rejected her, the woman built the moment into a mountain of a grudge—Mack's joking words about ransoming him the foundation.

According to Mack, that was also around the time he and Sam first slept together. Georgia had moved out of his place earlier that month, and had finally broken things off for good the week before. The pair found solace in each other, though neither would admit that. And, as time went on, they kept sleeping together despite the fact both continued to pursue other people.

For Samantha, that included Vasyl Kolesnik, the Ukrainian gangster with ambitions of becoming more. Kolesnik spent a lot of money on Sam, trying to impress her. Even though he wasn't the big fish she was trying to land, Sam cultivated the connection, effectively grooming him while he thought he was using her.

Once she had him in her thrall, she whispered in his ear about Elite's biggest, richest client.

But Kolesnik didn't know how to pull off the kidnapping for ransom. He was effectively a lackey for bigger criminals who used brute force and intimidation to make their way in the world. So, it was Sam who had to put the plan together. The original idea had been to set up some sort of honey trap, throwing Ukrainian prostitutes in Rainer's path until he took the bait, something he never did.

"Good thing there aren't a lot of hot black Ukrainian prostitutes," Georgia had grumbled.

Rainer had patted her ass consolingly, assuring her it wouldn't have worked. Especially since his social life had come to a grinding halt after the Elaine incident.

The honey trap stalled, Sam had brought Mack into the inner circle, somehow convincing Kolesnik that they needed him to figure out a new path because Mack was a genius when it came to strategy.

Mack's idea was much simpler—watch Rainer until the right opportunity presented itself. After learning what bank he did business with, it wasn't difficult for Sam to make friends with one of the bank receptionists. Dishing about the handsome multi-millionaire was a favorite pastime for single females everywhere he went.

But Kolesnik didn't like the idea of being edged out by another man. Aware he'd sooner get a bullet in the back of the head than a dime of the ransom money, Mack decided to bow out early. Sam was more than willing to pretend she had killed him because he was a loose end, and as a show of loyalty to Kolesnik.

The gangster was so pleased with Sam that he was more than willing to follow her lead for the rest of the plan. That included demanding any ransom be sent to a Cayman bank account. Kolesnik had no idea Mack had set up the account, or that all the funds would automatically be transferred to another bank in Switzerland once Sam had safely ditched him. Then Mack and Sam would split the money fifty-fifty.

But Georgia had ruined everything for them by warning Rainer.

Aware something had gone wrong after the men they had following Rainer ended up at Ephraim's house, Sam had decided to call things off, especially after Powell had tracked down and arrested Kolesnik.

Then Judy confirmed something Sam suspected—that Georgia and Rainer were together. A few weeks later, they were engaged. The fact that grease-monkey Georgia had succeeded where she had failed had pissed Sam off enough to resurrect her plan, only now there was no need to kidnap Rainer.

They had a far more accessible target.

"You mean Sam was there to grab *me*?" Georgia asked incredulously when Powell broke the news a week after she returned home from the hospital. "I assumed they took me only because they couldn't get to Rainer."

They were curled up on the couch at home while Powell sat in one of the armchairs to their left.

"The tranquilizer dart was filled with a mix of ketamine and zylaxine—a potent sedative," his security chief explained. "But the dosage wasn't high enough for someone of Rainer's size. It was calibrated for a much smaller person."

Georgia's mouth twisted. "Then why did she wait until Rainer had come home?"

Powell lifted a hand. "In a word—Waters. We think she knew there would be a guard with you. She slipped the same drugs into his drink —the camera footage has her offering Water's a coffee after she prepared one for herself during her chat with you. The camera angle was off so we don't have a recording of her spiking it, but that's the only time she could have drugged it. You were under the Corvette at the time and missed the exchange."

She scowled. "I remember hearing the coffee machine going off a few times, but my mind was on my work. I was only half-listening to her. Tell Waters I'm sorry. I'm the one who told her to help herself when she saw the machine and mentioned needing a pick-me-up."

Powell's shoulders straightened. "Waters is resigning."

Georgia gasped, leaning forward. "But it wasn't his fault!"

Rainer pursed his lips, but didn't argue when Powell shook his head. "He knew better than to accept a drink from a possible suspect. As it stands, Samantha couldn't have known the guard would be Waters. He is the largest member of the team. The drugs she slipped into the drink didn't work fast enough for someone of his muscle mass."

"He is hulk-sized," Georgia added morosely.

Powell's lip twitched, but he merely nodded. "Samantha must have been waiting for Waters to pass out to force you out of the garage. But because she miscalculated the dosage, Rainer had enough time to get home before the sedative kicked in. I think she meant to be long gone before he arrived, bringing the rest of the security detail with him."

"Then I stopped to socialize and Waters finally passed out, giving her away. Once that happened, she was angry enough to switch targets back to me."

Rainer wrapped his arm around her. "It wasn't the smart move. My lawyers would have given her the run-around while cooperating with the authorities. It would have been much easier for her to get the ransom if she'd taken you instead because I wouldn't have done that. To get you back, I would have given her anything, no argument."

"Aww." Georgia curled into his side, her hand flattening against his chest right over his heart. "But I still don't think Waters should lose his job."

"It's his decision to leave, and I respect it," Powell said, not adding what he'd told Rainer earlier—a guard who second-guessed himself was not one you wanted watching your back.

"Don't worry about Waters," Rainer added. "There is no need for concern. He has other opportunities he can pursue."

She turned to him. "Like what?"

Rainer rubbed the indentation between her brows with his thumb. "A private security firm I know is hiring. They'll be happy to have him if he's open to it."

But when they asked him what he wanted, Waters surprised them by asking for a recommendation for a completely different job.

EPILOGUE

A few weeks later, Rainer went downstairs to check on Georgia and her new assistant. She was still working in the apartment building, while the warehouse construction crew threw up a few walls to create an office space for her and Judy.

The receptionist felt terrible for telling Samantha about their engagement, but both Rainer and Powell had absolved her of responsibility. It wasn't as if Rainer had intended on hiding his relationship with Georgia. Sam would have eventually found out about their impending nuptials without Judy's help.

Georgia saw him and smiled, coming to stand next to him as Waters tried to cram his bulk in the narrow space under the Corvette.

The damage to the machine had been superficial and repaired quickly, the white-and-teal paint job gleaming under the fluorescent lights.

"I was going to ask how your new assistant was doing," Rainer muttered out of the corner of his mouth as Waters made a second attempt. "But now I see..."

Georgia tsked before rushing over to push some buttons on the car lift. The humming of the moving rotors filled the air as the car was levered up another foot.

She tapped the hood twice. "All good?"

Waters gave her a thumbs-up sign, getting to work with his usual chattiness.

"See, I told you the car lift was a better investment than the pit," Georgia said coming back to stand next to him. "And the big guy is doing great. I'm letting him change the oil on the car for practice, but he can stop if you feel like taking it for a spin."

"On second thought, I better not drive it, or I'll want to keep it."

Georgia wagged a finger. "You have enough cars."

"Bite your tongue," Rainer chided before capturing the finger to press a kiss to the tip. "There is no such thing."

She nudged him with her hip. "You're lucky I washed up after installing a new fuel line."

Rainer laughed, trapping her against him. "I do love the smell of gas."

Georgia wiggled her rear in retaliation. "As long as you don't eat it."

He was going to point out Waters would still fit better in a pit, but decided Georgia was right. Waters would probably overflow a standard-sized pit as well.

"You will need another creeper," he pointed out. "A wider one."

"True," Georgia acknowledged, turning to watch her assistant work. "But I think he's worth it. He's been a huge help moving the heavy equipment."

She gestured to the Super Berlina waiting in the wings. "And we're going to need to take that entire engine apart sooner rather than later because Judy is ninety-five percent sure she's found a buyer at our asking price."

"With quality work like this, they will sell themselves. Wait and see."

"Well, don't tell her that," Georgia admonished. "She's excited about closing her first big sale."

Rainer stopped to admire the sleek lines of the Berlina, which was halfway through its restoration. "It's beautiful, but why haven't you touched the Talbot yet?"

He jerked his thumb at the corner, where the third car was parked under a tarp. "I thought you'd be all over it after we moved it over here."

"I'll get to it *after* I finish the vehicles I plan to sell. Besides, Ephraim doesn't mind the wait—after all, he got his way. Regardless of which one of you claims the car, the Talbot is staying in the family."

"I hadn't thought of it that way," he said. "But as much as I would love to call that baby mine, I think you were right the first time. It should be a gift to him."

She took his arm, pressing against him. "Thanks. But I'm sure he'll lend it to you if you ask nicely."

"Like a teenager asking to borrow the car," he said with a laugh.

Slinging a wrench over her shoulder, Georgia gave him an assessing look. "I bet you were being driven around in limos as a teen."

"Guilty."

"Well then, you can have the teen experience now. Better late than never."

He laughed. "Trust me, I get enough of that every time we have dinner and he gives me the hairy eyeball like he knows what we get up to once he's gone." He broke off with a wry shrug. "I'm hoping that part of the teenage experience ends sooner rather than later."

"Oh I think it will—probably around the time we get married."

"Another good reason to move the wedding up."

"It's next month." She laughed. "That's soon enough. Besides, I have a business to launch. But no worries. With Waters helping, it won't be long before we are done with all three cars. Once they're finished, there will be plenty of time to have a proper honeymoon."

"That's great, baby. But you want to know the best part of having an assistant?"

"What is it?"

Rainer threw his arm around her shoulder, propelling her toward the elevator. "Well, as the boss, you get to delegate and leave your junior assistant to wrap things up so you can knock off early."

Guilt flashed across her expression, but she took his hand with a wry grin. "I think I'm beginning to understand how Mitch became such an ass. Power corrupts."

His laughter trailed behind them. "Don't worry babe. As long as you don't make him clean the bathroom, you're heads and shoulders above the Mitchs of the world."

"We use the bathrooms in the lobby," she reminded him. "And you know the cleaning service takes care of those."

"Then half my job is done and so is yours." He tugged her inside the elevator, then pressed the button for the penthouse. "Besides, I have a surprise for you."

Rainer covered her eyes before allowing Georgia to walk inside the apartment.

When she saw the Bugatti W16 on the display table, she jumped up and down and screamed. "Oh my God, you found one!"

Walking around the table with her hands over her mouth, she admired the engine from all angles. She bumped into the shelf behind her, the one with a pre-Columbian Aztec Calendar and the Chinese jade carving of a phoenix.

Her exuberance faded as she looked back and forth between the two. "Are you sure you want this out here in the living room with all of these museum pieces?"

The penthouse was no longer the empty post-modern stage it had been when Georgia first arrived. At first, the differences were subtle. Adding choice pieces from his art and antiquities collection didn't warm it up as much as he thought it would. Not without the other changes Georgia made.

Despite her assertion that she didn't do soft, George had done just that. Only soft was the wrong word. Vital. That was a better one. George brought life to the space around her.

It was the little things, like adding things the rust-colored satin pillows that brought out the gold in the bronzed horns of a Minotaur from Crete, or the brown rug she found that complemented the wooden bowl from Oceana.

Once she was more comfortable making larger changes, they painted the monochromatic blue and grey walls over in cheerful earth tones. It made a world of difference. Each room felt warm, as if the walls had soaked in the bright California sun in different degrees. The straight lines and precise angles of his furniture blurred as they were replaced by pieces that were less edgy and more welcoming.

His interior decorator would have had a heart attack, but Rainer didn't care. He felt more at home here than anywhere else he'd ever lived. Of course, that might just be because of the woman who was looking at the engine like she wanted to strip naked and dance around it like a pagan reveling at a solstice.

Rainer put his hands on his hips, contemplating the sweeping whirls of steel on the table. "Well, it's either here or the bedroom, but, honestly, I don't want to have to compete with this beauty for your attention."

Deviltry sparked in her eyes. Georgia stepped into his arms, wrapping her own around his waist. "Take your clothes off…and it doesn't stand a chance."

Rainer threw his head back and laughed. "Hands down the best compliment I've ever gotten," he said, squeezing her to him. "But there's another reason I think this should stay in the living room."

Backing up without letting go, he leaned over to pick up a box from the couch.

Georgia's lips quirked. "Christmas lights?"

The string was the old-fashioned bulb kind, cheerfully multicolored instead of plain white. She touched a bright red bulb.

"Christmas is around the corner. We can wind the lights around the table since we won't have a tree," he said, tearing open the box.

A hand stopped him. "Why wouldn't we have a Christmas tree?"

Rainer's drew his head back. "I assumed you didn't celebrate it. Weren't you raised Jewish? Or is Ephraim one of those flexible Jews? Did you not put up a menorah?"

"Oh, we did, but we also had a tree because yes, Ephraim is flexible. He sort of had to be since he was married to Diamond. She was a die-hard Catholic to the end."

"So, you had both a tree and a menorah?" he asked, the hopeful note undisguised. He sounded like a kid again.

"Yes." Georgia grabbed the box of lights, taking over the job of unwinding them.

"Good." He then went to a big box he'd dropped on the other side of the couch. Raising his arm, he withdrew an aged gold Menorah the size of a small Buick.

Georgia's smile was indulgent. "Let me guess. It's an antique?"

"You know I like things with history," he said, moving to set the menorah on the table next to the window. "We can find a better place for it once we decide where the tree is going."

He rubbed his hands with glee, deciding to order it right away.

The nine-foot-tall Blue Spruce was delivered later that night. It was going to take them multiple days to decorate the entire thing, so he quit soon after hauling out the ornaments from the closet. He snatched Georgia off the ladder she was using to hang the rest of the lights, then stripped her bare in front of the Bugatti engine.

She braced her arms against the table as he knelt in front of her, worshiping with his mouth and hands. When she climaxed, he gathered her limp body to him, burying his cock in her before carrying her to the couch. There he urged her to ride him while he took her mouth until she shuddered, moaning his name.

They stayed on the couch after, her back to his front, his now-soft length still nestled in her clinging heat. Drowsing, she admired the lights they'd managed to hang before their mutual hunger overtook them.

"So, I think we can add another thing to the list," she said.

"What list?" he asked, tracing the skin of her thigh with his fingers.

"The record of all the things that make you hot," she explained, peeking over her shoulder at him, teeth flashing.

"Hmm, well, that list is getting longer all the time. Highlights include you in my office wearing coveralls, you in my arms in a romper, or you tied to my bed naked." He raised an arm to point at their unfinished work. "Also, you on a ladder."

"I was actually thinking of smells." A finger went up.

"The scent of gasoline," Georgia continued, adding another finger. "And now we can add the smell of pine."

He huffed, about to deny it, when he reconsidered. "You know, you may be on to something. I have always been partial to those little air fresheners."

Georgia cracked up, laughing so hard that her little shakes aroused him again. This time, their loving was slow and sweet, but no less potent.

They spent hours on the couch, whispering promises and secrets while their bodies rocked together, giving and receiving bliss. When Georgia came apart, he caught her, following her into a languorous slide into a gratified oblivion.

After, her hand crept behind her, grasping his hip to keep his close. "Do you think we'll always be like this?" she asked.

He sighed, snuggling her. "Just until the fires burn out."

Startled, she twisted her neck to look back at him. "When do you think that will be?"

He let his head dip forward, lips pressing to the soft skin next to her ear. "A few years after never..."

THE END

UP NEXT IN THE R&R SERIES!

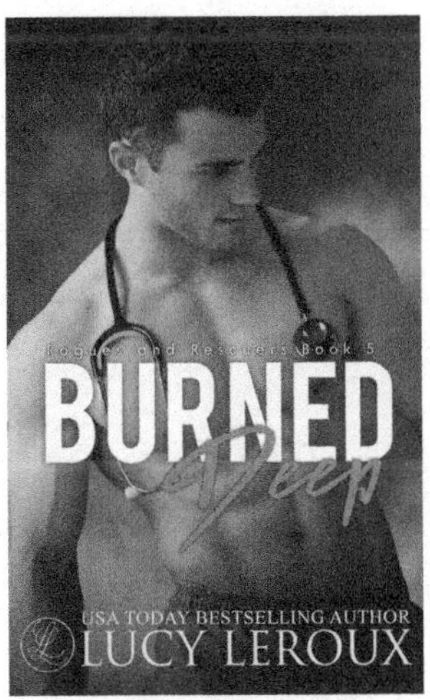

Rogues and Rescuers, Book Five

He's in the business of saving lives. She's in the business of taking them...

Doctors without Borders physician, Donovan Carter is no stranger to pain and suffering. After the love of his life dies while he's in medical school, he dedicates his life to helping and saving others. But when an overseas conference brings him face-to-face with the one woman who owned his heart, Donovan is hellbent on getting answers.

Faking her own death may have destroyed a lot of people—including herself, but it was necessary for Sabrina Morales to survive. Now, it's even more important to avoid Donovan at all costs, especially since he's ruined her mission. The last thing Sabrina is going to do is let him back in her life. After all, his family is the reason she's now a cold-blooded killer.

Thanks to Donovan's meddling, Sabrina's in more danger than she imagined. And once he finds out her secret, can she stop him from getting himself killed?

Coming Soon!

ABOUT THE AUTHOR

A 7-time Readers' Favorite Medal Winner. USA Today Bestselling Author. Mom to a half-feral princess. WOC. Former scientist. Recovering geek.

Lucy Leroux is the steamy pen name for author L.B. Gilbert. Ten years ago Lucy moved to France for a one-year research contract. Six months later she was living with a handsome Frenchman and is now married with an adorable half-french 5yo who won't go to bed on time

When her last contract ended Lucy turned to writing. Frustrated by a particularly bad romance novel she decided to write her own. Her family lives in Southern California.

Lucy loves all genres of romance and intends to write as many of them as possible. To date she has published twenty novels and novellas. These includes paranormal, urban fantasy, gothic regency, and contemporary romances with more on the way.

www.authorlucyleroux.com

amazon.com/author/lucyleroux
facebook.com/lucythenovelist
twitter.com/lucythenovelist
instagram.com/lucythenovelist
bookbub.com/authors/lucy-leroux

Made in the USA
Middletown, DE
03 March 2024